Blues in the Wind

Blues in the Wind

by

Whitney J. LeBlanc

RIVER CITY PUBLISHING

Montgomery, Alabama

 Published in the United States by River City Publishing LLC, 1719 Mulberry Street, Montgomery, AL 36106.

Library of Congress Cataloging-in-Publication Data:

LeBlanc, Whitney J., 1931-
Blues in the wind : a novel / by Whitney J. LeBlanc.
p. cm.
ISBN 0-913515-47-7 (alk. paper)
1. Creoles—Fiction. 2. Louisiana—Fiction. 3. Blues musicians—Fiction. I. Title.
PS3612. E25 B57 2001
813'. 54—dc21

River City publishes fiction, nonfiction, poetry, children's books, and art. We celebrate the bond between literature and the visual arts by providing a forum for leading authors and artists in our region and nationwide. In this spirit, the cover art was painted especially for this book by Steve Lowery.

Designed by Lissa Monroe.
Manufactured by Vaughan Printing in the United States of America.
2nd Printing

To request a catalog or to order any of our books, phone 1 (334) 265-6753.
Also visit our web site at www. rivercitypublishing. com

Contents

Chapter One 9
Chapter Two 15
Chapter Three 33
Chapter Four 39
Chapter Five 51
Chapter Six 63
Chapter Seven 69
Chapter Eight 81
Chapter Nine 91
Chapter Ten 99
Chapter Eleven 125
Chapter Twelve 137
Chapter Thirteen 147
Chapter Fourteen 159
Chapter Fifteen 177
Chapter Sixteen 185
Chapter Seventeen 201
Chapter Eighteen 221
Chapter Nineteen 233
Chapter Twenty 247
Chapter Twenty- One 259
Chapter Twenty- Two 281
Chapter Twenty- Three 303
Chapter Twenty- Four 319

Dedicated to my children.

Acknowledgments

I wish to thank Janice Bell and Ledell Smith of the Camille Stivers Shade African American Library Collection at Southern University. Their help in locating material on Frank Yerby and Southern University was critical in providing important historical references. A special and loving thanks goes to my lifelong friend Roberta Shade Tyson for her assistance and advice. Many thanks and much gratitude to Ashley Gordon, my editor. She was a warm, gentle wind guiding me to reveal what I was saying in my heart. Gratitude and thanks to Wayne Greenhaw and the staff at River City Publishing for their vision and belief, a rare and precious quality in the world of publishing—Al and Carolyn Newman, Tony Baine, Jim Davis, William Hicks, Lissa Monroe, and Tangela Parker. Love and appreciation go to my wife, Diane. Her faith, encouragement, and prayers lighted the path to completion of this work.

—Whitney J. LeBlanc

1

AUGUST 7, 1934, was hot and muggy. In the Deep South the heat clung to skin with the tenacity of a black shroud, leaving in its wake a residue of sticky moisture. Normally the fading of the sun brought welcomed relief. But today was different. The heat of day still hung over Estilette, Louisiana, well into the early evening hours. Relief came slowly with a reluctant release of the captured warmth from the bayous, creating currents of air that sporadically pushed away the stubborn shroud.

Tot's Tavern was a little distance beyond where the gravel of the respectable part of town turned into a dusty road. The well-worn path, through cocklebur and stinkweed, guided blues lovers to a ramshackle, weather-beaten shack, hidden beneath a grove of moss-dripping oaks and chinaberry trees. There was no sign on the building, but everybody knew where to find this hole in the wall.

Johnny "LightFoot" Broussard was the night's interlocutor, an honor bestowed on any volunteer willing to introduce the local blues players. The interlocutor was a master of ceremonies, but because most times the audience engaged him in a repartee akin to the era of minstrels, the title of interlocutor stuck. LightFoot jumped at the chance for this esteem whenever others were hesitant or failed to show. He liked the blues. It was his music. It made him feel good. The trials and tribulations of the blues stories made any problem that he thought he had seem trivial. LightFoot was favorably inclined to playing guitar for any blues singer who needed a side, which was the main reason that Tot wanted him around and gave him free drinks. LightFoot also played the harmonica, which he liked best. He carried it in his pocket, where it was handy whenever he had an urge to play.

The blues people had named him LightFoot. His left leg was shorter than the right, and he walked on the ball of his foot that left a half-print in the dust. It was a nickname given out of affection. He had attracted a small loyal following of blues lovers. An accordion player named Freddie expressed best what was generally felt. "Man, when LightFoot play the blues it's like a bolt of lightnin' just struck the roots of a tree. It go way down deep. He can *play* some blues. He can play the train so real, the peoples along his path can set their clocks when he pass by."

Tonight LightFoot didn't play. He only made introductions. And there were no challenging wisecracks from the audience, perhaps because it was hot, so beer drinking was taken seriously. The smoke-filled air was at a standstill, and the same could be said for the slow grind dancing, a prelude to what was sure to follow.

LightFoot made an introduction. "This here is my last act of the evenin', then I gotta get on home to sleep off this Early Times. I want y'all to meet Clarence Garlow. He just twenty-three years old and he from Welsh, over there by Jennings. Nobody ever heard tell of Welsh 'cause it's even smaller than Estilette. Clarence has been playing music since he was eight years old. He live in Beaumont now and was visiting his peoples in Welsh, so he come by here to play his fiddle. I want y'all to make Clarence Garlow feel at home."

Then LightFoot stepped down from the small triangular platform in the corner and headed for his usual seat at the bar. Tot stood on the opposite side, wiping the countertop as he spoke, "One for the road?"

LightFoot chuckled as he looked back over his shoulder at the stage. "Might as well. I wanna hear if this Garlow fellow can play the blues with a fiddle." Tot filled LightFoot's glass with Early Times and headed to the other end of the linoleum-covered bar, refilling other glasses along the way. LightFoot felt a hand on his shoulder; he turned to see Ventris Pugh settle in on the stool next to him.

"Vent, I ain't seen you in a coon's age. Where you been?"

"Around. You doin' the thang tonight?"

"What you mean, man?"

"Interlockin'."

"That's my last act up there now. It's gettin' late and I gotta get on home."

"Man, you gotta put my cousin on."

"Your cousin? I ain't knowed you had a cousin."

"He just got outta jail and he need a little bread to tide him over."

"Shit, man, it's too late."

"It's just 'bout eleven o'clock and my cousin's got hellhounds chasin' him, and if'n you can get the bottom of the basket covered, he'll play."

"What the hell you say? I told you it's too late."

"Ahhh, come on man."

"Where's your cousin, anyhow?"

"He sittin' over there. His name Leadbelly."

"You say Leadbelly?"

Tot came over to get Ventris's order. "What you talkin', Vent? Leadbelly in jail."

"He just got out today," Ventris announced proudly. "He singed for the governor and got his pardon. He over dere."

LightFoot turned his head to where Ventris was pointing, "Man, why didn't you say your cousin was Leadbelly?" LightFoot knew the name. Although he had never seen the man, he knew that Leadbelly had received an early release from a thirty-year prison term in 1925 by singing for the governor of Texas. Leadbelly was a legend. Now he had been released early from prison in Louisiana by singing for another governor.

LightFoot asked, "What he sing for Governor O. K. Allen?"

Ventris beamed with pride. "The song he wrote special for him. A man named John Lomax recorded it while he was in prison and took it to the governor. Went somethin' like:

> In nineteen hundred and thirty-two
> Honorable Governor O. K. Allen I'm appealin' to you.
> I left my wife wringin' her hands and cryin'
> Sayin' *Governor O. K. Allen, save this man of mine.*"

LightFoot was up like a flash, weaving his way to the table where Leadbelly sat drinking gin. LightFoot extended his hand to the blues legend; the big man squeezed it like a grapefruit.

BORN ON a plantation outside Mooringsport, Louisiana, Leadbelly's given name was Huddie William Ledbetter. There were many stories about how he got the nickname. There was the obvious corruption of his given name. Another possible source was his unusual strength. And still another story was inspired by the buckshot wound in his stomach. Whatever the truth, Leadbelly lived a charmed life. He was hot-tempered and mean, always in trouble with the law for murder or attempted murder. His reputation was known far and wide. Most sensible people stayed out of his way, but the foolhardy or unaware who challenged him got their comeuppance. LightFoot was neither, and he realized the opportunity that had fallen into his lap.

After a few minutes at Leadbelly's table, LightFoot hopped up on stage. He brought with him a half-bushel potato basket and held it up over his head. He yelled with excitement, "I want y'all to know that Leadbelly's sittin' over yonder. He just got outta prison and if'n the bottom of this basket is covered with dollar bills, I might be able to entice him to play the blues. I'm gonna pass it around."

The people went wild. Everybody in the tavern knew the name Leadbelly. Word spread like wildfire to those getting it on outside under the trees. In no time at all the entire place was packed wall to wall. The crowd even included a half dozen white men, there seeking sexual pleasures, who forgot all about any other attraction except hearing Leadbelly.

The bottom of the basket was covered when it got back to LightFoot. He had never seen anything like it. Tot was grinning ear to ear as he scurried from one end of the bar to other, doing land-office business. LightFoot made his introduction and Leadbelly took the stage.

A fifth of gin and a water glass were placed on the floor next to Leadbelly's chair. He played up a storm! The people stomped their feet, beat on the tables, danced and hollered. Anyone listening from the outside would have thought a riot had broken out. But it was only the joy and pleasure from Leadbelly's performance. At the end of each piece he turned up the bottle of gin, took a long slow swallow, wiped his mouth with the back of his hand, and then started strumming the next song. Every now and then he talked a little.

"My parole man say I gotta stay in *Louis-i-ana* for a year. I'm gonna spend a few days in Estilette, eating ham hocks and turnip greens. Then I'm gonna go to Baton Rouge where I'll meet up with John Lomax, the man who give my song to the governor, and we gonna criss-cross this here state and *re-cord* the blues."

But Leadbelly said there were two other things he wanted to do first, two things he had not done for four years while he was in Angola prison. "I gotta go see my peoples in Mooringsport, and then I'm gonna stick my thang in some jelly-jelly."

All the while Leadbelly was still strumming the guitar. He flowed right into singing "Jelly-Jelly," or any other song that fit what he was talking about. He sang most of his best-known songs: "The Boll Weevil," "Cotton Fields," "Goodnight, Irene," "Good Morning Blues," and others. But the two songs that brought down the house were "Governor O. K. Allen" and "Governor Pat Neff Blues." The water glass sat on the floor unused during the entire performance, but the gin bottle was empty when he sang his last note.

2

THE LARGE, TWO-STORY house sat on a graveled road in the respectable part of town, not very far away from the tavern. It was within walking distance, but far enough away that the goings-on could not be heard in the wind. The white clapboard had been painted only twice in the twenty years since it was remodeled from the remains of Joseph Broussard's plantation. It was a comfortable house with large windows, lace curtains, high ceilings, and nicely papered walls.

Phillip Fergerson waited to receive whatever breeze might happen to stir the still warm air. Martha, his wife, had tied back the curtains to let the cool air run through the whole house. The children were asleep upstairs. Phillip and Martha's bedroom was downstairs, along with a room for LightFoot, who was Martha's brother. There was also a modest bathroom with hot and cold running water, an unusual facility for houses occupied by colored people in Estilette. A long narrow hallway ran down the center, connecting a living room, dining room, kitchen, and "Papa's room." It was in Papa's room that, in the mornings, Phillip drank his cup of coffee and read the newspaper.

Phillip was restless and ill at ease tonight. He stood waiting for relief from the heat. Although he could not hear the blues from the other part of town, he listened as the bullfrogs croaked rutting songs to each other, delivering their subliminal message that nighttime was the right time for making love. And so it was for Phillip. It had been many months since he and Martha had made love for the sheer pleasure and enjoyment of each other. He had wanted that to happen for a long time. And for many years after the children were born, he wondered what happened to the intimacy they once shared in the nighttime. He suspected Martha's religious beliefs were more important than their sexual enjoyment. It wasn't that he disagreed with her about the divine purpose of the sacrament of marriage, but, unlike Martha, Phillip needed to have his "nature" satisfied. He also knew there were other feelings to be derived from closeness, from communication, from love between Martha and him.

In keeping with her strict Catholic upbringing, Martha believed the primary purpose for making love was to conceive children. She practiced the rhythm method, and when she figured her time was near, she would say to Phillip, "It's that time again." For the next week Martha prepared for the ritual of lovemaking. She would first take a douche, prompted by a strong belief that "nigger" women smelled bad. Not wishing to be included in this number, she bathed her body with scented oils and placed a dab of Evening in Paris behind each ear. Then she would put on a satin gown she saved especially for these occasions. Martha felt it was a sin to appear unclothed in front of her husband, so she dressed in the dark or alone in the bathroom.

Phillip too was convinced that he should not appear naked in front of his wife. He dressed privately in a special nightshirt rather than his usual pajamas. To consummate their union, he had to work his way up and under the gowns, fighting rolls of cloth like horse collars around their waists. Phillip hated this ritual. He would rather feel Martha's skin next to his. But Martha would not allow the immorality of nakedness to damn her soul to hell. She did like the feel of Phillip's index finger lightly stroking her swelling nipples, which strained against the tight satin covering. She was turned on by the tease—crossing boundaries of cloth, discovering private parts in the dark. Yet she never let on that this gave her pleasure, for fear the disclosure might tempt the wrath of God.

Phillip and Martha already had four children, the youngest being twelve, so the days of permissible lovemaking were few and far between. These nights were the only time they kissed. Their lips eagerly embraced each other with love-starved hunger from foreplay until Phillip fell off to sleep.

Tonight he stood at the window hoping the rutting songs of the frogs would have an effect on Martha. "Unlike the frogs and mammals, we don't have a mating season," he thought. "But you'd think that we did, the way she acts. A man likes to have a good fuck every now and then." He smiled at the word "fuck." Martha's reaction, if she knew he even thought the word, much less said it, was a humorous picture.

A squeaking of the bedsprings interrupted his nightdreams. Martha shifted her position.

"You gonna stand in the breeze all night long?" she asked.

"Sorry. I was just thinking."

"You always thinking about something. What is it now?"

Phillip turned and looked at Martha sitting propped against the pillows, bathed in the filtered moonlight. "I was thinking that maybe I was smelling Evening in Paris."

Martha laughed a mischievous and naughty laugh that Phillip had not heard in a long time. "You saying you want to try for another son?"

"No, I'm not saying that. You know we're both past the stage of having youngsters."

"What are you saying, then?"

"That I'd like to feel close to you again."

"Come scratch my back."

Sex play often began with Martha requesting her back to be scratched. It itched often, but during the day, when the need arose, she set her back against a doorway and moved her body up and down against the frame. When she was feeling horny, a phrase that existed only in Phillip's thoughts, Martha would say, "Come scratch my back."

He laughed, headed toward his side of the bed, and kissed her long and hard. She felt a spontaneous urge to have Phillip's thumb and forefinger softly caress the erogenous button growing on her breast. Maybe this passion was brought on by the heat of day, or a subtle suggestion from the frog chorus, or maybe the tender rays of filtered moonlight. Although it was not a rhythm-method-approved night, Martha felt a desire to have Phillip's body pressing against hers. There was something in the sound of his voice that caused her to want him on top of her. Perhaps if he continued to scratch, and they continued to talk, it would happen and God might forgive her. Martha believed that, if God had forgiven Phillip for his relationship with another woman many years ago, He might also be in a forgiving mood tonight.

Martha rolled over Phillip's hand that was now pressed between her body and the sheet. It was a move intended to plant ideas, rather than to better hear the quiet words that came out of the darkness. Phillip turned in her direction.

Martha rested in a shaft of moonlight. "God, she is beautiful," he thought. Her deep-set, gray eyes were framed by gossamer black hair, which cascaded over the white pillow. A delicate creamy skin told her true racial identity. She was Creole, a marginal class creation of the French, Spanish, and Negro-Indian blood mixtures found in southern Louisiana. Not regarded as white by whites, she did not consider herself Negro.

Memories of her father's voice interrupted Phillip's thoughts, as his gaze lingered on her face. "My boy, you too black to date my baby." He remembered those words like the sting of a wasp. Even though Phillip was a "teasing tan," his skin was not "white" enough for Joseph Broussard.

PHILLIP HAD first seen Martha in church. Their eyes met as she passed his pew after receiving communion. He had never seen her before that Sunday, although he regularly attended Mass. Perhaps it was because she was only a young girl when he had gone away to Southern College four years earlier. When he saw her that first time she was twenty, he twenty-four. For several Sundays afterwards, they exchanged glances as she passed on her way back to her seat. Finally, he was able to muster up the courage necessary to approach her papa about dating.

Joseph Broussard was a poor, proud Creole. It was important to him that his grandchildren also be Creole. At first Phillip did not pass Joe Broussard's brown-paper-bag test: "If you darker than the bag, get back. If you white, then you're all right." This was recited to all who expressed interest in his daughter.

Phillip ignored Broussard's remark about his color and said, "I'm only teaching until I have enough money to go to medical school." Phillip aspired to be a doctor. He and a friend, Frank Johnson, made the pledge years earlier while in college. But when Phillip saw Martha, everything he planned got turned around; instead of going to medical school, getting married to this beautiful Creole girl became his main priority. A colored man darker than a paper bag marrying up with a lovely, light-skinned lady was an accomplishment of the first order. Phillip was smitten.

And he was smart. The possibility of having a doctor in the family made all the difference in the world to the proud, uneducated man sitting on the porch of his crumbling plantation house. So Phillip got Joe Broussard's blessings on a proposal of possibility. He and Martha were married a year later. He still planned on being a doctor, but the thought moved to the back of his mind. As the years passed and his family grew, he thought less and less about going to medical school and more and more about his son, Bobby, becoming the doctor in the family.

Phillip's thoughts shifted back to the present; he gazed at Martha in the moonlight. Perhaps this night would indeed turn into a lovemaking night. They were sharing feelings, mostly about the children, which always brought them closer.

"Vel can hardly wait till she's eighteen," Martha said.

"I know. She thinks she's grown already."

"Be easy with her. She thinks you like Lala better'n her."

Martha also believed that Phillip loved the youngest daughter, Lillian, more than Velma, the eldest, because Lala was prettier. She was indeed lovely, as if created in the likeness of an artist's portrait from the Romantic period. Her beautiful, blue-gray eyes were delicately etched in an exotic mask of *café au lait* skin. Her elegant, thin nose and mouth were framed by silky black hair, which hung all the way to the middle of her back.

Vel's appearance was the opposite of Lala's. Her skin held a pasty pallor. Her hair was short and nappy; her nose and lips were unmistakable throwbacks to the strong African genes of Phillip's ancestors. And as the Creole standard of beauty influenced both Martha's and Phillip's judgments, there was little chance that either would consider her beautiful. There were also aspects of Phillip in Velma's behavior. She was stubborn and headstrong. She had a will of her own and was determined to do things her way. But unlike her father, she had an inclination to do the forbidden, anything that was off limits and tempting.

Martha's intuition about Phillip was right; he did love beautiful women. But whether he was partial to one daughter because of her looks was a subject still to be debated. Martha had never before questioned Phillip's preference of the two girls, and she was careful to not appear to question it now.

Phillip was defensive. "Now, you know that's not true," he argued. Although Phillip denied he had a preference, the tone of his voice and the look of his eye suggested otherwise.

Martha felt she should soften her earlier comment. "I know you love all your children the same. You just treat 'em different."

Phillip was silent for several choruses of crickets and bullfrogs. And when the full meaning of her statement had passed, he spoke softly, "I talked with Mr. Fontenot today."

Martha was irritated that he was trying to change the subject. Why else would he want to talk about the superintendent of schools in the middle of a conversation about Vel? This was the one thing she disliked most about Phillip. In the early days of their marriage, he was more considerate of her feelings. Now he had to have everything his way.

She knew that Phillip was a smart administrator; he had discovered that allowing too many opinions from others was not the best road for a strong principal to travel. So, over the years, Phillip learned how to take control of situations at school; she often lamented that he brought these skills home. Now Martha was trying to talk about Vel's approaching birthday, and Phillip wanted to talk about Mr. Fontenot. She was determined, however, to keep their conversation peaceful; the last thing she wanted was a fuss to spoil the spell that was headed toward lovemaking. She relented and continued with his conversation. "Well, what did you and that ol' white man talk about?" she asked.

"I told him I needed another teacher. And since my daughter Velma had finished high school, I could use her to teach third grade, come September."

Martha kissed him excitedly. "Oh, Phillip! What did he say?"

Phillip looked at her with hope dancing in his eyes. "He could only pay her twenty-five dollars a month."

Tears slid down Martha's cheeks. "She's got a *job*. Lord, that's the best present you could give her."

The sound of a train joined the cricket chorus that filtered in with the wind. Their lips met again. Phillip's hand found a path under the cotton nightgown and gently caressed Martha's breast, transforming her nipples into petrified reservoirs of pleasure. She rolled closer until she could feel the ramrod growing between his legs. The state of their pleasure grew higher and higher.

It did not last long.

A crash of falling objects and their dog Trixie's barking interrupted the train whistle. Phillip turned away in disgust. "That wasn't no train. That's your brother coming home drunk again."

The mood was irrevocably broken. There would be no lovemaking this night. "Go shut up that goddamn dog." Phillip's voice had lost the gentle affection that was there earlier.

Martha felt Phillip should be the one to get up and look after the disturbance in the hallway—he was the man. But she got up reluctantly and put on her robe, the disappointment in her heart slowly growing to anger. At the door she stopped and asked impatiently, "You coming?"

"He's your brother," snapped Phillip.

Martha glared at her husband. She bit her tongue to hold back the wrath better directed at LightFoot. She always thought of her brother as John, his given name, rather than LightFoot, the name he got in the juke-joints.

Martha turned on the light. John was sprawled out on the floor, laughing a low chuckle, more like coughing than laughter. The revealing light ended Trixie's barking, and she was now licking wet kisses on John's face. He pushed Trixie away sufficiently to look up and greet Martha. "Hey, big sister. I tripped."

"What you trying to do, wake the dead?"

"Where'd that table come from?"

"Who do you think you are, coming in at this hour?"

"I see you been movin' furniture again."

"The smell of alcohol is so strong that Trixie couldn't even smell it was you." The tone of her voice stopped John's laughter, and he struggled to get up. He righted the table and began picking up the whatnots from the floor.

"There ain't enough room in this narrow hallway for this table."

"When you gonna stop drinking and carousing?"

John sarcastically repeated Martha's words. "When you gonna stop drinking and carousing?"

"Don't you trifle with me."

"Then why don't you mind your own goddamn business?"

"Don't you use that low-life language in my house."

"It might be your house, but it's settin' on my half of the land."

"You always drunk, like those no-count niggers you run around with."

"Ain't nobody studdin' you. Just shut up and get on back to bed!" John stumbled past Martha on the way to his room.

She followed, watching his every move. "You can hardly walk, you so drunk," Martha yelled.

John's voice came out of the darkness as he fished around in the air trying to find the strip of cloth that served as a light pull. "You always meddling in somethin' don't concern you."

Martha stood with folded arms, surveying the disarray illuminated by the naked light bulb swinging from the ceiling. "This room smell just like a hog pen," she spat.

"Then why don't you get your ass out?"

Martha slapped John viciously across the left side of his face. He staggered back and fell onto the bed. In all the years of living with his sister's temper he had never returned her aggression. In spite of the fact that any man he knew would have hit her back, he was not going to start now. He lay there for the next few minutes, suffering Martha's assault.

"How dare you talk to me that way. You *common*, that's what you are. You embarrass the whole family with your drinking and running around with low-class niggers. You going on thirty-six years old and ain't done nothing with your life. And who do you think you are anyway, to come in here drunk and insult me in my house? You got some nerve. I saw that Ellis woman at the store the other day and she had the gall to say to me, 'I think it's nice that LightFoot's playin' music at Tot's Tavern now.'"

Her indignation fueled her tirade. "The nerve of that woman. To tell me that, when she know I don't cotton to that gut-bucket music or you going to them juke-joints. That's got to stop. You just drinking yourself into poor health, and you already a cripple."

John got up from the bed slowly and limped past her. He headed down the hallway toward the living room, intentionally bumping the table. Martha followed, getting louder as the fury of her passion mounted.

"Where you think you going?"

"Out."

"At this hour?"

"Yeah, away from you."

"You need to get yourself back in that bed, drunk as you are."

"You need to shut the hell up." John opened the front door, then he turned and delivered his own barrage. "I don't know how Phillip can stand you. You fuss all the time. Nothin' and nobody's good enough for you. And on top of that you pretend to be such a good

Catholic, always running to church . . . but you ain't nothin' but chicken shit." He slammed the door and walked out.

Martha jerked open the door, followed him onto the porch, and yelled after him, "I know where you going. You just gonna find yourself in a whole peck of trouble, you mark my words."

LIGHTFOOT HAD lived with Martha and Phillip for the ten years since his accident. He fell from the steeple of the white Catholic church when some scaffolding broke. The doctors at St. Landry Parish Hospital were in a hurry; they also had injured whites that they had to look after. The delay in setting LightFoot's left leg caused it to heal two inches shorter than his right, leaving him crippled. So it had fallen to Martha to care for her brother after he left the hospital. The Catholic church continued disability payments to the injured white workers for life; the injured colored got none. They did get their hospital bills paid, however, and the two who were killed were buried for free. But that was all.

Not able to find steady work in his profession as a bricklayer, LightFoot did odd jobs in construction and whatever else he could pick up. He continued to live with his sister to help make ends meet. In spite of all these hardships, he was not angry or bitter. He was the same easy-going, fun-loving person that he had always been. Martha was convinced that John's fall from the steeple was a sign from God that his lifestyle of, as she had worded it, "drinking, carousing with women, and playing gut-bucket music" was sinful and needed to stop.

UPSTAIRS, ROSALIE, the middle girl between Vel and Lala, stood at the window watching as her Uncle Johnny disappeared into the shadows of the moonlight. The "Going Home Blues" that echoed from his harmonica was also swallowed by the darkness. Rosa was plain, with an inner beauty that surfaced through her innocent, searching eyes, which believed everything they beheld.

Lala turned in the bed and focused on the silhouette at the window. "What you doin', girl?"

"Looking."

"At what."

"A shootin' star."

Lala got out of bed and stood next to Rosa at the window. "I don't see none."

"It's gone now."

Lala observed the rosary beads spilling out between the fingers of Rosa's hand. "You been praying for them."

"Did you hear?"

"I couldn't help it."

"Why don't Mama and Uncle Johnny get on?"

"He like the blues and she don't."

"What's wrong with liking the blues?"

"Nothing that I can see. But I guess it's because low-class colored people like 'em too. And you know how Mama feels about that."

"Yeah." Rosa looked up at the sky again. "Look, there's another one."

"Ohhhh, shucks, I missed it."

"They say it's good luck to make a wish on a star."

"And I know what you been wishing for."

A slight breeze brushed Rosa's face and she could swear that she still heard the echo of Uncle Johnny playing the blues. She looked inquiringly at Lala and softly asked, "I wonder why the blues is always sad?"

"It's not always," answered Lala. "Sometimes it's about good times between a man and a woman. And sometimes it's jest about feelings that can't be told no other way."

"How you know that?"

"Uncle Johnny. He gimme the beat." Lala began to snap her fingers and sing "I Got a Good Feelin' Blues."

Velma abruptly sat up in her bed on the far side of the room. "Y'all shut up and go on back to sleep."

Rosa obligingly headed to her bed; but Lala hollered back, "You shut up yourself."

"If I have to get up, I'm gonna slap the devil out of you."

"You think you so much 'cause you gonna be eighteen."

Rosa gently pulled Lala toward her, but Lala wouldn't be calmed. "It's time for you to get married and get your butt outta our room anyway."

"I'm not gonna take no more of your sass." Vel was up like a shot. She slapped Lala. Lala slapped back. The two girls continued to exchange blows.

Rosa tried to separate them but she was pushed down on the bed. She cried and begged them to stop but they fought on. Rosa ran downstairs yelling loudly, "Papa! Mama! Lala and Vel up there fighting. They gonna kill each other . . . you gotta stop 'em!"

Martha pushed herself out of bed one more time. Vel and Lala had fought their way downstairs and into the dining room, each blaming the other for striking the first blow. Martha was in the middle of sorting out the dispute when Phillip entered. "What's going on here?" he demanded.

The three girls spoke at once. Phillip raised his voice above the din, "Quiet down . . . there's been enough fussing in this house for one night."

Martha took offense. She crossed her arms and asked, "And what's that supposed to mean?"

Phillip could tell Martha was primed for a fight. "Nothing, woman," he answered.

"Naw, go ahead and say it. You talking about me."

"I didn't say nothing about you."

"You might as well. You thinking it."

"What makes you think you know what I'm thinking?"

"I know my brother drinks. But unlike some other people I know, I got to let him know how I feel about it."

The focus of the fuss had changed directions as usual. The girls, feeling responsible, dropped their heads in embarrassment. Even Trixie looked up, then buried her head down in her paws.

"I didn't say a word about your brother," yelled Phillip.

"As God is my witness, when he come home playing that harp you said, 'That wasn't no train. That's your brother coming home drunk again.'"

"Well, he was."

"He's not as much of a drunkard as Luther."

"Woman, I told you to keep my brother's name outta your mouth. You use any chance you get to twist the knife and castigate my family." A sore spot had been touched; salt poured into the wound.

Five years earlier, Phillip's brother, Luther, got in the middle of a domestic dispute. Jake, his poker partner, and Luther had been drinking heavily. Jake's woman, anxious to stop the game and go home, repeatedly picked up the cards from the table. After Jake warned her several times not to interfere, she did it one more time. Jake jumped from the table in a fit of rage and began beating her. When Luther tried to stop it, Jake turned on him and pulled a knife. Luther tried to take it away and Jake was killed in the struggle. Luther was cleared of charges, claiming self-defense. The grateful young girl became Luther's woman.

Martha hated the stigma this event cast upon the family. She continued her attack, savoring her advantage over Phillip. "All that drinking and fighting over a low-class nigger-woman. Now Luther's got a nigger-woman too." Phillip raised his hand. Rosa screamed. Vel ran out of the room yelling, "I'm gonna get the gun." Lala grabbed the cut-glass wax-fruit bowl, spilling the fruit, which rolled off the table and bounced on the floor one piece at a time. She held the bowl at the ready.

This was not the first time Phillip was pushed to hit Martha. But it was the first time he raised his hand to her in front of the children. Phillip stopped his hand in midair, recapturing his sanity. He looked around at the faces of his family and slowly lowered his hand. He turned and headed for his bedroom, kicking a wax apple out of his path. It ricocheted off the dining room wall and came to rest spinning at Lala's feet. When Vel entered pointing the pistol, Phillip grabbed it out of her hand and continued down the hall. Trying to contain his fit of rage, he wondered, "How long am I gonna have to put up with this crazy woman?"

Upstairs, son Bobby lay in his bed, staring into the darkness, listening to the commotion. There was nothing he could do. There was nothing he wanted to do—except stay out it.

3

LIGHTFOOT KNEW that his nickname riled his sister, but he didn't know until tonight that she harbored such strong resentment. He had been in a celebrating mood. "Hell, I wasn't that drunk and that damn table didn't belong there in the first place," he thought. He was not about to let Martha spoil the memory of Leadbelly's first night out of prison.

LightFoot beat the spit out of his harp and stuck it into his pocket. He continued walking and thinking in silence. Tonight he'd met a blues legend. "Barely a day out of Angola and he walks into Tot's with Vent. No one even knew he had a cousin in Estilette, but there he sat big as sin, drinking gin." LightFoot felt both joy and sorrow. Joy because he had just seen a living legend. Sorrow because he realized that he was not as gifted a bluesman as Leadbelly. Maybe if God had given him the same troubles and a raspy voice, he could also be famous. Then again, he was grateful that his troubles were small, even those with his sister. He only played the blues because it made him feel good, not because he had to get out of trouble—like Leadbelly. At any rate, he knew that he would never be as widely known. This was a night filled with conflict; but soon he would get some rest. He was getting close to Naomi's house, where he would spend the night.

Naomi was LightFoot's woman. She was everything that his sister Martha loathed. She was night-black with nappy hair. She hadn't finished high school, and perfectly fitted Martha's description of "low-class." She even practiced voodoo. But to LightFoot, she was everything he needed. She listened to his problems and understood his desires. She was kind and gentle and the best pussy he ever had. Her butt was round and firm and flowed generously down to merge into beautifully shaped thighs. Her breasts sat erect like ripe luscious mangoes. And she moved with the ease and grace of an African princess. LightFoot adored her. Except for the never-ending turmoil that it would surely bring to his life, he would marry her. But LightFoot disliked discord. He had heard fussing all of his life. His mother and father fussed. Martha and Phillip fussed. So in order to avoid the mess and maintain the peace, he was content to keep his relationship with Naomi restricted to the dark of night.

LightFoot walked into Naomi's living room. Candles were burning everywhere. The air was filled with the aroma of basil and thyme mixed with rose incense. Naomi stood in the doorway, one hand on her hip and the other on the doorframe. She wore nothing but juju beads. Bessie Smith sang "I'm Wild About That Thing" on the radio. LightFoot was surprised. "Has she been waiting for me all this time?" he wondered. Naomi seductively approached her bewildered prey, dancing slowly. By the end of the song, she had maneuvered her victim into bed, leaving a trail of his cluttered clothes on the floor.

THE LIGHT of day forced a shaft of sunlight through a torn section of the windowshade. The gentle warmth settled on LightFoot's face and nudged him awake. He looked around. In spite of morning-after stupor, he knew where he was. The aroma of coffee with chicory wafted from the kitchen. Naomi walked into the room, carrying two blue and white cups. Her infectious smile revealed her perfectly formed teeth. She breathed, "Good morning, sunshine." Then she sat on the bed and extended a steaming cup. LightFoot took a deep swallow of the thick black liquid that burned a path down to his stomach. He smiled in loving appreciation.

"How'd you know I was coming over?"

"I put on a spell."

He laughed and kissed her lightly on the cheek. "No, really. How'd you know?"

"It's true. Basil chased away the evil spirit."

"And that's how you knew?"

"And the thyme brought the good."

For a moment LightFoot was worried that Naomi really had the power to put a hex on him. Then he laughed in relief. He did not believe in the power of voodoo; although there were those who said there was little difference between the prayers of a Catholic to a statue and the conjure of a voodoo priestess to a fetish. He could not see how a spell could control behavior anyway, but there was something mysterious about it all. Still, he wondered how Naomi knew that he would be coming over. He racked his brain to remember if he had promised her he would come, and later forgotten.

Naomi cut through his speculation. "Honey, it ain't no big thang. It's just a matter of time 'fore your good Catholic high-falutin' sister kicks yo' ass out for good." She continued with a wry smile, "You's my man, and you likes the blues and drinks too much, and I'm your woman."

"You're right about that."

An unexpected voice caused LightFoot and Naomi to turn toward the living room door. There stood Martha holding a plate covered with a napkin, her hand on her hip. She said, "I brought you some breakfast. Figured you would need it after last night."

LightFoot jumped up from the bed. "How the hell did you get in here?" he demanded.

Martha immediately turned away, shielding her eyes with an outstretched hand, "For God's sake, cover yourself."

"You got no damn business in here," he snapped.

Naomi took the sheet from the bed and wrapped it around his shoulders. She said in a soothing voice, "It's all right, hon. The door was open."

"That don't mean shit. She got no right to just walk in somebody's house like that."

Naomi picked up the trail of clothes from the floor and then took the plate from Martha's hands. "This sho' is nice of you. Would you like to stay and visit with us?"

This was more than Martha had bargained for. She looked at Naomi for several seconds. Then she glanced around the living room at the candles, charms, dolls, bones, statues, and other voodoo paraphernalia. She closed her eyes and shook her head. "No, thank you. I'll be going. I just wanted to make sure John had a good breakfast." With those words she walked out the front door.

For several seconds Naomi and LightFoot stared in her direction. LightFoot shook his head, saying, "I don't believe what I just seen."

"Honey, them white folks think they can do anything they want."

"But she ain't no white folks."

"She think she is. "

"She's trying to make up for last night. "

"You think she'll live that long? "

LightFoot put on his clothes while he pondered the deeper meaning of Naomi's statement. Naomi headed to the kitchen with the plate. "Come on in here and eat this food. At least you know it ain't got no goofer dust in it. "

4

MARTHA AND PHILLIP'S son Bobby had to heat water to take his bath. The tank only held fifty gallons, so anyone who bathed after Vel was in trouble. She cared little for anyone else's hygiene but her own.

As the water warmed up, Bobby watched with pleasure as Vel struggled to hitch up the buggy in the back yard. From his vantage point at the kitchen window, he pressed his lips against the glass and wiggled his tongue. Before Vel could see him, the sound of his papa's footsteps made him quickly wipe away the wet imprint from the window with his sleeve. Bobby knew that his papa wanted him to act "more grown up."

The footsteps stopped and Papa's voice turned him around, "Hurry up, boy. I got a lot to do today."

"I'm hurrying, Papa."

"Got to drop your mama off before I go to town. You waiting on breakfast?"

"No, sir."

"Then why you just standing at the window?"

"I'm waiting for the water to heat."

"That girl used up all the water again?"

"What we gonna do in town, Papa?"

"Never you mind. Just make haste."

Bobby moved to the stove and reached for the kettle as he carefully eyed his father. He watched Phillip pour himself another cup of coffee. Tall and distinguished-looking, Phillip was the picture of self-assurance. He was dressed in a suit, white shirt, and tie. As usual, his pocket-watch chain was looped across the front of his vest. The thumb of his left hand rested in the lower vest pocket while his right hand lifted the cup to his mouth. He blew into the cup before taking a sip. Bobby figured that his father was planning to take care of important business; there seemed to be a lot on his mind. Phillip turned slightly to look in Bobby's direction, and Bobby quickly picked up the kettle and headed for the bathroom.

Vel had always been the one chosen to hitch the buggy. She was the oldest and the first to learn. She was also the fastest because she hated it and figured that the sooner she finished, the less time she would be around that "smelly ol' horse." Betsy, the horse, seemed to sense Vel's distaste; every time Vel connected the breeching straps to the buggy hitch, Betsy would drop another load. Vel was getting tired of the routine and the smell. She was twenty years old, had been teaching third grade now for more than two years, and she was still hitching the buggy.

"Why don't one of the others do this chore for a while?" she thought. "Why am I always the one?" She simply did not believe her father when he said that she did it best.

She could hear him clearly: "The bellyband harness has the right tension when you hitch the buggy."

"He's punishing me for something, or maybe he just don't like me as much as he likes Lala," she reasoned. "Lala should be doing this servant's work anyway. But no, the reason why she don't is always the same—she takes too long. And Rosa is afraid of horses. But Bobby. Why not Bobby?"

Martha appeared on the back porch, dressed in her nurse's attire. It was not the regular uniform that practical nurses wore. She made it to follow her usual style of dress: all white, high collar, tight bodice and full material above and below the waist, with a mid-calf hemline. On her head was an abbreviated version of a cap. The starched scalloped crown was made to look more like a tiara than nurse's apparel. The look of purity was completed by the white crocheted shawl draped over her shoulders, although the weather did not promise to be chilly. She watched Vel for a moment then asked, "You not finished yet?"

Vel eyed her mama and sarcastically replied, "Almost."

Martha sat in a chair on the porch and rocked while she waited.

"Mama, Bobby like to ride Betsy, so why don't Papa make him hitch the buggy?"

Martha's first thought was to run down the list of Bobby's chores—feeding the chickens, slopping the hogs, and milking the cows—in contrast to Vel's one chore. Instead she asked, "Chile, would you rather clean the mess that horse make?"

"No, ma'am."

"Well, then."

The division of labor was all well and good, but Vel was a grown lady-teacher and hitching the buggy was undignified. Plus she was dating now and she didn't want any of her admirers to happen by while she was hitching the horse. So in spite of not getting any support from

Mama, she made up her mind that this was the last time she would do this chore.

"Looks like Betsy made her usual mess."

Phillip's voice scared Vel. She turned to see him standing on the porch next to Mama. It sounded like he was making comments on her private thoughts. No matter what else Vel felt about her father, she was afraid of him. Even when she stood up to him in defiance, she trembled.

Phillip walked up to and pulled on the bellyband. "You did a good job."

"Thanks, Papa."

"This is the last time you'll have to hitch the buggy."

Now she was sure that he had read her thoughts. Or maybe he was he just saying that to mock her?

Martha tapped her foot impatiently, "If y'all ready, can we get started? I got to meet Dr. Rossini." She was anxious to leave so there was no opportunity for Vel to get any further explanation. Martha called to Bobby inside the house. "Bobby, come on."

Bobby ran out, dressed and ready. A handsome beanpole of a boy on the brink of manhood, he was dressed in a white shirt and tie and a pair of dark brown pants. He didn't know why he was told to dress up, but he suspected there was something special going on.

"Boy, get that mess cleaned up so we can go," Phillip commanded.

Martha interrupted, "Mister, I'm late. He can do that when he gets back. Plus he's got on his good clothes."

That was the final word on the matter. When Mama called Papa *Mister*, she was serious. Phillip made no further delays. Vel watched as the three took their seats in the buggy.

The carriage was an impressive one. The buggy body was mounted on accordion springs, which sat on four white spoked wagon-type wheels with hard rubber rims. A leather tufted bench seat was in the front, another in the rear. Phillip occupied the driver's position on the left. The reins passed through openings above a low leather padded wall that separated the carriage from Betsy's backside. Martha sat on the front bench seat next to Phillip. Bobby occupied the entire back seat. He had freedom to slide from side to side behind or between Mama and Papa. The leather-fringed top, supported by four metal posts fastened to the floor frame, protected the riders from sun and rain. In the back was a leather covering with a window-like opening through which the driver could see if he turned around. The sides and the front were open.

With everyone in place, Phillip turned Betsy onto the graveled street. Vel brushed her skirt free of dust stirred up by the horse's hoofs. She pulled her compact out of her skirt pocket and refreshed her make-up and patted down her hair. She was on her way to spend the day with Viola.

Viola and Vel were lifelong friends. Viola's mother, Gertrude Auzenne, and Martha were also lifelong friends. Gertrude had fallen on hard times when her husband died and she was forced to support her family of four by taking a job as a seamstress at Winsberg's department store. Although Martha and Gertrude no longer associated with each other socially, their daughters remained fast friends. Today they were going to the movie theater to see *The Great Ziegfeld.*

THEY RODE in silence. Betsy clip-clopped through the colored section by way of Court Street. During Reconstruction the whole area had been called Niggerville. After the Emancipation Proclamation, a large number of freed slaves had remained in the area, having no place else to go. In 1870 the town took the name of the rich family—Estilette—that had acquired most of the acreage from former plantations.

Now, in 1936, Estilette boasted a population of 25,000, but only 9,000 were colored. Racism and a lack of work caused the shift in population. Many of the freed slaves went to Mississippi because of the greater need for cotton pickers. And many left out of fear. After the acquisition of the vast acreage of land by Judge Estilette, the property was resold to whites eager to recover from the war, and Estilette rapidly became the heart of racism for the parish. The Southern Pacific Railroad track was the dividing line. The white folks lived on the north and the east sides, and the colored folks lived on the south and west. Over the years few things had changed; although the scars of the past had scabbed over, much of the hurt still remained.

Most of the colored-owned businesses were located on this gravel section of Court Street. The dry cleaners, a bicycle shop, barber shop, beauty shop, a cafe, and the grocery store made up the shopping district. As they passed the Sugar Patch Cafe, Martha looked at the group of men standing and sitting in front.

"Why they got to always hang out like that?"

"They don't have work," Phillip answered.

"I know times are rough but that's not why they hanging 'round."

Bobby leaned forward, eager to get in on the conversation "Why then, Mama?"

"They selling illegal liquor in there, that's why."

Phillip was silent. Martha continued after a pause. "You would think they get enough to drink at them juke-joints."

Bobby's curiosity was still unsatisfied. He was a tenth grader thirsting for knowledge any way he could get it. His chin remained cushioned on his mama's shoulder.

"What's a juke-joint?"

"A place of ill repute where they play gut-bucket music and no self-respecting Negro or Creole would be caught dead there."

Phillip cleared his throat. Bobby was familiar with that sound. He had heard it many times when his father was about to correct something somebody had said, or was getting ready to say something that nobody else knew.

"*Juke*, J-U-K-E, is a holdover from an African word meaning evil or disorderly. When the blues music started being played in public, these places were called juke-houses because the good church-going folks considered the music sinful. Now they call them juke-joints. I don't know what your mama's talking about, saying no self-respecting Negro would be caught dead in one. I consider myself self-respecting and I've been in quite a few in my time."

Martha laughed and playfully brushed Phillip's shoulder with her hand, "Oh, Phillip." Then she turned to Bobby, "Don't pay no attention to Papa. He's joshing."

"I'm not joshing. Last week I was in a cafe that had a juke box playing music."

Bobby could tell from the low chuckle and quivering shoulders that his father continued to enjoy the joshing. What he did not understand, however, was the ironic sarcasm neatly hidden by his father's use of humor. It also eluded Martha. Phillip liked the advantage of knowledge. Phillip smiled. He had made his point, whether or not they understood it.

Martha, who had been looking in the direction of the cafe, abruptly turned straight ahead and said, "That's ol' Judas."

"Who, Mama?"

"That old man walking with a stick in front of the Sugar Patch."

Bobby sat up and turned his head quickly.

"Don't let him see you looking."

"How I'm gonna see him if I don't turn around?"

"That's Silas," Martha explained. "He used to oversee for Grandpa. My papa trusted that man and Lord knows I don't know why. I'm sure that nigger killed Papa."

Phillip cut his eyes at Martha. The spirit of joshing rapidly faded. The reins cracked down on Betsy's back and the carriage lurched forward. Phillip spat out, "It was an accident."

"That's what he say. But I never believed it." Martha resumed explaining to Bobby. "One day my papa took Silas hunting. It was just he and Papa. And he brought Papa back dead. Face was blown off. I never did like that nigger since."

Phillip kept his eyes facing forward. He knew Martha didn't want to hear what he had to say about the matter. He said it anyway. "The sheriff investigated and said Mr. Broussard shot himself accidentally when he stumbled and dropped his shotgun."

"Silas lied. I know he killed Papa."

Bobby had never heard this story before. None of the children had. It was never talked about, and the only reason it was a topic now was Martha's chance sighting of Silas.

Bobby was full of questions. "Why would Mr. Silas want to kill Grandpa?"

"He didn't like him. Used to talk behind his back." Martha was now committed to tell all. "He used to say, 'Mr. Joe ain't nuttin' but po' trash who think he white. He ain't got nuttin' but that broken-down plantation house and forty acres.' Papa worked hard to keep up that place but it was just too big. And Lord knows he give Silas enough work, but he wasn't nothin' but an ol' Judas."

Bobby was shocked. "Why isn't he in jail, then?

"I don't know. But I do know he hated my papa. And after all Papa did for that nigger."

Phillip brought the whip down on Betsy's rump. "That's enough."

They rode on in silence, the gravel crunching under the wheels and hoofs. When they crossed the railroad tracks the sound changed to the rhythmic drumming of hoofs against asphalt. They had reached the white part of town.

The people passing on foot, in buggies, wagons, on bicycles or in motorcars waved greetings—white and colored alike. It seemed everybody in Estilette knew Professor Fergerson and his family. Phillip had been principal of the colored school for ten years and that meant all of the colored people in town knew who he was. Whites knew him by reputation if not through other dealings.

Bobby watched his parents. A few minutes earlier they seemed so friendly, and now they were silent strangers. The shift came while talking about Silas. He believed that they loved each other, but sometimes their actions, like now, they did not show that they did. Then his mama began laughing.

"Lord, Phillip I forgot to tell you 'bout Mrs. Rossini's new house girl."

"The one with the gap teeth?"

"Yes, that's the one."

Both of them were laughing. The untold story was so amusing that Martha held Phillip's steering arm as she rocked back and forth with laughter. A moment before, Bobby had decided his parents were angry with each other. Now he was confused.

Martha took a deep breath and turned to Phillip. "Last week while I was over waiting for Dr. Rossini to come back from making his rounds, me and Miz Frannie was drinking coffee and she told me a story that made me split my side laughing. She told me this new gal she got working for her been cleaning going on three weeks and never opened her mouth. One day Miz Frannie told her to figure a way to clean the chandelier. Well, the gal commenced to hissing and whistling and Miz Frannie could hardly understand a word she said. Then she noticed that wide gap in the gal's teeth. Miz Frannie asked her why she didn't do something about having her teeth fixed. The gal say, 'I am doing somethin' about it.'"

Phillip whacked Betsy across the rump one more time. He looked at Martha, who was still giggling.

"Then Miz Frannie asked her which dentist she was seeing and the gal said she wasn't seeing no dentist, she was taking Miz Esther's Teeth Oil. Miz Frannie wanted to know what that medicine was supposed to do. And the gal said when she drank six bottles the gap would close up and her teeth would grow back together. Lord, Me and Miz Frannie laughed and laughed."

Bobby could see his father's shoulders start to shake. Martha continued, "Then Miz Frannie said, 'I sure am glad you not like the other niggers around here. You don't believe in all these silly snake oil cures. I can have a decent conversation with you and if I didn't know better I'd think you was white.'"

Phillip spoke for the first time since he ended the conversation about Silas. "Francesca Rossini's not that white herself."

"That's cause she from southern Italy. They dark-skinned."

"Probably mixed with North African."

5

THIS STATEMENT brought them into the driveway of the Rossini house. Martha got out and walked in the back door, announcing herself as she entered. Bobby took his mother's seat in the front, next to his papa. He was anxious to know more. He knew that his father would oblige, especially now that they were alone.

"Papa, why did Mama get so mad when she was talking about Silas?"

"Your mama is still angry about things that happened a long time ago. She's disappointed because her life didn't turn out the way it was supposed to."

"I don't understand."

"Well, maybe it's time you do."

Phillip headed Betsy toward the business section of town. Bobby had it figured out now; they were going to buy him a suit. This had happened every year since he turned twelve. They would go to Winsberg's, the largest department store in town. Bobby would be fitted for a three-piece suit, the extra pants being his choice of any that would go with the coat.

Phillip cleared his throat. Bobby knew that this was another of his papa's habits when he was getting ready to say something that no one else knew. "Your great-great-grandfather, Grandpa's father's father, was named Antoine Broussard. He was a rich free man of color and he came to this town in 1845. He bought four thousand acres. That's about six square miles of land. And then he bought two hundred slaves to work the place."

"He had slaves?"

"Yep. Under the Black Codes of 1724 he had the same rights and privileges that were enjoyed by any other free person. Where we live now is where the mansion house was. The four thousand acres stretched from Bayou Courtableau all the way to where the courthouse is now."

"Our family used to own all of that?"

"Your mama's family."

"What happened to it?"

Phillip knew the oral history of the land. He had heard it many times from Joseph Broussard, who had heard the stories passed on from his ancestors. He felt it time to pass it on. Bobby was old enough now to hear and understand. "When Antoine Broussard bought all that land from Kenneth Estilette, it was overrun with honeysuckle, pecan, willow, and moss-covered oaks. He recognized the potential of the rich black soil and had his slaves clear and cultivate the land. Then he built levees and canals to control the water. And when the surrounding land was flooded, his bottomland was dry. He planted cotton, sugar cane, and sweet potatoes, and shipped his crops to New Orleans. In fifteen years he had tripled his wealth. As he grew richer and richer, Kenneth Estilette watched and got madder and madder.

Phillip seized this opportunity to pass on the history of land thievery, the likes of which was replicated all over the South. He continued, "After the Civil War and during Reconstruction, Judge Estilette had second thoughts about a man of color owning so much land. And on top of that, he had sold Antoine what he thought was worthless land, but which made Antoine a very rich man. So Judge Estilette said the land was sold by mistake. And he began to dig up covenants and ordinances which made land ownership by a person of 'mixed blood' illegal, although it wasn't illegal at the time of the sale. Over the next few years Judge Estilette got back all the land except the forty acres that your grandpa owned."

"Wow. I didn't know any of that."

"Your mama doesn't like to talk about it. That's why she so angry. She could be a very rich, Creole, society lady with many servants."

Bobby didn't know what to say, but there were many questions tumbling through his mind. Was the town named after the judge? Was the judge related to Stephen Estilette, the newspaper publisher? What happened to the plantation house? What's the difference between Creole and white? But he remained silent. On this short trip he had received more information than he knew what to do with. He decided he should think about it for a while before asking any more questions.

Phillip's voice interrupted Bobby's thoughts. "You still thinking about going into medicine?"

"Not really."

"What does that mean?"

"Nothing."

"Nothing?"

Bobby could tell by the tone of his father's voice when he got peeved over word games that avoided straight answers. "I think I might want to do something else."

"Like what?"

"I don't know."

They had just passed J. B. Sandoz and two blocks away was Winsberg's. Phillip directed Betsy to take a right turn at the next corner. Bobby knew then that he had given the wrong answers and had lost his suit. His father had changed his mind about going to Winsberg's. After an interval, filled with only the sound of Betsy's clip-clopping, his father said, "I never got the chance to go to medical school, and I thought maybe that you would."

Hoping to salvage whatever he may have lost, Bobby said, "I didn't mean that I wouldn't go to medical school. Right now, I just don't know."

"But you are going to college."

"Oh, yes, sir."

With that answer Phillip stopped Betsy in front of the Planters Bank. He got down, tied the horse to the hitching rail and said to Bobby, "Come on." Bobby knew something important was about to happen. This was the first time his father had ever taken him to the bank.

A half dozen white people were lined up in front of the three-barred teller windows. Phillip got in line. Bobby stood beside him. He noticed the heads of several whites turn in their direction. Their gazes were not as friendly as those of the people they had passed on Main Street. When it was Phillip's turn in line, he slid a passbook under the bars to the teller on the other side and said, "I'd like to draw out seven hundred dollars, please." Bobby paid particular attention to his father's intonation of the word "please." The white man behind the bars was only a few years older than Vel, but Bobby noticed the politeness with which his father had spoken.

The teller looked at Phillip, then at the book. He said nothing, then turned and walked away. The teller headed in the direction of a man sitting at a desk in the back near the vault. The sign on the desk read *President.* The man behind the desk stood and looked in Phillip's direction, then he approached the window with the teller trailing behind.

"Phillip?"

"How you do, Mr. Mayer?"

"This is a lot of money you want to take out."

"That's right, sir."

There was a pause, as if Mr. Mayer was waiting for Phillip to explain why he wanted to draw out such a sum; but Phillip stood tall and erect without another word.

"Well, you certainly have more than enough to cover this withdrawal." With that statement Mr. Mayer gave the passbook to the teller and headed back to his desk.

Phillip put the money in his pocket and left the bank with Bobby at his heels. Phillip guided Betsy east on Union Street until they got to Landry. They clip-clopped north on Landry Street. Bobby was afraid to ask where they were headed or for what purpose, afraid to break the safety of silence. Finally, they stopped in front of the Bordelon Motor Company. Then it was clear.

"You buying a car! " Bobby spurted out as if an unseen force had prompted him. Phillip looked at him, smiled, and then headed for the entrance door. Bobby ran behind and caught up.

They walked into the showroom area and looked at the six models of the latest Ford motorcars on display. Phillip knew exactly what he wanted. He picked out a beautiful four-door sedan and the two of them circled the car a couple of times. Two white salesmen watched suspiciously, but didn't approach them. Phillip stood quietly by the sedan. Bobby got nervous. He knew the white men did not want to wait on colored people. He wanted to yell out to them, "My papa got the money to buy a car. " He looked at Papa for a signal of what he was going to do. Phillip remained proud and silent.

After ten minutes of waiting, Phillip walked out of the showroom with Bobby close behind. They headed into the service area. Bobby struggled to keep stride for stride with his father. Phillip walked past the oil change area, brake repairs, and tune-up. Every white mechanic they passed stopped work to watch the march of the colored men who had no business in the service area. Phillip stopped in front of major motor repair and greeted the only colored mechanic in the place, Henry Eaglin, who looked up from connecting spark plugs. "Well, how you doin', Professor?"

"Just fine, Henry.

"What can I do for you?"

"I'm looking to buy a car. "

"Professor, a man like you shoulda had a motorcar a long time ago. "

"I was waiting until they had more models to choose from. "

"You come to the right place. We got a gang of 'em out there. "

Phillip chuckled slightly, "I know. Now I'd like for somebody to wait on me."

"I understand." Henry toweled off his hands. "Lemme see if I can rustle up somebody to help you."

Henry threw his towel into the car engine with defiance and headed into the showroom. Phillip and Bobby followed some distance behind. They stopped just inside the showroom door while Henry walked up to the two men who had observed Phillip earlier. After a few seconds, Henry and one of the men headed in Phillip's direction. Henry spoke in his around-white-folks voice, "Mr. Briley, this here is Professor Fergerson I was telling you 'bout." Henry made a special effort to emphasize the word "Professor." And then he continued in the traditional manner, "He sho' would like to buy one of our motorcars."

Phillip understood what Henry's manner and style was about. Bobby was perplexed. Phillip extended his hand and said, "Mr. Briley."

At first Briley was not too eager to return the handshake but there was not much else he could do if he wanted to make the sale, and he had not had a sale all week. He took a couple of steps to his right, blocking the line of sight from his buddy salesman, and met Phillip's hand with a limp response. "Professor, you see something you'd like?"

"I sure do."

"Well, we'll just have to get you over to the bank to get some financing."

"I'll pay cash."

That statement left Briley speechless. A wide grin spread across Henry's face, and he knew it was time to leave or he might just bust out laughing. "I guess I'll get back to my work. See you later, Mr. Professor . . . Mr. Briley."

Phillip made arrangements with Henry to drive Betsy and the buggy home. Then he and Bobby drove out in a brand spanking new 1936 DeLuxe Fordor sedan. Phillip headed the dark blue motorcar out onto the highway toward Lafayette. They spent most of the day driving through one little town and then another. It was dusk when they got back to Estilette. Martha almost fainted dead away when she walked out of the Rossini house and saw Phillip and Bobby waiting for her in a Ford motorcar parked right behind Dr. Rossini's Packard.

Martha walked circles around the car, oohing and ahhing and marveling at features she had only seen in magazines. She stood in front of the chromed grill and exclaimed, "Look just like the strings on a harp." She slid her hand over the chrome horn rings and oval headlamps. Then she walked around to the back, tracing her hand along the offset seam from the hood to the trunk compartment. She leaned over to look at her distorted image reflected from the chrome bumper. Then she stood on the running board and opened the passenger-side door. She sat down, taking in a full breath of the new car scent. And with her next breath came, "You gotta teach me to drive."

CONSIDERING THAT the country was in the midst of the Great Depression, 1936 was a good year for the Fergersons. And because Phillip had paid cash for the Fordor, a rumor took wing that they were the richest colored people in town. This year was also a schooling time for Bobby. He did not know it, but Phillip had intentionally guided him into situations that would teach him the ropes of life. In the breeze of summer twilights, Bobby sat for hours on the screened front porch, where Phillip held forth with whomever, listening to talk about world matters. Much of the time Phillip's exchanges of ideas and debates were with Leo Roberts, the county agent. Leo was the eyes and ears of the colored farmers of St. Landry Parish. He knew their feelings, attitudes, and ambitions as well as what crops they planted. So between the two of them, all matters about the educated and the uneducated were stirred in their cauldron of town gossip.

Leo had a master's degree in agriculture from Iowa State University. He and Phillip had met there during Phillip's sabbatical. The friendship that developed prompted Leo to apply for the position of Negro county agent for St. Landry Parish. Prior to his application, the needs of the Negro farmers were handled by the white county agent, which meant they were not handled at all. Phillip had encouraged Leo to accept the challenge of addressing the needs of the Negro farmers, just as Leo's hero, George Washington Carver, had done. Now their discussions were continuations of the subjects they debated in school.

The girls would spy through the window and wonder why Bobby just sat there not saying anything. Martha said, "He just sopping it all up like a sponge." Lala would sit unseen so she could listen from the inside, wanting very badly to join the men on the porch. Martha routinely made a pitcher of lemonade and some teacakes, put them on a tray, and instructed Lala to take the tray to the men. Lala welcomed the chance to get a first-hand hearing of the gossip around town and the goings-on in the world. The other two girls were simply not interested.

Every morning Phillip took his seat near the window in his room and read the *Times Picayune* while having his coffee. This and Carter G.

Woodson's *Negro History* were the only readings outside of his school work that he ever got the chance to do. But they provided all the information he needed for sessions with Leo.

"Roosevelt said that one-third of the nation is ill housed, ill clothed, and ill fed."

Leo jumped on the new subject as he received his cool glass of lemonade from Lala. "And that's the truth. As a matter of fact, the number is higher than that for colored people around here. A few days ago I was over near Krotz Springs. The CCC is building a levee to hold back the Atchafalaya River over there. There was a group of about thirty or so men workin', and only two of 'em were colored. I parked my truck and got a root beer from the general store. I moseyed on around the side under the Stanback sign, where several colored men was talking, and I joined 'em."

There had been a round of introductions, but most of the men had known Leo already. The men went on complaining that they had been waiting to get work for six months. "There was a time when them damn crackers wouldn't do nigger work. Now that the gov'ment's paying, niggers can't get no work."

"*No* kind of work."

"I'm still waitin' for my forty acres and my mule."

"Just like I been waitin' on them jobs from the CCC."

"Keep on waitin'," said one of them, kicking the dust for emphasis.

Leo was afraid that this idleness might turn to hopelessness. The men were aware that the CCC was paying good money and the white people were getting most of the jobs. Leo commiserated with Phillip, "There just ain't no justice for colored people in good times or bad."

Phillip argued that the answer was not in the temporary work of CCC but rather the ability of colored people to rise to the level of white people in all areas. "As long as white people think of colored people as niggers, and colored people act that way, they'll be niggers. Colored people have to show them that we are just as good as they are in everything, and white people will stop expecting us to be niggers. Look how Jesse Owens showed up those so-called supermen in Germany last week. Now that was *not* the performance of a nigger."

Leo was quick to add, "He sho' wasn't pickin' no cotton."

The two men had a good laugh. Bobby and Lala did too.

6

THE FERGERSONS DROVE to church in the motorcar on the first Sunday after it was purchased. Since there was not enough room in the car for LightFoot, Phillip said to him, "John, if you like, you can hitch up Betsy and ride to church. As a matter of fact, since we won't be using the buggy any more, consider that it is yours to use whenever you want."

"I 'preciate that, Phillip," answered LightFoot. "But I would like to take a ride in your new car sometimes, when you're not too busy."

Vel was the most grateful of all the family for this new form of transportation; she never had to hitch the buggy again. Now her only chore was to be first in the car. Each member of the family rushed to stake their claim for a seating position. Vel got the left window seat in the back, Lala the right; the middle was for Rosa, who would have to lean constantly one way or the other to look out. Bobby chose the seat in front between his mama and papa, "so I can watch and learn every move Papa makes."

That first Sunday Phillip headed in a direction different from his usual route. Martha looked past Bobby at Phillip. "Mister, why you going this way?"

"To avoid the gravel. I don't want rock dings on the car." He cut across from the asphalt of Main Street to the paved, tar-covered bricks of Church Street.

As they passed Sacred Heart Church, Lala announced, "That's the steeple Uncle Johnny fell from."

"Hush, girl," admonished Martha.

"I remember it, Mama. I was six years old, and . . ."

Phillip interrupted, "Your mama don't like to hear talk like that." He knew this subject brought unpleasant memories to Martha; he also knew that she didn't want to come this way because she had just called him Mister. Rosa made the sign of the cross when they passed the graveyard. The graveyard served both the white and the colored congregations. And the burial arrangement maintained the separation of the dead souls in the same manner that they had lived. There was a huge statue of the crucifixion on a hill in the center; the white were buried in the front of the statue and the colored in back. Soon after passing the graveyard entrance gates, the car bounced across the Southern and Pacific railroad tracks and into the gravel. Phillip drove at a snail's pace for the remaining five blocks to Holy Ghost Church. There was less gravel to contend with here than there would have been had he taken the shorter route.

Phillip was head usher for the eight o'clock Mass. He directed the worshipers to vacant pews, and passed out Mass cards so the congregation could follow the service in Latin. In the summertime he had the added responsibility of adjusting the windows to catch the breeze. If it was stiflingly hot he passed out the hand fans with "Lastrap's Mortuary" printed on the front, a reminder that this was the only white funeral home that buried colored. But his most important responsibility was to take up collection. He had been instructed by Father Pat to pass the long-handled basket slowly in front of the reluctant, "as a reminder that God expects their help to carry on His work." LightFoot helped with collection when he was there. He did not attend the eight o'clock Mass regularly. If he came home from a Saturday night in the early morning, he went to an early Mass on the way home. Or he would get a couple hours sleep and then go to the late High Mass, which he didn't like because it lasted too long. But always he would go to Mass. Today he helped Phillip take up collection. While they were preparing the offerings to be delivered to the altar, LightFoot whispered, "You see that?"

"What?"

LightFoot pointed to the bulletin board over their work area. Phillip read the message.

> The following parishioners have failed to tithe ten percent of their yearly earnings to Holy Ghost Church. This list is a reminder that all should do their part to support the work of the church. (Signed) Father O'Neill.

Phillip saw his name on the list. He was furious. Questions pounded away in his brain. How did Father O'Neill know how much he was putting in the collection basket? There had been a request that everyone write their names on envelopes provided for this purpose; but he never used the envelope. He simply dropped his weekly donations in the collection basket. How did Father know how much he was earning? And why would he embarrass anyone by putting this on a board for all to see? He was so upset, LightFoot had to complete the consolidation of the collection and deliver it to the altar alone.

FATHER PATRICK O'Neill had been the pastor of Holy Ghost for more than ten years. He was an energetic and persuasive man. This was his first assignment and he had been welcomed with open arms by his predecessor, Father Sean McCann.

Father Mac had come to Estilette in 1898 to establish a mission for colored Catholics. Prior to his arrival, the colored were allowed to occupy a few back pews at Sacred Heart. So the white people were extremely happy over the arrival of Father Mac. In fact, he had been assigned because the pastor of Sacred Heart had requested that the bishop make provisions for the growing population of "our colored faithful. " A wealthy white parishioner even donated a barn as a place of service and as a residence for the new priest. After the mission was established, the colored were not allowed to attend Sacred Heart at all because they now had their own place for worship.

The building of the new Holy Ghost Church was a marvel of cooperation. Father Mac solicited lumber and material, happily given by white businessmen, and inveigled a labor force from Creole construction workers, eager to have their own church. Within his first four years Father Mac had built a fine church and a comfortable rectory. He no longer had to say Mass in a barn or sleep in a hayloft. Several years later he was able to get an elementary school and high school built in the same manner. As the years passed, the work of providing for the parish became more demanding. Father Mac, getting on in age, was frequently visited by the gout. Consequently, the bishop sent Father Patrick O'Neill to help. It seemed that Father Pat was a duplicate image of Father Mac. They solicited the white Catholics so often, one parishioner was heard referring to them as the Irish Mafia. "They usually get what they want by hook or by crook, " he said. "To them, the end justifies the means. But they mean well, and if it keeps the coloreds in their own church, I don't mind helping."

When Father Mac died, Father Pat took over as pastor. For years he petitioned for an assistant priest but the bishop ignored his requests. So his only alternative of providing for his flock took the form of mandatory tithing, which he used to pay lay personnel to help with the business of running the parish.

Phillip's appearance in the sacristy that Sunday morning was a surprise to Father Pat. Everyone knew the priest had a busy schedule on Sundays. He said four Masses, and between each he would meditate. The parishioners did not usually trouble Father with business matters, except emergencies.

When Father Pat slipped out of his cassock and turned to greet Phillip, he assumed that Phillip was on a mission of urgency about church business. Phillip's personal urgency was still burning inside him. He confronted Father Pat with indignation that had been building since he saw the bulletin. Phillip laid out his complaint as he had rehearsed it in his mind. Of course, Father Pat explained and reaffirmed his policy of tithing. "Since ye can afford such a splendid automobile, surely ye can afford to do your duty to help support God's work."

"Father, my financial business is not your concern."

"Phillip, my good man, ye are a member of me flock and all of your dealings are my concern and the concern of God."

"Why would you put my name on the board like that for everyone to see?"

"I don't remember seeing that your name was on any envelope."

"I don't use the goddamn envelopes. I put money in the basket."

"Now, Phillip. I can't allow ye to take the name of the Lord God in vain."

"It's just an expression. It doesn't mean anything."

"To me it does."

"I'm sorry, Father. I'm upset. But you had no right to publish my name like that."

"Now I think maybe this conversation is over. I've got another Mass to say."

"That Mass doesn't begin for at least another thirty minutes."

"Still, I refuse to discuss the matter any further. Especially in ye state of mind. I think now you should leave the sacristy. I have more important matters to look to."

"This is important to me."

"Phillip, ye have said enough. Please leave."

"I'll leave, all right. Good-bye."

Phillip stormed out of the sacristy vowing never to return. He had been "put in his place" by another white man. When this was done by a man of the cloth, whom Phillip expected to accept all God's children as equals, it was an unforgivable sin.

Phillip's family was sitting in the car waiting. Martha could tell by the enlarged blood vessel pounding in Phillip's forehead that something had happened, but she dared not ask what. She knew Phillip would tell her when he was good and ready, and not before. They sped home in tense silence. Gravel flew in all directions, dinging the car and peppering Betsy, LightFoot, and the buggy as the car zoomed past.

7

COCK-A-DOODLE-DOO sounded. Then another. And another until there was a chorus of calls and responses announcing daybreak.

Butchering Day. Mid-October was hog-killing time. This provided the meat needed during winter. On his farm in the back part of the acreage, Phillip had penned up two hogs for this purpose. By enclosing them it was possible to monitor their food intake: corn for fattening, and a diet of nutrients to improve the quality of the meat.

Everyone had a special assignment. Bobby collected and stacked firewood. He then built a roaring fire around a large black cauldron filled with water. LightFoot constructed a long table out of pine board, supported it with sawhorses, and covered it with oilcloth. This was where they would lay out and cut up the meat. Then he cleaned the meat-grinding and the sausage-stuffing machines and mounted them on the table. Martha washed the pots and pans needed to hold the various cuts of meat. A group of four neighbors, including Naomi, did the many jobs of scalding, scraping, slicing, grinding, making lard, and cleaning guts. Everyone helped except the girls.

Martha was definite about her wishes on this matter. "It's not ladylike for them to be helping outside on butchering day. I'd prefer that they stay inside."

Phillip did not argue the point, so Rosa and Lala took their seats at the window where they could see everything, except the killing, which they hated to watch. Vel was nowhere to be found, since she no longer wanted to be associated with farm life in any form. Even when she was in school she would exchange her lunch of biscuits for a lunch of store-bought bread. She disliked homemade farm food as much as she disliked hitching the buggy.

The victim hogs waited foot-bound in the wagon for the slaughter. BookTau had hauled them in from the farm at daybreak. He was the strongest man in Estilette. Six feet ten inches tall, weighing 270 pounds, he could lift anything that wasn't nailed down. He was in his mid-twenties with the mental age of a ten-year-old. BookTau would do anything that he was told, without question, and he enjoyed playing children's games. Most folks in Estilette said he was not "all there," but no one in their right mind would make him mad because he could change quickly from pussycat to lion. He chewed tobacco, never wore shoes, and had a husky laugh that could be heard for a country mile.

While everyone waited for the water to boil, LightFoot took out his harp and played the "Foot Stomping Blues," BookTau's favorite. He danced up a storm. A light wind brought this early morning discord into the kitchen where Martha was washing and scrubbing pots. She walked to the window and looked at the command performance that was now accompanied by clapping from the butchering team. A cloud of dust, stirred up by BookTau's huge feet, drifted over the circle of gyrating bodies. Martha shook her head in disgust and walked away from the window. She was standing with her arms folded across her chest when Phillip and Bobby entered the kitchen.

"Is all that gut-bucket music and dancing necessary?"

"They aren't hurting anything."

"They kicking up a dust that'll get all over the meat."

"It'll settle by the time the hog is butchered."

"You know I don't cotton to this kind of carrying on."

"I know, Martha. Just stay in the house, then."

"Why's he gotta have that voodoo woman here?"

Phillip washed his hands in the sink. Martha continued stacking the pots and pans.

"Mama, where is the voodoo woman?" Bobby asked.

Phillip cut in before another word was spoken. "John asked me and I told him it was all right."

"You know I don't like that black woman."

"Woman, shut the hell up."

"I don't want that voodoo woman in my house."

"I'm getting sick and tired of you puttin' on airs, and I don't wanna hear none of your damn mess today."

Then there was silence. That was final enough. Now it was clear to Bobby that the "he" was Uncle Johnny. But this was the first time he had heard Naomi called "voodoo woman." Phillip wiped his hands and threw the towel on the table with anger, saying to Bobby, "Get those pots and pans and take 'em outside." Bobby immediately obeyed. Phillip grabbed the pot of coffee off the stove and stormed out behind Bobby, leaving the screen door quivering. Martha, hands on her hips, looked after him, shaking her head. After a few seconds she came back to life, reached on the shelf, got a coffee pot, and started brewing more coffee.

Leo arrived as the first bubbles broke the surface of the boiling water. He unwrapped his razor-sharp knives, pulled a hair from one of the hogs, held it between his thumb and forefinger, and sliced it in midair. He was ready. One of his duties as county agent was to supervise and teach the proper techniques of butchering. He was an expert in this. He went from farm to farm demonstrating his special skill.

WHEN THE time was right, Leo killed the first hog. Hitting the jugular in the neck was tricky business. It had to be exactly right for the blood to come gushing out. The blood was caught in a pail, to be taken immediately into the kitchen, where it would be mixed with rice dressing and made into *boudin*, a blood sausage.

The body of the dead hog was put on an inclined platform and boiling water was poured it over until the bristles were soft enough to be scraped off with sharp knives. Next Leo uncovered the Achilles tendons in the back legs and wedged in a spreader pole that held the legs twenty-four inches apart. At this point, BookTau was called. He picked up the three-hundred-pound slaughtered beast like a ten-pound sack of flour and hung it from a limb in the chinaberry tree. The team cheered. LightFoot played a salute on his harp that prompted BookTau to hide his face, run around in circles, and giggle like a six-year-old.

Leo slashed the hog from the anus to the head with one smooth motion of his knife. The internal organs slid down into the waiting washtub. Then the various butchering operations took place. Every portion of the hog was used—the tradition from the time of slavery.

Lard, cracklings, sausage, roast, ham, bacon, chops, liver, pig's feet, hog's head cheese, brains, chitterlings, and boudin were the most popular by-products. Nothing was wasted; they used everything but the grunt. Even the bladder was blown up for Bobby to use as a kickball.

The second hog was killed. Phillip selected special cuts from both animals and put them aside. Then he divided the remainder of the meat from one hog among the people who had helped. He kept all of the meat from the second hog for use by the family. This would be salted or smoked, to last without refrigeration through the winter.

The final chore was the gut-bucket. And it *was* a chore. The intestines were cut in five-foot lengths and the contents dumped. They were turned inside out with a peach-tree stick so that any remaining feces could be thoroughly washed away. Then the guts, as they were called at this stage of the operation, were soaked in vinegar. The stench was overpowering. It was hard to imagine how anyone who had breathed in this foul odor could eat chitterlings. But many did, with great delight. Martha did not eat them, nor would she cook them. She believed that "only niggers ate chitterlings," and insisted that this delicacy be given to the people who helped.

Butchering day ended with an earthen jug of cherry bounce, a sweet liqueur, being consumed under the chinaberry tree. Lala ventured out by this time and sat next to her papa on the bench. Phillip did not let Lala or Bobby drink cherry bounce. "Y'all too young to drink liquor, but you can have some of your mama's lemonade with the cracklings." The team stayed as long as the light from the fire and the contents of the jug lasted. Bobby liked this part of butchering day best because of the stories—folk tales as varied as the people on the

butchering team. Some of the stories were raunchy and some were risque, but Papa let him stay. Phillip figured he was old enough at sixteen to hear about life.

BookTau jumped up. "Me first! " Phillip laughed and agreed. Each year BookTau wanted to be first and he always told a tale that only he found funny. The others would laugh anyway. Some indulged him, and some even laughed *at* him, though they were careful to disguise their reaction so he would not know. BookTau stood up to perform.

> "Little Sally Walker, sittin' in a saucer,
> Weepin' and cryin' for someone to love her,
> Rise Sally, rise, wipe yo' weepin' eyes,
> Put yo hand on yo' hip, let yo' backbone slip,
> Shake the pussy to the east,
> Shake the pussy to the west,
> Shake the pussy to the one who you love the best. "

He howled at the end of his story, twisting his hands down between his legs like a naughty little boy. The laughter of the others was mixed with shock and surprise. Phillip looked at Lala to see her reaction. She was embarrassed.

Lilly Ellis stood up with her cup of cherry bounce wavering in her hand. "Lemme tell y'all about this lady wanna-be. She was born way back in Devil's Swamp. Her papa was an ol' Cajun man and her mama was his servin' girl. This here child look just like a white, and if nobody knowed any better they'd'a thought she was white. She growed up to be pretty as a picture, and she found herself out of place. She didn't want to be a nigger, and the white folks who knowed her wouldn't treat her like white. So the *onlyest* thing she could do was leave. She cut her hair and caught a freight train to New York City, hoboing like a boy. When she got there she got a job waitressin' in a fancy restaurant. In no time a-tall she was married to a fancy white-man lawyer. She was happy 'cause this made her what she wanted to be—a white woman. Well, child, guess what? She had a baby, and that baby come out jet-black like her mama. That white man divorced her butt so fast she never saw the light of another day in New York City. She come on back home with her white-black baby 'cause she couldn't be what she wanna be."

Lewis Richard, pouring his fourth cup of cherry bounce, loudly proclaimed, "That remind me of these two niggers playin' the dozens. The first nigger say to the other, 'Yo' sister so ugly she got to pull a sheet up over her face so sleep can sneak up on her.' The other nigger say, 'That ain't nothin'. Yo' papa so ugly he got to sneak up on a glass of water to get a drink.' The first nigger say, 'Yo' wife so ugly the wind won't even blow in her face.' Then the other nigger say, 'Yo' mama so fat, when she walk down the street the peoples walking behind her think they followin' a wagon pullin' two bales of cotton.'"

LightFoot was next. "That ain't nothin'. Now lemme tell ya'll about the blues. They say the man who started the blues was named W. C. Handy from Memphis, Tennessee. But the blues was started long before that in the dives and the sin-houses. It was a way for colored people to sing away their pain and troubles, most of which come from the evils of the white man. Now you take the stories of John Henry and the boll weevil and the Titanic. It was like this . . . John Henry, he outdid the white man's steam engine with just a hammer and his bare hand and his mighty strength. He was a steel-drivin' man. And then there was the boll weevil, who lived off the cotton.

He was like the niggers, always looking for a home. And don't forget Shine. He was on the Titanic. It was going down and the captain's daughter come to Shine and say, 'Shine, save poor me.' Shine say, 'You better jump your white ass in the water and swim like me.' Shine jumped in the water and met up with a shark. Shine said, 'You may be the king of the ocean and the king of the sea, but you got to be a swimming motherfucker to outswim me.' And Shine swam on."

Naomi stood silhouetted against the flickering flames, munching cracklings. She said, "I wasn't gonna say nothin', but since LightFoot opened his mouth, I'm gonna tell y'all how to attract a lover. First, you got to write his name on a piece of parchment paper with some dove's-blood ink, and then pin that paper to the bottom of a voodoo doll's foot. Then stand the doll on a clean cloth that's been boiled for two hours in bluing water. Then you gotta anoint the doll with love oil and sprinkle it with love powder. Now then, you take some love incense and light it. And while the love incense is burnin', recite the Forty-fifth and Forty-sixth Psalms. Wrap the doll in a red cloth, *bright* red, and hide it in a dark place. When yo' lover come through the door, and he *will* come, get the doll and bury it in a secret place. And I want ya'll to know that how I got LightFoot."

LightFoot jumped up and began chasing Naomi around the fire. "Wait till I catch up with you!"

Naomi playfully avoided his attempts. "I'm gonna *have* to wait . . . if you ever gonna catch me."

BookTau got up and joined the chase, "I'll help you, LightFoot!"

Naomi yelled, "Naw, that ain't fair . . . two against one."

Everyone around the fire was laughing and having a good time. Martha and Vel watched from the kitchen window. "Look at 'em out there, drunk as they can be."

"Mama, why you let Lala go out there?"

"Your papa let her go. Sometimes I don't know about that man." Martha went back to stuffing the boudin mixture into the sausage casing, with Rosa's help. Vel continued watching the activities around the fire.

When the laughter died down, Leo said, "Now I gotta say somethin'. We been tellin' lies and havin' a good time . . . and all that is well and good. But we got a couple of youngsters here and they need to learn something about history and about what is going on in the world right now. And this is for you, too, Lilly and Lewis and BookTau. You not too young to hear this either. Phillip, you already know all about this."

"Yeah, I know," Phillip answered. "You've told me this before. So I won't listen."

Leo shoved him playfully, took a sip from his cup, and continued. "During the Reconstruction time, Congress made a proposal to take land from the Confederate kingpins and give it to the freed slaves. That never did pass Congress, but the freed men made up a slogan, 'We gonna git forty acres and a mule.' Now what this meant to them was that they would be able to make a living doing what they was good at doing—farming. They had been farming all their lives. They had raised all the big money crops: the cotton, the corn, the tobacco. And they had raised all the food to feed the entire country for over two hundred years. They didn't get their forty acres and a mule, but two men saw the possibility of agriculture being the way for the colored man to raise himself."

Leo paused, then continued. "One was George Washington Carver and the other was Booker T. Washington. Carver was the first Negro to go to Iowa State University. That's why I went there. He studied agriculture. That's why I studied agriculture. Booker T. Washington started Tuskegee so he could educate the head, the heart, and the hand. Booker T. said to us Negroes, 'Cast down your buckets where you are.' He wanted us to learn by doing. He wanted us to raise our own food and our own livestock. And that's just what I'm doing, teaching colored people how to raise their own. And we doing that right here, right now—tonight. Phillip raised these hogs back there on his farm and he's sharing the meat with us."

Phillip raised his cup in a salute. "That's mighty nice of you, Leo, but you not getting my forty acres."

BookTau jumped up. "'Fessor, can I have the mule?"

Mr. Bobo raised his hand like a schoolboy asking permission to speak. "Since ya'll going back in memory, I 'member somethin'." Mr. Bobo had not said a word all day, just gone quietly about his task of making the crackling. He was the oldest person there and his face told the story of a hard life. He lived alone back of the farm and worked the land for Phillip. Mr. Bobo was the only name for him that anybody ever knew.

"It was nineteen hundred and twenty-two. May sixth. I'll nebber forget it. I was a grown man . . . forty-five years old, when it happened. Now I'm fifty-nine . . . older than the 'fessor here, but he know what I'm talkin' 'bout. They had them a lynchin' in Kirvin, Texas. Them white folks took three colored mens from the sheriff and burned 'em alive. Dere was over five hundred white folks dere, standin' around watchin' and laughin'. "

Silence. A long pause. Everyone waited for him to go on. The fire crackled.

"Dat's all I know. Never did know no mo'. Just heard tell 'bout it but it never left my mind. So it's good to hear the memory of those two mens that Leo was talkin' 'bout. I'm gonna try and 'member that, too. "

Lala walked over, kissed Mr. Bobo, then headed toward the house. Bobby ran to catch up with her.

Phillip watched them disappear. He turned back to the others. "We've heard stories about mean and evil white folks, but I want ya'll to know they got some dumb white folks too. Over in St. Thomasville they had one stoplight. Every night the sheriff sat on the other side of the light behind the Nehi sign and waited to arrest anyone who ran the light. One night a Negro from Baton Rouge drove through and ran that red light. The sheriff pulled him over and walked up to his Chevrolet and said, 'Nigger, you just ran that red light. ' The colored man said, 'I'm sorry, officer. I saw all the white folks going on green, so I thought the red light was for us colored folks. ' The sheriff said, 'You supposed to stop on red. I'm gonna give you a ticket and you goin' to jail. Now I want you to write yo' name and address on this here ticket and you report to the courthouse on Monday. ' Well, the man took the ticket and began writin' like the sheriff told him. On Monday when the sheriff met the judge, the colored man was nowhere to be seen. The judge asked, 'Where is the man you charged with running the red light?' The sheriff said, 'I don't know, your honor, but I got his name and address right here on my ticket. ' The judge looked at the ticket, then he looked at the sheriff. The judge asked, 'Did you write this ticket?' The officer said, 'Yes sir, Judge, your honor. I wrote him up.' The judge said, 'What's written on this ticket says, "Go to hell, you ignorant white son of a bitch." Case dismissed!'"

Phillip's story broke up the gathering. BookTau enjoyed it most. LightFoot gave him a rhythm and BookTau began dancing and slapping his legs. Mr. Bobo got up slowly and headed toward home, back of the farm.

Lilly loaded her arms with meat and chitterlings and said, "See ya'll. Good night."

Naomi slipped her arm through LightFoot's and led him away. He kept playing his harmonica. BookTau followed the blues into the night. Lewis drained the jug into his cup and mumbled, "Cherry bounce for the road."

Leo sat quietly. Phillip stared at the stars, hoping to see the explanation for what Mr. BoBo remembered—for what he, Phillip, did not understand. The fire faded.

8

THE NEXT DAY, Phillip put several pieces of meat wrapped in brown paper in the trunk of the car. He called Bobby to ride with him. They drove to Dr. Rossini's house. Bobby stood alongside his papa, arms loaded with meat, waiting for the knock to be answered. Mrs. Francesca Rossini came to the back door. Although she recognized Phillip, she greeted him through the closed screen door, then left to call her husband. Dr. Rossini came lumbering into the kitchen talking to his wife, himself, and Phillip, all at the same time. He opened the door and invited them in.

Phillip said, "This is my son, Bobby," whom the doctor had not seen since a case of the mumps. "He's almost finished high school, and he's thinking about going to medical school." Bobby was sure this was the main reason he was brought along. Dr. Rossini made a cursory response, as if he believed that the announcement about medical school was a wishful fantasy. Phillip stacked the packages on the table and the doctor thanked him.

The doctor asked, "Anybody over at your place got any aches and pains?"

"We're all doing fine, thank you, Doctor."

"Tell Martha I'll be needing her soon. I've got a patient waiting to be discharged and she'll need some house care."

Martha was beholden to the doctor. The employment that had started as nursemaid to his children turned into her training as a nurse. This occupation provided cash, which Martha kept in a secret place for a rainy day. After a brief exchange about the weather and additional comments about Martha's valuable assistance, Doctor Rossini walked to the door, a sign that it was time for them to leave.

"Thank you for the hog meat, Phillip."

"You're more than welcome, Doctor."

"I really appreciated that Christmas goose last year."

"And you got another one coming this year."

Doc stood in the doorway as Phillip and Bobby climbed into the car.

"Nice looking car you got there. Nineteen-thirty-six?

"Yes, sir."

Phillip proudly turned the key, starting the smooth sounding engine, and backed out of the driveway.

At the next stop Bobby asked, "Who lives here?"

"Mr. Fontenot."

The same routine was enacted, except this time the back door was opened by a colored maid.

"How you doin', 'Fessor Fergerson?"

"Fine. And you, Ida?"

"O.K. Mr. Fontenot next door. Come in. I'll go get him."

Phillip and Bobby entered the kitchen and sat at the table. Bobby's eyes wandered slowly around the room as he compared what he saw with his family's kitchen. "They have running water," he thought, "we have running water. And they have electric lights just like us. Their stove is gas; ours is gas. They have a Frigidaire; we have an icebox. They have an oval table; we have a rectangular table. Their floor is tile; ours is linoleum." Bobby concluded that there was not much difference between the environments in which each family lived. "They the same as us," he thought.

Phillip and Bobby sat waiting. Finally the front door slammed and Mr. William Fontenot walked in. Phillip and Bobby rose. Mr. Fontenot extended his hand, which Phillip shook.

"Nice to see you, Phillip."

"Mr. Fontenot, I'd like you to meet my son, Robert."

Bobby stood next to his father and politely greeted Mr. Fontenot. Fontenot bade them to sit down at the table with him. Phillip presented the gifts for which Fontenot expressed his gratitude. He then called Ida to store the meat.

"How are things going with the school?"

"Just fine, Mr. Fontenot."

"You need anything?"

"Not really, but I was wondering . . ."

Bobby eyed Ida as she leisurely made space in the Frigidaire. He knew she was listening, although it did not seem she heard or cared what was being said. Perhaps by sunrise the next day, colored people all over town would have heard that "Uncle Tom Fergerson give some hog to the white folks to keep his job." This was the same type of distortion that Bobby sometimes overheard on the playground. He knew this was not an accurate description of his father's character, no matter what it seemed like to somebody else.

Phillip outlined the program to which he had given much thought. He called it In-Service Teacher Training. He explained, "Many of the teachers in our colored schools have only a high school education, and it would be beneficial to the school board if they got additional training."

With these words, Phillip's mind shifted to a conversation he had had with Felix Mack, a pioneer of education. Over a supper of warm French bread, butter, and syrup, the sage of strategy in getting white folks to do his bidding had laid the groundwork. Phillip remembered his saying, "We are the only ones who will improve our own education."

Mack went on to tell of a series of classes for teachers begun in his town of Opelousas ten years earlier. "We've got to keep it quiet, though, or the white folks'll get nervous." Mack laid out the entire plan as it had gradually evolved from Southern College in the mid-twenties. Phillip was listening intently. Mack began laughing and pointed his finger. He said, "You just poured syrup in your coffee."

Mack stirred circles of soft butter into his plate of honey-colored goodness, which was his favorite supper meal. He said, "And don't forget to make it sweet for them. Make 'em feel they gettin' lagniappe. Before they know it we'll have this program going over the entire state."

Now it was Phillip's turn to try to establish a program; he could do no less. He proposed to Fontenot that the college at Scotlandville send a professor to conduct classes for which the teachers could get credit toward a bachelor's degree.

Fontenot listened carefully. He was quiet for a long beat and then asked, "When would this take place?"

"On Saturdays during the school year."

Fontenot blew on the lenses his glasses, shook out his handkerchief, and carefully wiped each lens. Holding them at arms' length toward the light, he asked, "Who would pay for this?"

"Each teacher would pay an enrollment fee to the college that would cover the expenses and salary for the instructor."

Fontenot's face brightened and his questions followed more quickly. "Where would these classes be held?"

"At my school, if it's all right with you."

"How long?"

"Until the requirements for a B. A. degree are met."

"Any other requirement from the college?"

"Summer school at the college for three years."

It was clear to Fontenot that Phillip had done his homework. He had no reason to doubt Phillip's intentions. He had built his school from a one-room elementary to twelve grades housed in two buildings. And Fontenot knew that Phillip knew his place, so to speak, so it was not likely that this was a scheme of one kind or another.

Phillip scratched his head—Mack had told him this technique worked—and then he said, "The school board would be getting better teachers with no increase in salaries."

Fontenot looked off into space. After a few moments he said, "Let me think on it. I'll take it up with the board."

Phillip remembered the last admonition from Mack. "Don't push. Let 'em take their time. They don't want to feel that niggers tell them what to do or when." Phillip felt that a good first step had been taken with the delivery of the hog.

Fontenot walked Phillip out, saying, "I want to see this new car that Father O'Neill told me about." Phillip realized then that Father

Pat had gotten information about his salary from William Fontenot. After showing Fontenot the car, Phillip drove out of the yard, deep in thought.

BOBBY LOOKED at his father's face. He knew that preoccupied fixed stare had something to do with the remark that Mr. Fontenot had made about Father O'Neill. Bobby wanted to start a conversation but didn't know exactly how to go about it. Finally after several minutes of silence he asked, "Do you think Father Pat ever says Mass at Sacred Heart?"

Phillip laughed. That question interrupted his reverie. "I don't think so, although I do know that he and Mr. Fontenot play golf at the Cedar Lane Country Club where they probably tell each other nigger jokes." Phillip paused. Should he say more? Should he share with his son what he felt in his heart? That white people are united in one common cause—to keep colored people in their place. Maybe Bobby should learn this from his own experiences. And when he does, maybe he will feel differently. So he decided to only say, "Anyway, that don't give either one of them the right to discuss my salary."

Bobby knew that his papa was consistent about honesty. Right and wrong did not change with the color of a person's skin, nor did a claim of "in God's name" twist a wrong to make it right. Bobby was learning about his papa, but he wondered how long it would be before he went back to church. This was not a good time to bring up this subject. Instead he asked, "When are you going to teach me how to drive?"

"Tomorrow."

Bobby did not expect to have driving lessons so soon after the stress and frustration of his mother's lessons, but he didn't argue.

They drove into the parking lot of *The Chronicle* to see Stephen Estilette. He was the owner-publisher of the town newspaper and the only white person with whom Phillip was on a first-name basis.

Bobby seized the moment, "Papa, is Mr. Estilette related to that Judge Estilette you were telling me about?"

"Judge Estilette was Stephen's great-grandfather. The town is named after him. Our families have known each other a long time."

The ties between the Estilettes and the Broussards went back many years, and Stephen and Phillip frequently talked of yesteryear. Stephen had inherited wealth, much of which, he readily admitted, came because his ancestors re-acquired the Broussard plantation from Martha's ancestors. But bygones were bygones for these two twentieth century victims of slavery, and each knew how far to go with the other.

Phillip and Bobby met Stephen in his office, and the three walked across the lawn to the Estilette house next door. Bobby carried the packages of meat. They entered the front door and walked down a hallway of highly polished oak into the kitchen. Stephen showed Bobby where to store the meat, took a bottle of wine from a rack beneath a cabinet, and said to him, "Bobby, when you finish, there is an orange soda in the icebox waiting for you. We'll be in the parlor."

When Bobby entered the living room, Stephen was describing the qualities of the Bordeaux wine that he'd purchased on his monthly trip to New Orleans. He compared it to other wines in his cellar. This particular bottle was imported from France and Stephen opened it to acknowledge Phillip's gift.

This was Phillip and Bobby's longest stop of the day, and Bobby learned from the conversation that this was a yearly affair. It sounded much like those that took place with Leo on the front porch. Bobby closed his eyes and listened; he heard no difference. When he opened his eyes he saw a white man and a Negro in equal discourse with respect for each other's opinions.

Bobby wandered around the room sipping his Nehi Orange and inspecting the original Audubons that hung on the walls. He stopped before an unusual pastel portrait of a father and son. Bobby turned, his face one large question mark, and looked at Mr. Estilette. Stephen answered without being asked.

"That is a painting of a white father with his mulatto son. It was done by Jules Lion, an artist who lived in New Orleans in the mid-eighteen-hundreds." Stephen got up and walked to the opposite side of the room. "Do you recognize this woman?"

Bobby shook his head slowly and then, with a burst of enthusiasm, as if he were in class, gave his best guess, "Aunt Jemima?"

Stephen laughed and looked at Phillip, who also enjoyed the ironic humor. "This is Marie Laveau, the voodoo queen of New Orleans. And although she is wearing a tignon, she's a long way from being an Aunt Jemima." Stephen explained this was one of several copies of the original by artist George Catlin. "No one really knows who owns the original, but I keep hoping that one day this will be declared the one and only."

Bobby looked at the painting with new appreciation. He thought of Naomi. She was the only real live voodoo woman that he knew. A dozen questions ran through his mind but this was not the time or place. His eyes remained glued to the painting.

Stephen returned to his seat and resumed his conversation about the possibility that Franklin Roosevelt would run for a third term.

When he and Phillip finished the bottle of wine, it was time for Bobby and his dad to leave. Stephen had to get back to work.

On the drive home, Bobby thought about the differences in the relationships between his father and the three white men. Ever since he could remember, his father had given presents from the butchering to white people, and he had wondered why. Before, he had agreed with what he heard on the playground. But now he had a new appreciation of his papa's cleverness. Papa was paying for services that he could not get any other way. From Dr. Rossini he got good medical care for his family. From Mr. Fontenot he got special consideration for his school and a job for Vel. Bobby wondered if this would also be his relationship with white people—the giving of gifts for privileges not allowed by segregation.

However, Bobby could not understand what special favors his papa got from Mr. Estilette. He could not believe it was friendship; they existed in different worlds. It didn't occur to him that his papa and Stephen Estilette simply liked each other.

Bobby enjoyed going places with Papa. It was always an adventure. Now he looked forward to learning how to drive.

9

EACH AND EVERY Sunday, when Phillip dropped the family off at Holy Ghost, Martha asked the question, "When are you going to go to church?" When he picked them up, Rosa presented a new list of sins that he had accumulated. It was a question of how long he could hold out before being forced by the family to make a decision to return to the fold. Not wishing to compromise the position he took against tithing, and still angry because he believed that Father Pat had discussed his salary with Fontenot, he could not make the decision to go back to Holy Ghost. He decided to go to Sacred Heart.

Mass had started. He attracted the attention of the late-coming white parishioners. They stopped in their tracks and looked at him as if he were a creature never before seen. In fact they had never seen a Negro drive a late-model motorcar into their parking lot before. He walked proudly into the vestibule, crossed himself from the blessed-water fount, and found a seat in a partially occupied pew several rows from the front. He joined the worship at the Confiteor.

Two ushers, who had seen him enter, whispered and nodded in Phillip's direction. They were joined, in the rear of the church, by a third, and soon there was a conference of several ushers debating how to handle this intruder in their midst. A decision was not finally reached until the reading of the epistle. One of the ushers walked down the aisle to the pew where Phillip sat, leaned over and whispered into Phillip's ear, "Niggers ain't welcomed here." Phillip looked up at the man and after a moment returned his gaze to his missal and continued reading the epistle. The usher looked back at the group and hunched his shoulders, as if to say, "What shall I do now?" The priest announced the gospel and everyone stood. The usher, not knowing what to do next, went back to the conference of ushers to get instructions. The group was definitely committed to the conviction that this man did not belong in this church.

The voice of the priest cut through their discussion, "The Gospel according to St. Matthew, chapter 10 verses 16 to 22: At that time, Jesus said to his disciples, behold I am sending you out like sheep in the midst of wolves. Therefore be as shrewd as snakes and as innocent as doves."

The hasty approach of two ushers toward the altar caused the priest to look up from his missal. He saw, for the first time, a Negro sitting in a pew near the altar, apparently the target of the approaching ushers, who were swiftly descending on him. Not knowing what else to do, the priest stopped reading. The ushers grabbed Phillip by the arms from both sides. Phillip resisted at first, but reluctantly gave in. The ushers pulled Phillip out of the pew and walked him out of the church as the priest and the congregation watched in silence. The trio reached the church door. Now fully dedicated to their mission, and aided by encouraging words from the group, the ushers pushed Phillip out the door and down the steps. Phillip struggled to keep from falling on his face, preserving what was left of his pride. He turned back and looked into the hate-filled eyes of the guardians of white Catholicism.

The priest now continued the gospel, "Be on your guard against men; they will hand you over to the local councils and flog you in their synagogues."

Phillip took a deep breath, swallowed his anger, and walked to his car with what dignity he had left. He sat behind the steering wheel and read the rest of the gospel. The last sentence echoed in his mind, as he drove out of the parking lot: ". . . and you shall be hated by all men for My name sake; but he who perseveres unto the end, he shall be saved."

Phillip wondered how the white ushers could hear the same gospel and still call themselves Christians?

REVEREND PAUL Promise was delighted to receive Phillip into membership at Mount Calvary Baptist Church. Martha was appalled. Vel stopped speaking to him. Rosa cried and prayed for him. Lala was embarrassed. Bobby tried hard to understand.

Phillip was weary of the hypocrisy in the Catholic church. He viewed the action of the ushers as maintaining segregation in God's name. He saw the church's failure to maintain equality of all men under God as a violation of God's law. He saw no reason why he should drive forty miles away to Lafayette, to attend a colored Catholic church, when Sacred Heart was only a few blocks away. No one else in his family saw the situation as he did, but Phillip hoped they would understand in time.

It was the first Sunday of October in 1937 and Reverend Promise was in rare form. His sermon was delivered as usual—with passion. This style of preaching was a new experience for Phillip, but after several months of attendance at Mount Calvary, he had grown to like the vocal intonations and colorful delivery.

Reverend Promise's voice was deep and strong like rolling thunder. "As you heard in 1 John, chapter 3 verse 15: Whosoever hateth his brother is a murderer. Now you know, 'brother' in the bible means mankind . . . and that extends to sisterkind. Today I want to share some words about hate and how it kills."

There was a long silence. It was clear that Reverend Promise was deeply moved. His voice now became a whisper, but was still as powerful as a chilling wind. He continued, "I just got word that one of our *ce-leb-ri-ties* is no longer with us. Last week, on the twenty-sixth day of September, Sister Bessie Smith, the Empress of the Blues, had a car accident and bled to death because not one, not two, but three white hospitals in Clarksdale, Mississippi, refused to take her in for treatment."

Remarks flowed through the congregation like a buzz of bees, "Oh, my God," "I can't believe it," "It can't be," "Jesus, say it ain't true," "Lord Almighty, what they gonna do next?"

Reverend Promise waited until the disbelief had spent itself. When there was silence, interrupted only by periodic sniffles, he continued, "Brothers and Sisters, she did not have to die. It was not her time. No Siree! God did not call Sister Smith to his bosom. But she went anyway. She went 'cause she was sent."

Phillip had not heard of Bessie Smith before, but she must have been special. He looked at the shocked, grief-stricken faces of people around him. In the silence that followed, he could hear the rustle of the hand towel that wiped the tears from Reverend Promise's face; but the Reverend kept the tears in his voice, increased the volume, and speeded up his rhythm.

"She was sent by hate. Just like Cain sent Abel home by hate, she too was sent by hate. She was sent by intolerance . . . just like Joseph was sent by his brothers to slavery, she too was sent by intolerance. She was sent by the haters. And the haters killed her as surely as if they had plunged a dagger into her heart. And it was a good heart . . . a wonderful heart . . . a heart that spoke to every one of us . . . a heart that spoke to you and to me . . . a heart that spoke the blues . . . the blues that came from her heart and her soul. Can I hear an *amen!*"

The church responded as one voice. Phillip joined the response without giving a second thought. Reverend Promise continued his momentous eulogy.

"Now, y'all know the blues is sung in the juke-joints and sin-houses, and it ain't rightly condoned by this church. And I want y'all to know it ain't my choice of music . . . But I'm gonna make an exception in the case of Sister Smith. Because she was a Christian and a child of God . . . and as the Empress of the Blues she traveled the bright highways of the land . . . and she traveled the dark back roads of Mississippi, singing for all to hear. She didn't have no prejudice. She sang for all who would listen . . . all of God's children. But those people . . . those haters . . . would not let her in. Those devils at the Mississippi hospitals let her bleed to death at the door. That car wreck didn't kill Bessie Smith . . . those white folks at the hospital killed Bessie Smith . . . hate killed Bessie Smith . . . *seg-re-ga-tion* killed Bessie Smith. *In-tol-er-ance* killed Bessie Smith. She's gone home now . . . she's in the bosom of Jesus. She don't have to worry about sitting in the back of the bus. She don't have to worry about going to the back door . . . or the front door . . . or any door, 'cause she don't have to worry about singing in segregation. The Empress is singing for King Jesus now. *Amen!*"

Phillip sat mesmerized. It was the most powerful sermon he had ever heard. In the Catholic church the priest retold the gospels as sermons but seldom were they related to everyday happenings in the lives of the congregation. This was the difference for Phillip. He was now a member of a church that related to the life of the people. He could never remember a time when the concerns of Father Mac or Father Pat had to do with what happened in the lives of the parishioners—except to ask for money.

That evening at supper Phillip said to LightFoot as he passed the potatoes, "Have you ever heard of a blues singer named Bessie Smith?"

"Yeah, I got some of her records."

After a moment of silence Phillip said, "Well, I hate to tell you this, but she's dead."

"She's what?"

"She died in a car wreck in Mississippi. They wouldn't treat her in the white hospital."

"How you know this?"

"It was announced in church."

LightFoot didn't say another word. He didn't eat another bite. He quietly got up from the table and walked out the door. Martha followed him to the porch and watched him head in the direction of Naomi's. She returned to the table, picked up her napkin from the chair and said with a sigh, "I don't know what he sees in that woman."

Phillip was silent. He knew if he tried to explain, it would lead to a fuss. Lala broke the silence.

"Papa, who is Bessie Smith?"

"The people at church tell me she is one of the best-known women blues singers there was. They say another blues singer called Ma Rainey discovered her, and she used to sing in tent shows, and she made a lot of records in the nineteen-twenties. They say she was only in her early forties, and they called her the Empress of the Blues."

Martha interrupted, "She wasn't nothin' but a gut-bucket singer."

There was something in the tone of Martha's voice that Phillip resented. He didn't favor the blues any more than she did but there was something intolerant in her voice that had to be challenged.

"Now why you got to go and say something like that?"

"It's the truth. Empress of the Blues, my Aunt Fanny."

"Martha, you don't know nothing about what you talking."

"I know if you hadn't joined them heathens you wouldn't be bringing these gut-bucket people up at my supper table."

The children stopped eating and looked from one to the other. Like always, the fuss was not about the initial conflict—the blues. It was about Phillip leaving the "true church." After several minutes, the children left the table, one at a time.

Martha continued, "Papa Joseph and his father, Antoine Junior, and his father, Antoine Senior, were all Catholics. And even though my great-great-grandfather owned slaves, nobody in my family has ever embarrassed me as much as you did by joining that church."

"And what does that have to do with a blues singer dying?"

Martha ignored the question and continued, "And over nothing. Every Sunday you put more than ten percent in the collection basket, and have been, for as long as I can remember. So I don't understand why you get so mad 'cause Father Pat wants you to put your money in an envelope with your name on it."

"'Cause that's all Father Pat care about—taking our money. He doesn't care about colored people."

"You know you are committing a sacrilege by going to that church, don't you?"

"At least I know the preacher cares about me."

"You gonna condemn your soul to hell."

"Why you so concerned about my soul? When you condemn your own soul with all your hateful words about anybody who's not Creole or white."

And so the supper was over. Phillip left the table with half his food left on the plate. Martha sat for a spell until she regained her composure, then she scraped away the uneaten food on all the plates and stacked the dishes.

BESSIE SMITH'S voice cut through the flickering shadows like a Bowie knife. LightFoot and Naomi sat on the floor, hearing the recordings for what seemed like the first time. Bessie held center stage in this incense-laden, candlelit room, as they both realized that she would not make any more recordings. The only words spoken by LightFoot were, "I never got the chance to see her."

10

JUNE 22, 1938, was a hot muggy night. Outside there was a breeze every now and then, so Phillip connected the radio to a long extension cord and set it up on the screened porch. Gathered around were those who didn't have a radio or those who preferred to listen to the prize fight with someone they knew. Bobby, his friend John Webster, and Emanuel "PeeWee" Hill from Chicago, and Lala, Rosa, Vel, and her friend Viola were there. LightFoot, Leo, and his wife Catherine, Henry the mechanic, and BookTau were also there.

Martha had decided that all she was serving was water. "There's too many people to squeeze that many lemons for." She put a big pitcher of water filled with ice for anyone who might want something to drink. The swing and the rocking chairs were full and some people had to sit on the floor and the steps, but everybody was settled and anxious by the time Phillip tuned the radio and settled in his chair.

Max Schmeling, the German superman, had defeated Joe Louis two years earlier. Louis won the championship from Jim Braddock one year later. Now the championship was on the line again with this return bout between Louis and Schmeling. The lighting bugs provided the only illumination and the voice of the announcer the only sound.

"Fifteen rounds of boxing for the heavyweight championship of the world . . . Round One . . . A right and left to the head, by Louis . . . a left to the jaw . . . a right to the head . . . and referee Donovan is watching carefully. Louis measures Schmeling . . . a right to the body . . . a vicious left hook to the jaw and Schmeling is down . . . the count is five, six, seven, eight . . . the men are in the ring . . . the referee stops it! The fight is over on a technical knockout . . . Schmeling is beaten in one round . . . two minutes four seconds of the first round . . . The *winnerrrrrr* and still champion . . . Joe Louis!"

The people on the porch went crazy. Other people yelled from across the street. Folks up and down Academy Street yelled. Every colored person in Estilette yelled the celebration of this quick, decisive victory over Schmeling and fascist Germany. First Jesse Owens and now Joe Louis had provided undeniable proof that colored people were as good and equal to anyone in the world.

A COUPLE of weeks later Bobby, John Webster, and PeeWee Hill, still wearing the pride of their first national hero, went to the picture show. PeeWee, John Webster's first cousin, lived in Chicago. His father had sent him to Estilette to spend the summer with his brother's family. He was sixteen, the same age as the other two boys, but he looked older and was more physically developed—the basis for his paradoxical nickname. He was a high school football hero, with the body of a bronze Adonis, which he proudly showed off every chance he got. PeeWee was also a braggart and a bully. He felt he could do anything better, and knew more about everything, than anyone else. He had won his share of Chicago street fights and boasted the fearlessness that comes from such victories. Having tasted freedom in the North, he was not accustomed to traditional colored behavior around white people in the South. He was vocally critical of what he observed of his cousin's ways. But mostly, in spite of his adult appearance, he was young and immature about the ways of the world.

The boys sat in the balcony of the Delta Theater and watched *Buck Jones Rides Again.* To their surprise and delight there was also a *World News* short that showed the Louis-Schmeling fight. The boys were so excited that they sat through a second showing just to see the knockout one more time.

Their liveliness carried them out of the picture show, down the outside stairway, and several blocks down the street. It prompted PeeWee to take off his shirt, pump up his arm, and say, "Look at my muscles. *I'm* gonna be the next heavyweight champ."

He and John Webster began a boxing match that progressed down the sidewalk. Bobby, not to be left out, took out the harmonica given to him by his Uncle LightFoot and played "America the Beautiful" as he followed their progress.

Tammy Fay Hicks approached from the opposite direction. She observed from a block away this weird ceremony that slowly inched its way in her direction. Tammy Fay was an attractive, highly imaginative white woman. She had been shopping. Perspiration from her store-to-store journey had caused her thin cotton dress to cling revealingly to her body. She carried several packages that she pressed against her bosom. A few feet away she stopped, observed the tomfoolery of the boys, and then said in a loud clear voice, "Will you boys stop clowning and let me pass?" Her voice did indeed halt the tomfoolery. Bobby stopped the music and John Webster moved aside, opening a path for Tammy Fay. PeeWee stopped where he stood, turned in her direction, and said, “Sure, lady, come on by.” For a brief moment Tammy Fay observed his nude chest glistening in the afternoon sun. Then she tossed her hair and started walking. As she passed, PeeWee said, “Just practicing to be heavyweight champ . . . wanna feel my muscles?”

Bobby’s eyes widened. John Webster’s mouth dropped open. Tammy Fay turned with such indignation that one of her packages flew out of her arms. She shot back, “Boy, you better shut your filthy mouth.”

PeeWee treated her remark lightly and laughed. He picked up the package, extended it to her, and said, “This makes your boy a *gentleman*. Now ain’t that somethin’?”

Tammy Fay snatched her package, gritted her teeth, took a deep breath, and walked away. PeeWee’s laughter cut through the air. John Webster said, “Shut up, man.” He grabbed PeeWee by the arm and pushed him the direction they were walking. Bobby picked up the shirt and flung it on PeeWee’s shoulder.

“Are you crazy?”

“No, why?

“You can’t talk to a white woman like that.”

“I talks to anybody, any way I wants too.”

CLOVIS HICKS, sitting in the draft of a small fan, was going through the motions of testing vacuum tubes at a workbench piled high with radio chassis. Clovis was Tammy Fay’s husband. It was really too hot to do much of anything, so he was mostly listening to *Folk Songs of America* on a radio tuned in to WNYC. The voices of Woody Guthrie and Leadbelly filled the cluttered space. He knew the Woody Guthrie voice but not the other. It didn't matter. They sounded good together anyway.

He leaned back, took a soda out of the icebox, closed his eyes, and let the music sink in. Tammy Fay entered the shop, threw her packages on the counter, and dropped into a chair near the doorway. Clovis looked at her, wiped away some perspiration, took a deep swallow from the soda and said, "I know it's hot out there. I got another Dr. Pepper in the box. You want it?" Without waiting for an answer he leaned back, got the soda, and handed it to his wife. She took a long drink, got up, walked to the open doorway, and looked in the direction from which she had come. She said scornfully, "That nigga got some nerve."

"What you talkin' about, Tammy Fay?"

She told her version of the incident. As she talked she got more and more agitated, pacing back and forth the length of the counter. Clovis noticed her dress clinging to her shapely body. The damp cloth pressing against her panty line followed the luscious shape of her ass. She always turned him on, with or without clothes, and he imagined that this had been the source of attraction for the "hot-blooded nigga." Tammy Fay's anxiety level had now reached a pitch that exceeded the seriousness of the incident. Clovis's questions and curiosity increased in emotion by the same degree. What had been a defiant breach of Southern tradition now became a warped and twisted fiction of sexual intent. She said with disgust, "And then he had the nerve to want me to feel that muscle."

That statement drove Clovis to the phone. He dialed frantically, and then reached under the counter for his revolver.

"Lee Jay, meet me out back. We gonna teach a nigga a lesson. I'll tell you on the way."

He hung up and rushed out the back door. Tammy Fay slid into the butt-shaped impression in the shabby wing chair made by years of waiting customers. She crossed her legs and assaulted the still hot air with impatient twitching. She fanned the top of her thin cotton dress back and forth, sending a cool breeze down between her bosoms. The slight smile that had arched her lips moments earlier now embraced the mouth of the Dr. Pepper bottle. Her violation would be avenged.

Lee Jay Clary was known for his short temper, especially in matters that involved "niggas." He was Clovis's partner in the radio business and did the pickups and deliveries while Clovis kept the store. Lee Jay lost no time getting out of Gator's Pit, two blocks away, where he had a cool beer on hot days. Clovis was waiting in the truck on the passenger side with the motor revved up. Lee Jay almost fell on the gravel rounding the corner. He jumped into the driver's seat and took off, kicking gravel against the wall of the buildings.

STILL IN lively spirits, the boys had crossed the railroad tracks, leaving the incident with the white woman behind. PeeWee playfully chased first John Webster then Bobby, stinging them with his shirt as a weapon. The late-modeled panel truck came to a quick reduction of speed, then followed slowly behind at a distance. Inside the truck, Clovis pointed in the direction of the boys and said, "That's him . . . the one with no shirt on."

The dark blue Ford truck pulled alongside the boys and slowed to the speed of their walk. Lee Jay yelled, "Hey, boy, come here."

Bobby and John Webster immediately recognized the sign of trouble and took off running in different directions. PeeWee's response to their shouted advice of "Run!" was to maintain his walking pace. The truck continued to follow along beside the proud, defiant "nigga."

Looking back from his hiding place, a safe distance away, Bobby saw a man with a gun in his hand walk PeeWee behind the truck. He didn't look for or try to find John Webster. He ran all the way home by way of back alleys, fields, and secret paths known only to the inhabitants of that part of town.

The reflection from the mirror on the wall near the stove revealed one of God's dissatisfied creatures. Vel was in the kitchen meticulously massaging her face with Presto Bleaching Cream, while she waited for the straightening comb to get hot. After the comb was smoking hot, she ran it through her nappy hair. The smoking sizzle, from a thick coating of Blue Seal Vaseline that kept her hair from burning, was the only sound of this transformation. This was a weekly necessity. She hated the fact that her hair was not as straight as Lala's. She wanted to have light skin and straight hair. Her features had come from her father's side of the family and she regularly prayed that she would wake up blessed with features from her mother's side. Since this prayer was never answered, she did what she could to acquire the look of a Creole.

Bobby got home at twilight, out of breath and trembling all over. He ran directly to the sink for a drink of water, interrupting Vel's activity. She got angry. It was not so much because he had seen her frizzy hair, but he had invaded her privacy. It was a family understanding that the kitchen was her private domain when she proclaimed that she was going to "fix her hair." She yelled, "Mama, Papa!

Bobby's home." It was her hope that this announcement would bring the wrath of punishment, because he should have been home several hours earlier. Bobby retorted, "Big mouth," and threw a glass of water in her direction. He ran out of the kitchen with Vel in hot pursuit, her face white with bleach and her hair dripping with water. Bobby ran, trembling, into Phillip, who was headed to the kitchen with his razor strap. Martha was right behind. Vel immediately pleaded her case of wet hair, hoping that her revenge would be served by seeing Bobby get a good whipping for being late. Phillip began his interrogation.

"Boy, what's wrong with you?"

Bobby ignored the encounter with Vel and told of the incident with the white lady and PeeWee's disappearance. Phillip listened with worried silence. When Bobby had finished his story, Martha said, "I knew that little nigger was trouble when you had him over here to listen to the fight."

Phillip asked impatiently, "How did you know that, Martha?"

Phillip was usually peeved when he called his wife by her name. At other times he addressed her as "Mama." This time he answered his own question with a question.

"Because he's black?"

"Yes, just a black nigger."

"The boy didn't do nothing, according to Bobby here."

"He insulted that white woman."

They were off and fussing—Martha blaming PeeWee and Phillip defending. Bobby could not believe what he was hearing. It seemed to him that his mother believed that PeeWee was wrong just because he was black. And then Vel joined in, "A nigger and a fly can't do nothing for me."

Bobby replied, "You're a nigger, too."

Phillip yelled, "Stop this nigger-this and nigger-that talk." He invoked his authority by sheer volume. No one dared challenge.

There was silence. Rosa and Lala appeared in the doorway of the living room, summoned by the turmoil. After several seconds, which seemed like minutes, Phillip said, "I know how the word *nigger* is used by the colored people around here. I also know what it means when it is used by white people, and I don't want to hear it used in this house any more."

It was clear from the disdain on Vel's face that her father was taking away her only expression of personal superiority. Vel and Martha were alike in this need. Although Martha did not exhibit any indication of being upset by Phillip's edict, no amount of protest from Phillip could convince her that it was not necessary to separate herself from "those other people." She would simply not let him hear her say *nigger*. By now any thought of punishing Bobby for being late was forgotten by Phillip. One by one the members of the family departed the kitchen to the privacy of their own thoughts about the implications of the incident.

Phillip was very disturbed by the incident that Bobby reported. For several minutes he sat on the porch in his rocker in the twilight, thinking. This incident could be very serious. Did it happen the way Bobby said? Was PeeWee abducted? Or was the entire event an exaggeration from Bobby's imagination? He had to be sure. He left the porch, got into his car, and drove to the Hills. John Webster, Sr., answered the knock on the door.

"Evenin', Professor."

"Evening, John. Your boy back home from the picture show?"

"Yeah, he got back about fifteen minutes ago."

"What about PeeWee? He back too?"

"No sir, he not back yet."

"Did your boy tell you about what happened?"

John turned away from the door while still holding the screen open and called into the house for John Webster. Then he turned back to Phillip and said, "Come on in, Professor."

Phillip entered the living room as John Webster appeared from a hallway that led to the rest of the house.

"You want me, Papa?"

"Where is PeeWee?"

"I don't know."

"What happened while y'all was at the picture show?"

John Webster looked at Phillip and realized that Bobby must have told him what had happened, so he told the same account of the incident with the white lady that Phillip had heard from Bobby. Phillip was convinced that the boys were telling the truth. Then he asked, "Did you see one of the men with a gun?"

"No, sir . . ."

John interrupted, "Professor, what's all this stuff about a gun?"

Phillip explained the best he could from the information given by the boys, without jumping to a conclusion. But as he now had it figured, Bobby was the only one who saw a man with a gun. According to the account that John Webster had given, he and Bobby ran off in different directions and he didn't stop until he got to the Sugar Patch cafe. Then Phillip concluded, "My boy said he stopped a short distance from the truck and looked back from a hiding place and saw a man with a pistol pointing at PeeWee."

John was now getting a little impatient with his son.

"Boy, why didn't you tell me this when you got back?"

"I didn't think too much about it. When PeeWee didn't show up at the Sugar Patch, I just thought he musta went on by Jessie Mae's house."

"Who's Jessie Mae?"

"That girl he's been messin' around with. She live over by the Tavern."

"How long he been seein' her?"

"About a week after he got here. They'd meet over at the Sugar Patch and if she weren't there he'd go by her house."

John seemed a bit more relieved now and shrugged his shoulders and said to Phillip, "You know, Professor, my brother been having some trouble with that boy. He think he's grown. He been chasin' girls all over Chicago and it looks like he doing the same thing here. But I know he can take care of himself."

Phillip left after asking John to let him know when PeeWee got back. On his drive home Phillip hoped and prayed that PeeWee was simply out sowing wild oats, and all the suspicions about being abducted were nothing to get alarmed about.

PEEWEE WAS not seen again. A week passed. His parents arrived from Chicago. His disappearance was reported to Sheriff "Cat" Bobineaux.

William "The Cat" Bobineaux had been sheriff for ten years. His nickname was earned during his early years of late-night roaming around. He was quiet, smooth, and secretive, especially with the ladies, but when riled he never lost a fight. It was his take-no-nonsense reputation that got him elected the first time. And he stayed in office because he was tough on "nigras," a fact that endeared him to the white population of Estilette. He was not afraid to be around the coloreds, as were many white people, and he did not insult them as most did. He treated colored people in the traditions of the South, which meant bending the law to fit the situation.

When John Hill called that he wanted to make a complaint, Sheriff Cat Bobineaux went out to the house to investigate. He sat on the porch and listened to the group of three colored men and two boys describe the incident with the white lady. Phillip and John Hill suggested that John Webster, Jr., and Bobby tell the sheriff about the men in the panel truck, the gun, and the alleged abduction of PeeWee. They also wanted the sheriff to know that a dark blue Ford paneled truck with *Radio Service* printed on the side had been seen in the colored section twice in the last week. From their description, Cat Bobineaux knew exactly to whom the truck belonged. However, he did not believe there was enough evidence to show that Hicks and Clary had anything to do with, as he put it, "that boy's disappearance. Just 'cause they was seen talking to the boy, that don't mean nothing. And your boy was too far away to say for sure that he saw a gun."

John Hill would not be put off so easily. He said, "Then why they driving 'round this section, then?"

"Pick-up and delivery."

"Now, Sheriff, you know as well as me, Mr. Hicks ain't gonna pick up no colored radios. They been looking for these other boys."

Tom Hill, John's brother, insisted that the men be brought in and questioned, to which the sheriff responded, "This here's a nice peaceful town. I can't go charging those men on these boys' say-so. We don't know if your boy's run away from home or what. There just ain't nothing to go on. He could be anywhere. Until we got something to go on, there's nothing I can do."

Tom Hill was not satisfied. He said that he was going to the FBI to see if there was something they might be able to do to help find his son. Sheriff Bobineaux scratched his head and rubbed his chin in thoughtful deliberation, then said, "Suit yourself. I doubt if they'll do anything until you can prove that somebody's been harmed. But if they order me to, I'll have those men picked up and have you bring your boys to my office to identify 'em and file charges."

The colored men on the porch understood the implications of what this meant. Their response was silence. With nothing more to be accomplished, Sheriff Bobineaux left the porch of the Hill house with a final word, "When your runaway boy shows up, give me a call."

The Hill brothers were boiling with anger and threatened to take the matter into their own hands. They had no doubt that redneck Clovis Hicks, and the man with him, had done something to PeeWee. After considering violent retaliation, they realized that this would not be the smartest way to handle the situation. Instead they decided to look for PeeWee on their own. They would spread out through the backcountry to see if they could find someone who might have seen something. In the meantime the Hill brothers and Phillip agreed that both Bobby and John Webster should be safeguarded. There was no doubt that Sheriff Bobineaux would alert the culprits that the boys who had witnessed the abduction had identified them.

ON THE drive home Phillip told Bobby to get a few clothes together because he would have to hide out until the situation cooled down.

Bobby was scared. Although he knew he had not done anything for which he should be frightened, he was. He could not get the image of the gun, or what seemed like a gun, out of his mind. After hearing what the sheriff said, he was no longer sure about what he had seen. He thought of PeeWee and how daring he was in the presence of white people, and he wondered whether it was wise for him to have been so brave. For the first time since PeeWee disappeared, Bobby cried. For the first time, he realized that PeeWee might not get to be heavyweight champion of the world.

It was about two o'clock in the morning when Phillip came to Bobby's room and told him to get dressed.

"Why, Papa?"

"It's time to hide you out."

"Where?"

"You'll know soon enough. Come on."

Downstairs his mother held him in her arms with fear in her heart. Bobby asked, "Can I tell the girls good-bye?"

Martha said, "No. I'll tell them you went to 4-H Club camp."

Phillip hurried Martha's good-byes and they were off. They drove for a half hour or more. Bobby could not figure out where they were going but he was sure they had passed the Planters Bank twice. He figured they were driving in circles. Bobby noticed that his father kept checking the rear view mirror to be sure they were not being followed.

Finally Phillip turned off the headlights and turned into Stephen Estilette's back yard. Phillip got out and headed toward the house, and when he got near the steps the door opened. The interior of the house was dark but there was enough light from the moon for Bobby to recognize the silhouette of Mr. Estilette, who came down the steps to greet Phillip.

Bobby climbed a narrow stairway to the attic concealed behind a closet door in the kitchen. Mr. Estilette explained that this was formally the slave quarters when his grandfather occupied the house.

"You'll be safe here. We'll bring your food, three times a day, and leave it at the top of the stairs. A knock on the door will be your signal. Your bathroom is right in here." He opened the door to a small room under the slanting roof that contained an ancient toilet and a face bowl of the same vintage.

"You should not flush or run any water until after dark. We'll be sure not to have guests in the house at that time."

Bobby began to get scared all over again. If his father and Mr. Estilette thought all of this secrecy was necessary, then he must be in real danger.

"Is John Webster gonna be here, too?"

"He's already gone to Chicago."

Phillip hugged him and said, "There's nothing for you to worry about. Things will settle down soon and everything will be all right."

Bobby was left alone. He did not take off his clothes because he knew he would not sleep. He lay on the small bed, looking out of the gabled window at the night sky, wondering why things had to be the way they were.

The days in his friendly prison went by slowly. He ate the food that was left and he slept. Then he read and he slept. Sometimes he just let his mind wander idly and did nothing. These were times when nothing made sense. Bobby tried to figure out why he was being hidden in one white man's attic to be protected from other white men who might want to do him harm. What had they done to PeeWee? And why? PeeWee had not done anything. Yes, he had talked back to a white woman, but he had not done her any harm.

For the second time in the week he had been there, he heard music. It was a lady singing the blues and it came from downstairs. The voice was a welcomed relief from the silence. The worst part of being in this prison was being alone and not having someone to talk with. For the first time in his short life of sixteen years he realized how necessary other people were to his everyday activities.

The aloneness was overwhelming and he closed his eyes and tried to sleep. The sound of music grew louder. He opened his eyes. He felt he was not alone. Someone else was in the room. He turned his head and looked into the face of a white girl holding a tray of food. He thought he must have been dreaming. He looked around the room; all was real. He sat up in the bed startled. The girl said, "It's all right. I'm Alexandrine Estilette."

"Why . . ."

Before he could get his question out, she interrupted.

"Why am I here? I brought your dinner. When you didn't pick it up, I thought something might be wrong. Are you all right?"

"Yeah. I was just takin' a nap."

Alexandrine set the tray on the table and Bobby took his usual place. She stood awkwardly watching as he began eating.

"Do you mind?"

"What?"

"If I . . . wait for the tray."

"No."

She took a seat. Bobby could still hear the music.

"Who is that singing?" Bobby asked.

"Bessie Smith."

"She dead."

"Yes, I know."

Bobby had never heard Bessie Smith before. He was amazed to hear her records for the first time in the home of a white person. Somehow it didn't seem right, especially after his mother had expressed so little concern over the news of her death. He was also embarrassed that he did not know more about her and had not heard her records. He knew that his Uncle Johnny had her records, and he knew that his mama felt that this gut-bucket music was not worth listening too.

"I have every record she made."

This revelation by Alexandrine was the twist of the knife. She valued Bessie Smith so much she had all of her records; he didn't even know who she was until his father brought the news of her death from church. He was curious about Alexandrine.

She told him she was nineteen and in her freshman year at Vanderbilt University in Nashville. That was the same city where the colored school, Fisk University, was located. And Alex, which is what she insisted that she be called, had attended several concerts of the Fisk Jubilee Singers. She was giving him more information about his own history than he cared to have her give. Nevertheless he found her fascinating. She was studying sociology and wanted to do her master's research on the marginal Creole groups in Louisiana.

Her personal revelations opened the door for some bragging from Bobby. He said he was planning to study medicine but he had not decided where. Alex was quick to furnish information about Meharry, the fine colored medical school in Nashville. Bobby was not sure he liked her. It was turning out that she knew more about colored institutions than he did. However, he realized that his growing antagonistic attitude was unfair. It was his responsibility to learn about his own history and it was clear, during the time it took to eat dinner, he had not done that very well.

Alex took the tray and headed downstairs. Because the record had long since ended, she promised to put on another and suggested that he leave the door open so he could hear better. It was ironic that they had never met before. She was only three years older, but knowledge of each other's existence had never been revealed, in spite of the fact that their fathers were friends. It was indeed a strange world that Bobby was discovering.

His aloneness was now filled with strange thoughts. In the brief time it took for him to eat dinner, he was attracted to a white girl who was interested in Negro history. Was this the reason why he felt a growing bond of friendship from such a brief encounter? Or was it because she had white skin? He knew many girls who were Creole and had skin as white as Alex's but he did not feel the same about them as he did about Alex. He was sure of one thing, however—there was no possibility of this relationship growing, no matter how compassionate Alex might feel about the Negro people. He closed his eyes and went back to sleep; hopefully to dream.

Two weeks later Bobby opened the door to get his breakfast. There was a folded newspaper next to his tray. He put the tray on the table and opened the *Estilette Chronicle*. The headline said MAN'S BODY FOUND IN BAYOU. Bobby got weak in the knees as he sat on his bed. He read the article.

> Yesterday the unidentified body of a man, who appeared to be nineteen or twenty years old, was found in Bayou Teche about ten miles from Port Barre. The body was tangled in catfish traps and appeared to have been bound by ropes to a heavy object. The fisherman who found the body said it had been badly eaten by alligators, and it seemed that the ropes had been bitten through, allowing the body to be carried by the current. Identification was difficult because of the action of the gators. However, there was no mistaking that the body was male and colored. He was wearing khaki pants and no shirt.

Bobby could not read anymore. It was difficult to see through the tears. He could barely make out the watery forms of two people standing in the doorway. He wiped away the teardrops. It was Mr. Estilette and Alex. Alex approached the bed, sat next to him and put her arm around his shoulder. She cried also. After a moment Mr. Estilette said, "Your papa's downstairs. He's come to take you home."

THE COLORED community was shocked. The names of the suspected killers, Hicks and Clary, were on the lips of everyone even though, as the sheriff had said, there was no proof that they were guilty. John Webster and Bobby had come out of hiding because there seemed little likelihood that the sheriff was ever going to arrest anyone for the murder.

Lynching was a new term for Bobby's vocabulary. He learned about it on the porch from the mouth of his papa and Leo.

"It was gettin' more frequent from the Reconstruction days, but lately it's leveling off. Last year there were eight, and the year Jesse Owens won, there were also eight."

Leo's comment was received with a long silence from Phillip. Then a clearing of the throat, and Bobby knew that an insight of significance was about to be uttered. He listened carefully. Phillip spoke slowly, "And this year, 1938, we've already had six, not counting PeeWee. Since Joe Louis knocked out that white fella we're liable to have more. It's only August; just wait and count."

Leo continued, "That don't make no sense a'tall. That boy didn't do nothing to that white woman."

"Except talk back. It's not necessary to do anything else. They only need a victim to blame in order to teach the rest of us to stay in our place. And Joe Louis showed 'em that our place was equal to theirs."

Bobby watched Leo's reaction to the thought-provoking statement and wondered what Leo would say. He did not have to wait long. "Seem like most of these lynchings take place over white women's claims that they have been raped, molested, or talked back to. It's like they hoping things were different so they wouldn't have to lie about it to they men folks."

Phillip cleared his throat again. "Bobby, don't you think it's about your bedtime?"

That ended Bobby's learning about lynching. He knew his papa did not want him to hear what they perceived was the real reason for the killing of PeeWee.

MOUNT CALVARY was packed. Since most of the family lived in Estilette, Tom Hill decided to bury the remains of his son here, even though all of PeeWee's friends, except Bobby and John Webster, lived in Chicago. Reverend Promise had plenty of grist for the mill of his eulogy and there was an ample supply of screaming and crying.

Martha sat stoically ill at ease, fanning herself demurely. This was the first time that she had been in a church other than Catholic. And she would not have been here this time if Phillip had not insisted that the family pay its respects to the Hills. "After all, Bobby and PeeWee were friends." Martha had been taught in catechism classes that it was a sin to enter a church of another faith, but under the circumstances she felt that God would forgive her. However, she was not sure that God's forgiveness would extend to Phillip. He had been christened Catholic. His father was Catholic and his great-grandfather, who was white, was a Catholic.

Reverend Promise began his eulogy, "They used to lynch us from a tree for everyone to see, but now, brothers and sisters, they do their killing in secret."

The memory of Phillip's family tree jumped into Martha's mind's eye, along the metaphor of the killing tree used by Reverend Promise. She remembered James, Phillip's great grandfather, a slave-holding Fergerson from Ireland. When his desirable house slave became pregnant with his child, he felt it his Christian duty to raise the boy, Phillip's grandfather, in the big house with his other children. He called the boy Chrispin, from the Latin word meaning curly headed. James allowed Chrispin all of the privileges and opportunities of his legitimate children and he was taught to read and write along with them.

When the children were teenagers, Chrispin got one of his half-sisters pregnant. Old man James Fergerson was so incensed that he made a deal to sell the boy to the most brutal slaver in the parish. Chrispin overheard the plan from a partially opened hallway door and ran away to Philadelphia. He forged freedom papers on his father's letterhead and lived and worked as a freedman. After the emancipation, Chrispin returned to Louisiana because it was home. He married a girl whom he had admired from afar while visiting a nearby plantation. Their son, Phillip's father, Henry, had two sons, Phillip and his older brother Luther. In Martha's way of thinking this ancestry made her and Phillip members of the same class, or almost. She was Creole, descending from the French, and he Mulatto, descending from the Irish. So it was a mystery to Martha why he would forsake his religious heritage to join a church of colored people.

She was not aware of the remainder of the eulogy or what had transpired in church during her thoughts. When she heard the name John "LightFoot" Broussard, she was transported back to present time. She saw her brother walk to the front of the church and stand next to Naomi in the choir. He played his guitar and sang.

The sky is cryin' E-man-u-ell is dead
The sky is cryin' E-man-u-ell is dead
They say he was young and talented
Kilt by someone mean-spirited

He ain't gonna be funnin' no mo'
He ain't gonna be goin' to the sto'
No mo' runnin' and playin'
No mo' wishin' and prayin'

The sky is cryin' E-man-u-ell is dead
The sky is cryin' E-man-u-ell is dead
The gators in the bayou been fed
A young boy's life has been bled

The mean and evil is a-celebratin'
There's one less nigga for segregatin'
Like his namesake befor'
He ain't alive no mo'

E-man-u-ell is dead
E-man-u-ell is dead
The sky is cryin'
The sky is cryin'.

The entire church came alive in a rare combination of pain, sorrow, and celebration. They clapped their hands to the music and shuffled up the center aisle, past the coffin and down the side aisles, singing, moaning, and crying. It was hypnotic. A spellbinding and eulogizing celebration/lament of ecstasy and rapture all rolled into one. It lasted for what seemed like hours, and Martha had never in her life seen a spectacle like this. She watched as her brother played and sang with a burning inspiration that ignited the very air. It was difficult for her to believe that John could have written this gut-bucket music, now being sung as gospel. She looked at Phillip. He was clapping his hands and swaying in time with the other mourners. So were Bobby and Lala. Vel and Rosa sat with folded arms, like Martha, in rocklike silence and watched in bewilderment. Martha was now more convinced than ever that she had little in common with these people.

It was raining by the time the service was over and Martha decided that she would not go to the cemetery. Phillip dropped her off at home and the children went with him to the interment.

Julia Donatto had been patiently waiting for Martha on the front porch for over two hours. Affectionately called Miz Julee, she was blind since birth, an accomplished pianist and an artisan with a crochet hook. To stay busy while she had been waiting, she was putting the final touches on a shawl for Martha.

A few years older than Martha, Julee had never married. It was rumored that Julee's father, a Creole fun-loving lady's man, had given her mother syphilis and she was born blind as God's punishment. Her parents had sent her to the school for the blind in Scotlandville where she remained until she was thirty. After their deaths, she returned to Estilette and lived in the large two-story house that she had inherited. She lived on the combination of a small cash inheritance and money she made from teaching music. She refused to wear the dark glasses that identified the blind, and the blue-gray membranes of her eyes, surrounded by the *café au lait* coloration of her skin, gave her face an eerie appearance. Many who spoke to her could not stand to look in her face; she was able to perceive this from the direction of their voices and she referred to them as insincere. Except for this oddity, her face was kind and gentle, accented by a large black mole in the middle of her chin.

MARTHA JOINED Miz Julee on the porch and described the entire funeral while they enjoyed sassafras tea. Miz Julee listened and her fingers nimbly continued the creation of the intricate patterns of the lacy shawl. When it was her time to speak, she tried to make Martha understand that blues music was only a means of telling feelings so indescribable that they defied all other means of expression.

"What you call gut-bucket music is a cry from the inner spirit."

"Inner spirit, my Aunt Fanny. It's just low-class nigger music."

Miz Julee could tell that her remarks about the subject were upsetting Martha so she decided to be silent. Martha poured another cup of tea and went on to another subject dear to her heart—Phillip's leaving the church. Miz Julee and Martha were lifelong friends and Martha did not hesitate to share her secret thoughts. As a matter of fact, Martha liked the idea of having Miz Julee as a sounding board for feelings that she would never share with anyone, not even her priest.

In the meantime, unknown to Martha, Phillip and the children had returned. The children went immediately to their rooms to change clothes. Phillip went to the kitchen, poured a cup of coffee, and headed to the front porch to join the ladies. When he reached the door of the living room, he overheard Martha say, "Since Phillip had joined that other church, he does not seem like the same person I married."

Miz Julee volunteered that there was little likelihood that, because he felt differently about Catholicism, it would affect his feelings toward his wife. Martha said, "The feelings that are changing are mine."

There was level of distress that was disturbing, and Miz Julee tried to ease the trouble that she heard in Martha's voice. She counseled, "You put too much faith in the Catholic church's ability to answer everyone's needs."

At this point Phillip made his appearance. He had heard enough. His presence made Martha uneasy because she did not know how much of the conversation he had heard. Julee also perceived Martha's distress and asked if Phillip might drive her home, ". . . now that the rain has stopped."

In silence the cup of coffee and the two cups of tea were drained, and the completed shawl draped over Martha's shoulders. Then Phillip drove Julee home.

11

THE NEXT TWO years passed quietly without further incident.

Phillip watched his family grow in directions that were not entirely desirable. He understood that parents are seldom satisfied with how their children grow, but it seemed that his children were missing the mark by too wide a margin. He felt disappointed in all of them. Vel hated black people, Lala attracted boys like the proverbial flies, Rosa was a slave to the church, and Bobby lacked self-confidence.

Vel had been teaching third grade in Phillip's school for four years. Before that she had been a proficient student. Pride would not allow anything less than being at the top of her class. However, scholarship was not the only attribute of a good teacher, and compassion and understanding were not Vel's strong points. As a teacher she did not have that special quality of caring that is usually associated with one who inspires young people.

Phillip was a good principal. He kept in touch with the nuts and bolts that held his school together. He was always around, watching, listening, and learning. One day at recess he walked past an eight-year-old sitting alone on a log from a fallen tree. Phillip noticed that the child was crying. He sat next to the young boy and asked what was the matter. The boy replied, "My teacher don't like me."

"Why do you say that?"

"She make me stand in the corner."

Phillip was inwardly amused because most teachers followed this practice to control unruly or inattentive students. But he wanted to know more and he continued to interrogate the young boy, who seemed eager to tell someone what he was feeling.

"Why does your teacher make you stand in the corner?"

"She don't like me."

"Were you disturbing the class?"

"Sometime."

"Have you been doing your homework?"

"Sometime."

Phillip looked inquiringly at the boy. There was fuzz from a goose-down pillow still woven into his hair. As he pulled the lint from the boy's head he noticed several buttons missing from his rough dried shirt. The boy's ears were caked with ashy flakes of dried skin; a telling sign that face-washing was not a morning habit. The parents were responsible, so the boy's unkempt appearance was not Phillip's main concern at the moment.

"Is that what makes you cry?"

"Naw sir."

"What then?"

"She don't treat me like the others."

Phillip now felt that he had stumbled onto a problem. The boy had noticed that his classmates were not given the same punishment for the same offenses. The boy realized that his behavior was treated differently. For him, this translated into the teacher not liking him as much as others in the class.

"Who is your teacher?"

"Miz Fergerson."

Phillip was silent. He took his handkerchief, dipped it in the bucket beneath the faucet that served as a drinking fountain, and washed the boy's face. His tears had made tracks through the ash of his skin. The boy's big eyes lit up with gratitude and his face sparkled with a new ebony patina. Phillip said, "I'll have a talk with your teacher." The boy ran off to join the other children, knowing that at least the principal of the school liked him.

Phillip looked around the school for Velma, who was scheduled for noontime duty. He found her in the classroom freshening her make-up. He sadly watched from the doorway until Velma caught his reflection in her mirror.

"Oh, Papa, you scared me."

"I've told you not to call me Papa at school."

To Vel this reminder was a slap in the face; thoughts of indignation whirled in her head and she responded sarcastically, "I'm sorry, Professor Fergerson."

"At the end of the day, I would like to see you in my office."

"Are you going to fire me—Papa?"

There was little point in responding. Phillip turned and left with a heavy heart. There was no doubt in his mind that the boy had experienced Vel's dislike of dark-skinned people. He did not know what to say or feel, except perhaps some guilt for allowing, at one time or another, her attitude to go unchallenged.

MOTHER GOSPEL, now seventy-five, had been playing the organ at church for the last fifty-five years. She could no longer strike the keys without the excruciating pain of rheumatism shooting through her body. Mount Calvary was without an organist, at least until Mother Gospel could train someone else. Phillip saw the opportunity to become a contributing member of the congregation. He volunteered the services of his daughter, and carefully explained to Reverend Promise that Lala was of another faith. This did not matter to Reverend Promise as much as it did to Martha, who was outraged.

"It's a sin to let your daughter play in a Baptist church!"

"It's only until somebody else learns the organ."

"It's bad enough that you left your church. Now you want Lala to join up with those heathens, too."

"Dammit, woman, that's not the point. You always harp back on that, no matter what."

Martha was dead-set against Lala playing for the choir of a Baptist church, no matter that she was being paid. Both Martha and Phillip had overlooked the fact that Lala was an adult with a mind of her own, and argued the situation without consulting her. Overhearing the fussing that had gone on for several minutes, Lala thought it was time to make her voice heard. She walked into the bedroom and said, "I don't mind."

Martha was speechless; Phillip said nothing. Lala welcomed the opportunity to speak her own mind. "Miz Julee taught me to play 'Amazing Grace' on the organ and I don't think that's a sin." Martha could not argue the point. Phillip smiled proudly, feeling that he knew all along how Lala would respond. Lala continued, "And I know how to play 'The Lord's Prayer.' It's the same for all the churches, except at the end. I wouldn't mind playing for Mount Calvary until they find somebody. Anyway, I could use the money."

Lala had welcomed the opportunity to learn Baptist music. Martha was not aware that Lala already had an acquaintance with syncopated rhythms. After getting lessons from her Uncle Johnny, she frequently picked out blues tunes on the piano. Phillip had heard blues notes while sitting on the front porch; Martha was not aware of the influence that her brother was having on her daughter's music. Martha, totally defeated on the matter, exhaled angrily and reluctantly agreed, "But only for the rest of the summer. When school starts you'll be too busy to be doing that, anyway."

With that the matter was brought to an end.

After finishing high school, Lala had followed the footsteps of her older sisters. She was in her second year as an elementary school teacher in Frilotville, a small community near Estilette. Martha was delighted for this assignment because it was in a Creole settlement. This was the environment that Martha wished for all of her children. Lala fit in perfectly. She liked the people and they liked her, and she attended their weekend *fais-do-dos*. She was popular and sought after; every weekend she had a different gentleman escort. Phillip resented this because these dances were segregated; only people whose skin color was lighter than the color of a paper bag were allowed to attend. Unlike Martha, he did not want Vel's attitudes about color to be cultivated in Lala. At this point he had not seen evidence of that. Lala liked everybody and did not mind being around the darker-skinned people at Mount Calvary. Phillip was pleased about this. However, in the back of his mind was a conversation he'd had with Leo.

In the small town of Estilette all the telephones were party lines. The Fergersons were on a three-party line with Leo Roberts and Lilly Ellis. Someone placing a call had to ring for an operator, who would then plug in the connection. If one of the other parties picked up during a call, they could listen in on the conversation. On several occasions Lilly Ellis had listened in on conversations between Lala and some of the boys she saw socially. This became the main subject of gossip in the small back-room beauty shoppe at Lilly's house. Lilly did not like Martha, in spite of the fact she was invited over every year at butchering time. "That's only 'cause she thinks she's too good to clean the guts," Lilly had said. When reminded that she always left the Fergersons' butchering with a healthy supply of meat, her response was, "At any rate, I likes Phillip. He's a good and fair-minded man." However, this was not enough to keep Lilly from taking delight in spreading the word about the overheard conversations. "That girl attracts boys like a dog in heat! She's as hot as a two-bit pistol. It's a wonder them phone lines ain't melted."

Leo's wife, Catherine, went home from getting her hair done and picked the phone up on one such conversation. It was not as bad as Lilly made it out to be, but as she said to her husband, "Where there's smoke there must be fire."

Weeks later the main conversation in Jimmy Boudreaux's barber shop was the juicy gossip from the beauty shoppe. When Phillip walked in for his haircut, the shop went silent. After the normal greetings from the five men waiting, a new safe subject became their main topic of conversation—the treatment of coloreds by local whites. Leo, who was in the barber chair at the time, decided he would wait until Phillip had his hair cut. He told Phillip, "I want to go out to the farm to check out your declining egg production."

On their way to the farm, Leo told Phillip there was gossip going around town about Lala. Phillip's immediate response was to question, "What did you hear?"

"Things."

"What things?"

"About how the boys are hot after Lala."

"You think it's true?"

"Yeah. And she's trying hard to keep 'em at bay."

"How you know this?"

"You'd know it to, if you'd heard what I heard. Just keep your shotgun ready."

Phillip did not like hearing this. He thought about restricting Lala's social activities. Not because he felt she was guilty of doing what the gossip alleged; he knew that the stamp of a "bad reputation" frequently followed a carefree young girl who was attractive and fun-loving. His greater concern was how others would perceive her actions. Because she was an adult, there was not much he could do about imposing restrictions.

ROSA WAS different. Unlike Lala she seldom sought or wanted the company of men. She did not like to go to parties or dances. She was devoted to church and family. She had been teaching at the Catholic school for three years. She liked going to church, singing in the choir, and playing the organ for special occasions like weddings or funerals. Every morning she made coffee, put the *Times Picayune* on the desk next to Phillip's chair in "Papa's room," and knocked softly on his bedroom door. "Papa, coffee's ready," she would say. Phillip would put on his slippers and robe, sit in his chair near the window, drink his first cup and read the paper. Rosa would get dressed, kiss Phillip on the forehead, and go to the six o'clock Mass. Since it was unusual to have music for the daily Mass, many people came just to hear Rosa play. On the weekends, she helped out at the rectory, cooking, cleaning, and answering the door.

Phillip did not like this. However, he was silent on this matter because it would very likely be interpreted that he was trying to get back at Father Pat over the tithing issue. What Phillip did not know would have made any distress over the tithing issue seem minor by comparison. Martha would have yelled to high heaven had she known about the developing relationship between Rosa and Father Pat.

Still upset over Phillip's leaving the church, Rosa confided her feelings to Father Pat. She always cried when she discussed the matter. Usually Father Pat suggested that they kneel together and say the rosary. They prayed that Phillip would be shown the error of his ways. In the two years since Phillip left the church, Father Pat had become Rosa's confidant as well as confessor. She was now sharing personal thoughts with him, as she would share with a best girlfriend. Father Pat delighted in this confidential relationship that he referred to as "the will of God." Rosa also felt the hand of God guiding her to Father Pat's counsel. The pain that she previously felt over her father's "renunciation of the church," as it was termed by Father Pat, was gradually lifted. This she attributed to Father Pat's intercession.

The only miracle left to witness was her father's return to the folds of the one true church. She and Father Pat prayed constantly for this in their sessions, which had now grown to include a litany and a novena. Father Pat arranged these private sessions to take place when the other ladies who helped at the rectory were not around. It all seemed quite appropriate to Rosa, who understood that they should not be disturbed during their times of counsel and prayer.

Rosa and Father Pat were comfortable in each other's company, so much so that it was considered a normal turn of events when, after accidentally spilling a cup of coffee in Father Pat's lap, Rosa immediately began to clean it up. Along with the tearful apologies, the gentle stroking of her hand wiping his pants awakened his suppressed maleness. Father Pat reached out and gathered the kneeling Rosa into his arms. He kissed away her tears while whispering assurances that no harm was done. Their lips met in a long, gentle kiss. Still on her knees between his legs, they embraced as would long-lost lovers.

Phillip did not see anything wrong with his daughter being close to God and working for the church. However, deep down inside, he harbored resentment. It seemed like she was free labor for the white priest-man. He thanked God that she was not headed in the same direction as her sisters; and he was content in the belief that no real harm could come to one so devoted and religiously centered. What he and Martha did not know was that Rosa and the church, in the flesh of Father Pat, were at one with God and each other.

IN SEPTEMBER Bobby would be ready for college. Whether he would study pre-med was still undecided. Phillip had suggested on several occasions that Bobby consider going to Meharry Medical College in Tennessee. He got no response. What Phillip did not know was that Alex had placed the same thought in Bobby's mind. Alex was in Bobby's thoughts more and more. She phoned several times to find out how he was feeling after his ordeal. On these occasions they talked about his growing interest in the blues. He described the events of

PeeWee's funeral in detail, and expressed pride in his Uncle Johnny's blues-dirge.

But beyond this there was little else he would do or say to advance a relationship with Alex. He dared not take any action that would arouse suspicion of his interest in her, because he knew that Mr. Estilette and his father would not approve. Still, the feeling that Alex's voice aroused in him led him to believe that a closer relationship was mutually desired. Somehow he had to get to Nashville, but he did not want it to seem too obvious.

Phillip no longer mentioned the study of medicine. He had no idea how Bobby would resolve his choice of a profession. If Bobby wanted a career in medicine, Phillip knew that he had to exhibit more self-confidence than was so far evident. Medical school had not been Phillip's first priority; he was distressed that it was not Bobby's either. By contrast, his friend Frank Johnson had put medical school before everything and everyone. He had graduated and opened an office in Kansas City by the time Bobby was born. Consequently, Phillip felt that the chances of Bobby becoming a doctor were as slim for his son as they had been for him.

Phillip knew that the girls spoiled Bobby. They did everything for him; made his special dishes, washed and ironed his clothes, made his bed, cleaned his room, scratched dandruff and washed his hair. Phillip and Martha were both disturbed by the attention. Martha felt it was an unhealthy sign for a brother to be so close to his sisters. She would often find Bobby with his head in Rosa's lap while she combed through his hair, scratching dandruff. It was all quite innocent but nevertheless disturbing to Martha. She had heard stories about brothers and sisters being lovers, especially among the Creoles. She secretly worried that there might be something in their physical makeup that made this tendency attractive to her offspring.

Phillip was disturbed because he felt that Bobby was too dependent on women. He wanted his son to be self-sufficient. Bobby was not the "strong man" that others of his age were; rather he was easygoing and passive. Phillip would have preferred that Bobby have more self-determination and be less dependent on the affections of women.

PHILLIP COULD do little else except love his children at arm's length. Love remained a distant proposition for the family; it was seldom manifested by a word or an embrace. As he watched his children grow in various directions, he turned inward. A more desirable direction should have been toward his wife. However, Martha was not the haven that Phillip's love needed. He felt she was narrow-minded, too centered on church and skin color, and supportive of the children's shortcomings. Seldom was there peace in the house. They had a fresh supply of fussing subjects provided by one aspect or another of the children's character. Their most effective form of communication was either fussing or silence.

From outside it appeared that the family was together, but this was not really the case. It only seemed that way because they were all, including John, living under the same roof. This would not be true for long however, because Martha was succeeding in "fussing" her brother out of the house, just as Naomi had predicted.

With all of this came a feeling of change in the air. Phillip did not know where it came from but he could feel the chill. He was not so naive as to believe everything would always be as it had always been. But he did believe that a person would be happy if he did what he believed to be right. He was not happy. He did not believe Martha was happy, nor were the children. If anyone in the family even remotely approached contentment, it was John. And maybe, just maybe, the key to happiness was in his nickname. LightFoot's life was unburdened by expectations, and was carried by the ebb and flow of the blues.

12

EARLY IN AUGUST 1940 William Fontenot called Phillip to a meeting of the school board. School was not scheduled to begin for another month, so Phillip felt anxious. It was not a routine planning meeting, nor had he ever been called to a board meeting before; he thought he was going to be fired. He entered the room, looked around at six stern silent faces, and was directed to have a seat. A cold shiver ran through his body as he sat alone on the opposite side of the table. The uneasy anticipation that accompanied the presence of white faces surged through his being. It usually meant that something unpleasant was about to happen. Phillip wondered what could have caused him to have this feeling. He was not guilty of anything, nor did he feel that he deserved whatever verdict this tribunal was about to pronounce. He had never experienced this feeling in the presence of Stephen Estilette, so he knew it did not come automatically in the presence of whites. Phillip felt confident that this feeling was not the result of paranoia, but rather an instinctive reflex to history; whites only gathered in the presence of a Negro for the purpose of opposition.

Fontenot introduced Phillip in a formal tone, "Professor Phillip Fergerson." Phillip noticed that the manner in which Fontenot responded to him was different in the presence of other whites than it was when they were alone. He was more stone-faced, distant, and less friendly. Phillip was not sure whether Fontenot was speaking to him or the board. He went on to say, "I have asked Phillip to come here to discuss a matter that has been on my mind for some time now. As you know, I have been concerned about the quality of education that our colored teachers have. As a result of my conversations with . . . er . . . you, . . . Phillip, . . . for over a year now, the members of the board have agreed that my idea for a program of extra education for our colored teachers would be a good thing. Now, we would like to know if you agree, Phillip, and would be willing to help us set up such a program with cooperation from the colored college in Scotlandville."

An angry shiver ran through Phillip's body. William Fontenot had taken Phillip's idea and made it his own. In the intervening two years since Phillip had presented the idea, Fontenot had not spoken about the subject at all. On several occasions Phillip wanted to ask about the program but thought better of it. He did not want Fontenot to feel, as Mack had warned, that he was being pushy.

Phillip was speechless. He did not know how to respond. There was little to be gained by correcting Fontenot and putting credit for the idea where it rightfully belonged—he knew that was professional suicide. He was trapped. He was now being asked to make his own proposal work to the credit of a white man.

History had caught up with him. He remembered Lewis Latimer, who had an idea for the first incandescent lamp, Norbert Rillieux, who had an idea to improve the making of sugar, and Garrett Morgan, who had ideas for the gas mask and the traffic signal. And there were others throughout history whose initial ideas were ultimately credited to white men. At least he and Felix Mack were in good company. But this did not make the bitter pill any easier to swallow.

He smiled graciously and agreed with Superintendent Fontenot that, "In-service teacher training is a great idea." He was trying to be clever and use the correct term for the program that he had proposed, but the subtlety went over Fontenot's head. He said he would be privileged to contact the college and set up the program. With that, the meeting ended. The six members of the school board drifted into a closed circle to discuss President Roosevelt's new minimum wage law. Fontenot worked out the details for Phillip's trip to Scotlandville as he walked him to the door.

IN 1913 DR. JOSEPH Samuel Clark was appointed president of the first institution of higher education for colored people. Originally located in New Orleans, the new college was relocated in 1914 to a picturesque site overlooking the Mississippi River, seven miles north of Baton Rouge in the small town of Scotlandville. Twenty-six years after the move, Southern A&M College had grown to a student body of nine hundred and a faculty of sixty.

After enrolling Bobby in his alma mater, Phillip made his way to the office of the president. Dr. J. S. Clark, now in his early seventies, looked like a brother of Carl Sandberg but he was definitely a Negro. Now in a position of President Emeritus and advisor, he listened carefully to Phillip's proposal. Felton Clark, his son, had taken over the day-to-day operation of the college two years earlier, and was committed to whatever his father's wisdom dictated. The relationship between Phillip and the old man went back to the time when Phillip had worked his way through school as Dr. Clark's chauffeur. The two had driven many miles over the state, during which many words about many subjects had been exchanged. In that time, Dr. Clark had become Phillip's mentor. Over the years he had followed Phillip's progress closely. He knew that after receiving his bachelor's degree from Southern, Phillip spent four summers and two semesters completing a master's degree, and further study toward a doctorate at Iowa State University. And while undertaking these studies he was also teaching and raising a family. The old man took pride in Phillip's accomplishments, especially his scholastic achievements.

So now a former student was bringing to his mentor a proposal to establish another center for in-service teacher training. Dr. Clark instructed his son, Felton, to carry out the program immediately. He turned to Phillip and asked, "Can you stay over tonight?"

"Yes."

"I would like for you to meet our new director of Extension Education. She will be at the reception."

"The reception?"

"Yes. The welcome-back family reception."

Phillip remembered that Dr. Clark considered his faculty as family. And at the beginning of each school year he opened his home for a gathering of that family. "Felton will make arrangements for you to stay in the new men's dormitory." This was the same dormitory to which Bobby had been assigned earlier in the day. Phillip was pleased that he would be able to spend an extra day to see that Bobby was settled in properly.

That evening he walked to the president's house, which sat majestically on Scott's Bluff overlooking the Mississippi River. He enjoyed once more what he remembered from his days as a student; the beautiful sunset glistening off the river and filtering through the moss-covered trees. The reception was already in progress.

Doctor Clark took Phillip by the arm and led him gently to the other side of the room. “I want to introduce you to Alicia Wallace, the lady you’ll be working with.” Phillip could not believe what he had heard. He asked to have the name repeated. He wanted to be sure that he had heard correctly. “Alicia Wallace—I think you’ll like her.” They moved in the direction of a group standing near the punch bowl. The lady turned in response to Dr. Clark’s greeting. It was, indeed, the women he expected. Their eyes met. Phillip took a deep breath, not knowing how to respond. Alicia was cool and in control. She extended her hand and said, “I think we’ve met before. I believe it was at Iowa State. Is that right, Professor Fergerson?”

“Yes, I do believe it was Iowa.”

Phillip had picked up her cue. Doctor Clark explained the reason for the introduction—his expectation to have the two of them work together on the new project. He wanted them to get acquainted, so he turned and left to greet other members of his family.

Phillip and Alicia moved away from the punch table for privacy. Neither could believe the coincidence of their meeting. It had been ten years since they had seen each other. During that year of Phillip’s sabbatical they had been lovers. At that time Alicia was suffering the pain of a doomed marriage that was plagued by social and educational differences, and Phillip was a long, lonely way from home. What had started as a friendship of mutual comfort turned into a deeper and more intimate sharing. When Phillip returned to Estilette, Martha knew, however it is possible for a wife to know these things, that he had been with another woman. Now he had run into that woman again, only forty miles from Estilette.

Much water had passed under the bridge and there were many years to be relived; they wanted to be alone. Each made an excuse for an early departure from the gathering. They met under the moss-covered oak in front of the administration building to plan the rest of their evening together.

Alicia suggested the Green Light Club in Port Allen, across the Mississippi River, away from the college. This was where she went when she wanted to enjoy herself—incognito. As a student, Phillip had heard stories that described the place as a "bucket of blood." Alicia explained that since the club was now on the circuit for up-and-coming blues singers, the owner did not allow any rough behavior. Phillip was curious. He had never been to a juke-joint before, and he thought it might be fun to hear some gut-bucket music.

They changed to plain, folksy clothes so they would not be identified as "hoity-toity niggers from the college." They were greeted at the door of the Green Light with a cover change because there was special entertainment tonight. A couple of blues people from Houston Texas, "Thunder" and "Lightnin'," were being featured. Thunder Smith was the pianist and Lightnin' Hopkins the singer and guitarist. Both were "working outside of music" and Phillip concluded that they played the blues as a sideline. He also learned that Lightnin' Hopkins had been to prison, a fact that was consistent with Martha's connection of gut-bucket music to "low-class niggers."

No matter how much Phillip's predisposition condemned the music, it made him feel good. He could now understand what John felt when he played the blues. This guy Hopkins was something else.

Phillip had nothing to measure the music against but he liked what he heard. And so did everyone else. He looked around at the faces of the finger-poppers, hand-clappers, and foot-stompers. They were all mesmerized. The music was a series of personal recollections and observations delivered like a conversation, to a steady repetitive beat. The people understood Lightnin'; he was talking to them about what he felt, and the music said what they felt but had not spoken. Phillip could feel it too. Lightnin' Hopkins spoke to him as well as to them.

Alicia was ecstatic. She was possessed. She yelled, swayed, rolled her hips, and waved her arms. She was feeling the spirit. She had let her hair down, and Phillip saw another facet of the sparkling person that he remembered. The blues had uncovered the true being beneath the veneer of education. Here it was—the common denominator that many colored people tried to deny. Lightnin' had knocked down the walls that separated *colored* from *Negro*. He sang "Come Back Baby." Phillip and Alicia danced. They rubbed bellies. Phillip looked into the soft, searching eyes that he remembered from yesteryear, and watched them change into sultry, mysterious, and inviting flames. Phillip could feel his nature rise against Alicia's leg. He remembered ten years earlier when he and Alicia had made love. She looked and felt more enticing as the night wore on. They partied as never before.

PHILLIP FOUND his nakedness tenaciously fused to Alicia's nude erotic body. It was different than being with Martha. Afterwards, Phillip lay on his back looking at the moving shadows of leaves on the ceiling. Alicia knew what was fluttering through his mind.

"Don't."

"Don't what?"

"Do that to yourself."

"What am I doing?"

"Feeling guilty."

Perhaps it was an expected feeling after being intimate with someone other than his wife, but Alicia knew exactly what was on Phillip's mind. She tried to console. She tried to exorcise the phantom that had taken up residence in his imagination.

Alicia said, "I won't make any problems."

"I wasn't worried about that." Phillip lied. The thing that he dreaded most was scandal—an intimate relationship made public. He and Martha had this in common. They would rather suffer in silence than allow unpleasant, unspeakable subjects to become public knowledge. Alicia attempted to explain how things could be, to ease his anxiety.

"Whether you were worried or not; we can remain close friends—as before."

Alicia emphasized the word *close*; it was both a comfort and a vexation to Phillip. However, he tried not to think about the bothersome aspect of the intonation. Alicia tried subtly to rekindle the desire that she believed still burned.

"I love you, Phillip, and I always have. And now that I'm divorced from that truck driver, I'd like to be with you whenever possible."

"But I'm still married."

"I know. But are you happy?"

Phillip was silent. What he wanted to say, he didn't want her to hear; nor did he want to get into a discussion about his marriage. Alicia spoke before he could answer.

"I'm sorry. I should not have asked that. If you feel comfortable seeing me again, I'd like that."

Phillip sat on the edge of the bed. "It's getting late. I should get back to the dormitory before daybreak."

It would not help his cause to be seen leaving Alicia's house, which was located on campus; especially after Dr. Clark had approved his program. Nor did he wish to have Bobby see him enter the dormitory at the crowing of the roosters. Phillip stood and began to get dressed.

He said, "When we see each other again, we must be discreet."

"I agree. And we can never let our feelings show while we're setting up this new program."

They agreed to be careful. Phillip kissed her one last time and went back to the dormitory feeling renewed.

In the early morning, two hours after Phillip fell asleep on the sagging dormitory cot, he was awakened by a knock on the door. It was Bobby. He had changed his mind about attending Southern College. He had been awake most of the night thinking about becoming a doctor. He had made up his mind that he would rather go to Fisk University to prepare for med school at Meharry. Finally, Bobby was being decisive—being his own man. He was setting his own priorities. Phillip was overjoyed. But he did not know that Bobby's decision had been motivated more by the prospect of being near Alex than it was by a desire to practice medicine.

Phillip was up and dressed in minutes, and they were on their way to Nashville.

13

BLUE'S TAVERN WAS jumping. Bill Blue was busy behind the bar. Usually he did not work the bar, but tonight he was short-handed and the crowd was in a drinking mood. He worked hard at two businesses—the tavern and a wood yard. In the daytime he cut down trees that he sold for firewood. At night he ran his tavern, which was larger than Tot's. It had a dance floor and a woman singer that made it the preferred spot, although the same clientele patronized both. Except for the nights of his chore as interlocutor at Tot's, LightFoot was found performing most often at Blue's Tavern. The blues makers preferred it because there was usually a larger crowd.

Bill Blue was a big man—six feet four and 230 pounds of pure muscle. Lifting logs and swinging the axe had developed his strength and biceps. He was not afraid of anything or anybody. The frequently told story that had became local legend was, "One day Bill was cutting cypress trees in the swamp and a gator swum up from behind. Bill wrestled that gator all over that green slimy water. While he held the gator's jaws shut with one hand, he dragged the son of a bitch to where he'd dropped his axe. Then with his free hand he split the gator in two. That gator never had a chance."

There was only one other person to witness this exploit—BookTau. There were those who doubted the story because BookTau could not always be counted on to tell it exactly like it happened. Nevertheless, no one could deny that Bill Blue had killed an alligator—the stuffed body was mounted over the mirror behind his bar.

LightFoot had just finished the second request for "Emanuel's Gone Blues," which had become a favorite since the funeral. It didn't matter that it was a memory-story of a lynching. It took on the spirit of all blues—a reminder that life was tough and time was short, so let the good times roll.

LightFoot sat in his usual place at the end of the bar. He nursed his usual Early Times and Coke. The music continued as another blues maker, Clifton Chenier, took the stage. He was young and played the accordion, which was a most unusual sound for the blues. His brother, who played a washboard in the Cajun tradition, accompanied him. Many in the place did not pay too much attention but Clifton played his heart out trying to make his songs as memorable as LightFoot's.

Bill Blue wiped off the bar in front of LightFoot and breathed out in disgust, "Here come that goddamned cracker." LightFoot turned his eyes in the direction of the door and there stood a familiar figure—Frank Miller.

Miller, a deputy, had the innocent face of a minister that became anything but virtuous when he spoke. He was not large or threatening so he carried his sidearm on duty and off. It gave him a feeling of power that his physical presence could not. His face was so familiar in the tavern that, when he entered, heads did not turn as they did when other white men entered. He liked the music and loved colored women—Vitalee Johnson in particular.

Vitalee sang the blues. She sounded good, and often said, "If singin' paid any money, I'd do it full time." She was fucking Frank full time, or whenever the urge hit him. Usually it was once or twice a week. Vitalee used Frank's urges to supplement her meager income from the bus station food counter. She was a real con artist and cunningly got money from Frank without making him feel he was paying for the pussy. This particular night Vitalee had sung and gone home early so she could be with her true lover-man.

Frank surveyed the room, straining to see through the dim smoke-filled light. Bill said, "That horny bastard is looking for Vitalee."

Not seeing Vitalee's smiling black face, Frank headed for the bar.

"Hey, boy, gimme a beer."

LightFoot looked into Bill Blue's tense face, knowing that he did not like being called out of his name—especially "boy" by a white man. Without looking in the direction of the affront, Bill got a bottle of Jax and slammed it down in front of Frank with just the right amount of force not to break. Frank got the message, threw a quarter on the bar, then spit out, "Where Vitalee?"

"She ain't here."

"I can see that. Where she at?"

"I ain't her keeper!"

"Boy, you getting smart with me?"

LightFoot knew that this second "boy" was not going to set too well with Bill. By this time their verbal exchange had brought silence to those within earshot.

"This is my place and I don't have to answer to the likes of you 'bout nothing."

"Nigger, I'll close this goddamn place down."

"Finish your beer and get your ass out."

"You wanna put me out?"

This was a question that Bill Blue could not let go unanswered. He came from behind the bar like a clap of thunder before a sudden storm. The patrons, knowing that shit was about to fly, moved out of the path of harm. Bill headed directly toward Frank. Frank pulled his gun and screamed as he backed away from the big black storm headed in his direction, "Stop, nigger. You're under arrest."

Bill continued bearing down as Frank backed into tables, stumbled over chairs, and pushed people out of his retreating path while still screaming, "Nigger, I told you to stop!"

Frank had built himself an impossible mountain to climb. Bill, not afraid of a gun, would not be intimated by a white face in his own place, and did not believe Frank had the courage to shoot. Frank, now forced to save face in front of a bar full of "niggers," pulled the trigger and pumped three bullets into Bill's chest. Bill dropped to his knees and fell dead on his face. Before the smoke cleared the place was empty.

ABOUT AN hour later Sheriff Cat Bobineaux arrived, with Frank Miller in the front seat of the patrol car. Several of the patrons, including LightFoot, had drifted back inside and were sitting at tables around the body, holding, in their own way, a private wake. Bill's body lay on the floor where he fell. He was covered with a patchwork quilt that LightFoot had borrowed from the lady next door. The sheriff entered with Miller brazenly following. He went over to the body, looked under the quilt, ran his hand across his chin and looked into the face of each of Negroes assembled. He cleared his throat and said,

“My deputy tells me he was making an arrest and this here Bill Blue resisted and attacked him, so he had to shoot him. Any of you people see anything any different?

Frank Miller turned and looked, from one side and then the other, at the bowed heads of the grief-stricken gathering. There was silence. The sheriff said, All right then, I’ll send the undertaker back to pick up the body. ”

With that, the sheriff left with Miller following. Bobineaux felt he had investigated the case. All he could find was a case of resisting arrest in which deputy Miller killed in self-defense. Not one witness, including LightFoot, dared to attest to the fact that Miller, who was off duty and had no cause to arrest, had insulted and then challenged Bill Blue. What would normally have been a fistfight between two men ended in the unwarranted death of the colored man.

LightFoot went home to Naomi. He tried, almost incoherent with grief, to relate what had happened. The plot was not new. A flood of anger, built up over years of sexual exploitation by white men, matched equally by their contempt and disrespect of colored people, had suddenly burst forth. It seemed there was no end in sight for repetition of this familiar scenario. But the ending was always the same. The white man could kill without fear of being liable. Naomi understood LightFoot’s pain. She went to the Victrola, wound it up, and played “Graveyard Dream Blues. ” LightFoot listened as tears sparkled in the candlelight. If only he could wake up to discover that what had happened was only the dream that Bessie Smith was singing about. His eyes grew heavy and he prayed for sleep.

The next day, word of the killing had run its course in Estilette. Each person believed whichever rumor suited their standing on the racial-social ladder.

The white people believed, "The nigras are always doing something against the law, and the only good nigra is a dead nigra."

The colored people believed, "That white man was in a place he had no business being, looking for pussy he had no business gettin'. So when he called Bill 'boy,' the scared little son of a bitch had to shoot to keep from getting his ass kicked. And the law ain't gonna do nothin' about it."

The Creole people believed, "Those nigger juke-joints ain't nothing but buckets of blood. They should close 'em all. The nigger got what he deserved, 'cause he was probably mouthin' off to the law."

At dinner that evening Martha was full of reckonings. The fact that LightFoot was witness to this tragic event caused the family to listen in silence to his account. He was appropriately graphic. He described the entire scene, down to and including the tension-filled air and the smell of gun smoke. When he finished Martha said, "I reckon that's too bad. That nigger shoulda known better than tangle with the law. I reckon now there'll be one less juke-joint."

LightFoot rose violently from the table and walked to the door. He stopped and turned. "That's it. I'm moving out tonight."

Everyone at the table was shocked. Each of the children protested. Phillip was silent. He alone understood the depth of LightFoot's exasperation with Martha's remark. She said in a tone that was patronizing, "Don't be silly. Sit and finish your dinner."

"My darling sister, it's not about eatin'. I'm sick and tired of hearing you talk about nigger-this and nigger-that. You act like anybody who's darker than you ain't got no right to live a'tall. And I'm sick and tired of you pretending you're white 'cause I know you ain't. I'll come back for my things."

With that, LightFoot was out of the door. The only comment came from Martha: "He'll be sorry."

MARTHA WAS right. LightFoot would be sorry. But he was not sorry for the reason she predicted. It was the war years—the early forties. Rationing of gas, meat, and sugar was making changes in every family. Because LightFoot was registered as a member of the Fergerson household, his ration stamp allotment was issued as part of the family's. He was now living with Naomi. Every month he had to negotiate with Martha to get his proper amount of stamps. He was sorry that this situation made it necessary to have to deal with his sister. Every month they would get into an argument over how many of which stamps he was due.

Since he didn't have a car, he felt that the portion of gasoline stamps from which he did not benefit should make up for a greater number of meat and sugar stamps. Every month the final amount of stamps would be decided by a whole new set of figures and reasoning. Every month he had to listen to speeches from Martha about "living in sin." Yes, LightFoot was sorry that he was forced to have anything at all to do with his sister. He knew the rift between them was over the blues and Naomi. And he was not about to give up either, so he had to weather the monthly storms if he expected to get any stamps. Since he was not married he could not legally get his stamps any other way.

Blue's Tavern had been boarded up for the eighteen months since Bill Blue was shot. One day LightFoot walked slowly past, looking and

thinking as he had done many times. He had a lot on his mind. When he got home he shocked Naomi with a proposal—"Let's get married."

She faced him with a hint of mischief dancing in her eyes.

"You tired of fussing with Martha?"

"Yeah, but that not the reason."

"What then?"

"Let's buy us Blue's Tavern."

The hint of mischief left her eyes and was replaced by a somber questioning of his sanity. "Man, is you lost your mind?"

With that she left the room. All discussion was off. As far as she was concerned, there was no way LightFoot could possibly have been serious. He followed her as she disappeared into the bathroom and closed the door. LightFoot stood outside and continued his proposal.

"I figures it this way. They got all them colored soldiers over at Camp Claiborne on maneuvers in them swamps all week long. And on the weekend they ain't got too many places to go to have a good time. We could take that little money you got saved up and my share of inheritance from the old place and go into biddness for ourselves. Course, in order to do that we gotta get married."

After the sound of a flush, Naomi came out of the bathroom with the hint of mischief restored to her face. She kissed him on the cheek and walked away, coyly throwing back over her shoulder, "If you can get yo' money outa your tight-wad sister, I'll marry you."

As far as LightFoot was concerned it was settled. They would get married, buy Blue's Tavern, and he would not have to deal with Martha over ration stamps any more.

LIGHTFOOT HAD a fifty-fifty share of ownership in the property on which Phillip and Martha had built their house. "With my share bought outright, y'all will have uncontested ownership of what's left of the Broussard estate." Phillip listened. LightFoot knew better than go to Martha with this proposal. Phillip, however, was not too happy when he realized that he would have to dig into his savings for the cash. But he certainly understood. He also realized that it would make the distribution of property to his children less complicated further down the road. Phillip promised to have the property appraised and to give LightFoot three-quarters of its value. Phillip would give the extra quarter as a wedding present. However, LightFoot had to promise that the gift would remain a secret between them. LightFoot agreed; Blue's Tavern was purchased.

LightFoot's construction skills were put to good use. He got some of his buddies to chip in and help him repair, paint, and fix up the old blues place. It was soon the talk of colored town. Word also leaked over to the white side of town. There was not much joy in Estilette over the prospects of "another nigra joint, for them nigra soldiers."

Sheriff Cat Bobineaux called the camp commander, complaining, "All these nigra soldiers are bound to cause trouble." The commander said there was little he could do to stop them. Of all the nearby towns Estilette was the favorite because, as he put it, "They like your high-yellar gals and that blues music." But he pledged a strong and vigilant military police force that would, "at the slightest hint of trouble, get the colored troops back to camp." Bobineaux took the attitude of wait and see, and left the matter alone.

LightFoot found out that he was not as free as before to play blues all night. He had to tend bar and look after all of the other "biddness" that running a place demanded. Maybe once or twice a week he would leave Naomi behind the bar and pick up the guitar for one song. But on a regular basis he had to bring in local bluesmen and others to play. Silas Hogan heard the word about the Blues Tavern reopening as far away as Scotlandville. He usually played blues clubs around Baton Rouge, but the lure of playing for the soldiers was very strong. Vitalee was now the regular singer and could easily adapt to the various styles of Silas Hogan, Clarence Garlow, or Cleve White. All of these bluesmen drifted in and out of Estilette from as far away as New Orleans.

Every bluesman or blueswoman who wanted to play or sing was welcomed; and there were a few in the service, like Roy "Professor Longhair" Byrd. No one really knew whether he was on maneuvers in the Louisiana swamps or on furlough from a nearby state. He was there in his uniform like all the other soldiers and nobody cared. The only thing that mattered was that he was sitting at the piano with whoever happened to need or want a blues-piano sideman. Estilette was never quite the same after the reopening of Blue's Tavern, now renamed The Blues Tavern, without the apostrophe.

The fact that LightFoot was now a juke-joint owner was a nightly one-person conversation in the Fergerson household. Martha could not figure out where the money came from to buy what she called "that place." She was not aware of the transaction that changed the title from the Broussard family estate to Fergerson community property. Phillip thought this was best, to keep down family conflict. He was even able to get the parish recorder to take a few extra dollars to accept only his signature on the deed. So Martha would shake her head and say, "I sure would like to know where that woman got all that money."

She figured that LightFoot had not contributed anything to the purchase because, "I know he ain't got no money."

Everyone listened but said nothing. Phillip never raised his eyes from his plate. Rosa and Vel simply didn't care. Lala was curious but dared not let her mother know she was interested. The lack of response did not deter Martha's conversation about the shame, gossip, and embarrassment to the family name. "Mama and Papa would turn over in their graves if they knew," she said.

One Friday night when Lala was supposed to go to a *fais-da-do* in Frilotville, she instead persuaded the Martel boy she was dating to take her by the tavern. The place had the usual fill of soldiers and single women. Since most of the eligible men in town had been drafted or had volunteered for the service, many women went places unescorted. The few men that were still around were either 4F or classified deferred because of vital occupations. The Martel boy fell into the category of farmer—a vital occupation. His family had large sugar cane acreage and he was the mainstay, since his father was going blind.

Lala was one of the few fortunate women who had a steady boyfriend. Most of the other women had to go places alone or seek out the companionship of weekend soldier-visitors. The term "loose woman" that had been applied to any female going out unescorted was now applied to so many that it began to lose its stigma. It was now more uncommon to see a woman walk into a public place escorted by a man than to enter alone. It was this uncommon sight that caught Naomi's eye. She walked behind the bar to LightFoot and said, "Guess who just walked in?" LightFoot looked toward the door and saw his niece standing at the edge of the crowd, like a chicken with a broken wing at feeding time.

"Lala, what you doing here?"

"Thought I'd come hear the blues."

"Your mama know?"

"Naw, and don't you tell her."

LightFoot had never laughed so completely in his life. It was a laugh full of utter enjoyment for the ironies of life. Here was the beautiful, silken-haired image of Martha's Creole pride standing in the midst of the field niggers. Called to worship by that same gut-bucket sound that spoke so loudly, the feelings of all who were called colored. The one thing that Martha wanted so badly to deny was now speaking in the soul of Lala.

"What's so funny, Uncle Johnny?"

"Nothing you will understand, chile. Com' on sit down."

He led her to a table in the front near the stage. She snapped her fingers, clapped her hands and kept time with the beat of the music. Her whole body moved with the rhythm of the blues, and in no time at all she was up dancing. LightFoot watched with pride. It made him feel good that at least one other member of his family had blues in the blood.

14

IT SEEMED THAT the release of suppressed feelings was the order of the day. Ever since Phillip had called Vel on the carpet about her unfair treatment of the dark-skinned boy, she had been sullen and indifferent. At school she hardly spoke to him. At home she was rude and abusive. Anything Phillip said to her would provoke a fuss. Martha noticed the discord and tried to salve the irritation but without success. There was little peace between them. Vel seemed to find any and every thing she could to antagonize Phillip. First it was her clothes. She changed her wardrobe drastically. Her dresses were tighter fitting, more revealing, and brighter colored. Phillip could no longer ignore what she was wearing to school and called her to his office. If he had not wisely waited until the end of the school day, the eruption would have embarrassed him in front of faculty and staff. Vel did not take his admonishment lightly.

"You don't have a damn thing to say about what I choose to wear."

"As long as you are in my school and living in my house, I do."

"Then maybe it's time that I left your damn school and your damn house."

Phillip was not ready to deal with this course of events. In the first place, Vel was using profane and indelicate language that she had never before directed at him. They were now yelling at each other. Vel had decided not to hold in her feelings any longer. She left the office in a fit of rage and headed home on foot. Usually she rode with Phillip, but everyone else had already left for the day and there was no one to ask for a ride, so she was forced to walk. Phillip was relieved that no one was around to hear the outburst.

For some time Vel had entertained thoughts of moving out. A few months earlier, she had overheard Miz Julee tell Martha that she was planning to take a teaching position at the blind school and was looking for someone to keep her house. Furthermore, Vel knew that Miz Julee was more liberal than her parents. Now was the time.

Vel took full advantage of the situation. When Phillip returned from his farm, where he went every evening after school, Vel was loading the last of her clothes in Viola's car. She gave him a cold good-bye and left.

It was not long after this that Miz Julee left to go to Scotlandville to take up duties at the State Blind School for the Colored. Vel now had the whole house to herself, which was completely to her liking. Miz Julee was so grateful that "someone responsible," as she put it, would be looking after her house that she only charged a monthly rent of fifteen dollars. Vel, twenty-six, living alone, really felt independent. For the first time in her life she did not have to answer to anyone for anything. She was footloose and fancy-free. And one of her fancies was to have lots of admirers. What better place to see and be seen by admirers than a movie theater box office?

Answering the call of the times, an enterprising white man decided to open a movie theater for colored. David Spitzer renovated the old opera house, abandoned by the whites when a new one was built. He opened a movie theater where colored did not have to sit in the balcony as they did at the Delta, and it was an instant hit. Vel was one of the first to answer his ad for "attractive colored girls to sell tickets."

Martha had a fit but there was nothing she could do but rant and rave. Phillip, as usual, was silent. He knew there was nothing he could say that would have any effect on Vel.

Vel enjoyed the admiration of the many soldiers who came to the early shows before hitting the juke-joints later in the evenings. As time passed she began to feel an attraction for some of them and struck up conversations. Sometimes she found a guy waiting outside to walk her home after the box office closed. This was especially desirable, because she was at liberty to invite him in for conversation or a drink if she chose to. One handsome light-skinned soldier from Chicago talked her into letting him sleep with her. It was her first time and she enjoyed it. At twenty-six she was no longer a virgin. Having been taught in church that it was a sin to have sex before marriage, surprisingly she did not feel particularly sinful. Rather, she felt good. She looked forward to seeing and walking home again with this special soldier who called himself Gabriel.

At nine o'clock the next night Gabe was waiting to walk her home. He stayed and talked, telling exciting tales about the big Windy City, until she fell asleep. The next morning she woke to discover that her personal belongings had been ransacked. Her wristwatch and fifty dollars were missing. She was furious, but there was no one she could complain to. She briefly considered reporting the thief to Sheriff

Bobineaux, but changed her mind when she envisioned how quickly such juicy gossip would travel all over town. She was angry and wanted revenge. A few nights later she enticed another willing body to walk her home. Over a beer she told him she needed to replace a watch that had been lost. It was a special and expensive present given by her parents for graduation. It would destroy them if they knew. She wanted to replace it but did not have enough money. If he would contribute a few dollars, she would be grateful enough to kiss him goodnight.

Every night there was another and another until she had more money than she'd lost in the theft. She enjoyed the charade and the accompanying sexual arousal. There was also a feeling of power. She was in control. She would never again allow her personal belongings to be at risk while she slept. Not only was she being paid back for her loss, but in the future she would be paid in advance for her affections. Thus began a weekend activity, the word of which quickly spread among the soldiers. In a short time Vel was the most sought-after young lady in Estilette. However, she was discreet and highly selective in choosing her clients. In all cases they had to be light-skinned, well-groomed, and mannered. She could not resist telling Viola about her newly discovered source of extra money for the latest fashions. Not long after that Viola joined Vel's enterprise, and they became the two most popular young ladies in Estilette.

THINGS WERE not as they had been. The number of people appearing at the supper table on a daily basis had diminished. Bobby was away at Fisk University and Vel was living at Miz Julee's. During the week Lala and Rosa were constantly busy correcting papers and making lesson plans, so a regular schedule of eating supper was difficult for them to maintain. Although Rosa was usually around on the weekends, Lala had persuaded her Uncle Johnny to let her "sit in" on sessions at the tavern. Lala liked the feel of being a blues musician and was now sitting in on a regular basis on weekends. She knew that there was no way she could explain to her parents, especially Martha, that she was a blues musician, so she had become adept at creating excuses for being away from home on the weekends.

So in an odd way, peace had finally come to the Fergerson household. There was no one around to fuss with or about. Phillip and Martha had now gotten into the habit of exchanging only the barest number of words. Supper was a scene of silence, broken only by the steady staccato rhythm of silver against china. Once in a while a "Pass the salt" would interrupt the evening rhythm, but usually there was silence. They had nothing more to say to each other. And after supper was finished, Martha put away the food and cleaned up the kitchen. Phillip usually found something to read, or he would simply sit and reminisce. An uneasy peace had settled in but it was not to be long-lived.

In a town as small as Estilette it was just a matter of time before anyone's most intimate act became public knowledge, and it was Lilly Ellis who took insidious delight in the revelation. She never liked Martha anyway, and she knew that Martha did not like her. She did not even care whether she was giving news that was already known or not. However, she suspected that Martha would not approve of the gossip going around: "Lala is playing piano at the blues juke-joint."

Martha pretended not to be alarmed. She was not about to let someone that she considered a "common nigger" see her upset over such idle talk. She thanked her politely and said, "It must be a mistake or hearsay. I'm sure her uncle would never allow her to do such a thing." In truth she was not sure. She would not put anything past her brother, especially since he had taken up with a common woman. As far as Martha was concerned, anyone who hung around with low-life riffraff was capable of anything. So there might be a slight chance that the Ellis woman knew what she was talking about. Martha had to find that out for herself.

The following Friday, as Lala was preparing to go out, Martha asked casually, "Lala, where you off to tonight?

"Fais-do-do in Frilotville."

Lala continued brushing her hair and added after a slight hesitation, "With Lester."

"He's a nice boy. I like him. Don't stay out too late." Martha's hands caressed Lala's hair as she planted a kiss on her forehead. "Your hair sure is pretty."

"Just like yours, Mama."

Martha did not question her any further. Lala had never lied to her. And since she only had the word of a woman she did not respect, she was not about to question her daughter about gossip from such a source. Lester came by to pick up Lala as usual. And after exchanging the usual pleasantries with both "Mr. and Mrs. Fergerson," as he called them, and updating them on the condition of his daddy's failing eyesight, Lester and Lala took off for the evening.

As the night wore on and turned into early morning, Martha became more and more uneasy. She kept going to the door and looking out. She was up and down so much that it caused Phillip, who was no longer accustomed to small talk, to inquire, "What's your trouble?"

Martha made the excuse of having indigestion, "And walking seems to help." Phillip returned his attention to the book he was reading, Carter G. Woodson's *Negro History*, and tried not to be disturbed by her movements. Finally, the early morning hour and Lala's failure to show up got the better of Martha. She told Phillip what she had heard from the Ellis woman. Phillip was silent. He didn't know what to say, and really didn't want to say anything. Not because he felt that the gossip might be true, but he simply did not want to get into a conversation with Martha over anything, especially something said by a neighbor she did not like. He looked at his watch, slipped it back into his vest pocket, and flipped open the book. Before he could resume reading, Martha interrupted, "I think we should go over to that place and see for ourselves."

"It's one o'clock in the morning."

"The fais-do-do is usually over by twelve."

"Maybe Lester had car trouble."

"She should'a been home by now, if she had gone to the dance."

"Martha, the girl is twenty-two years old."

"That mean it's all right for her to be in that place?"

"We don't know she is."

"That's what we need to find out. Come on."

Phillip was not too happy about the idea but he chose not to try and talk Martha out of going. Plus the fact he did not want her to take the car and go without him.

THE JUKE-JOINT was jumping. Soldiers and their women were crowded into every available chair and space. LightFoot was behind the bar serving drinks hand over fist. Naomi was waiting tables. With sweat falling into overflowing glasses like raindrops, the two of them worked steadily to keep up with the demand for liquor. Whenever he got a chance, LightFoot ran his index finger across his brow and flicked away the salty moisture. Although Naomi used her table towel for double duty, to dry the tables as well as her face, she did not get the chance to wipe often enough to keep sweat out of the drinks.

The music was loud, the beat was right. Lala was at the piano. "Schoolboy" Cleve White was alternating between guitar and harmonica. Word that Estilette was a soldiers' weekend playground had brought blues musicians from as far away as Baton Rouge, and "Schoolboy" was one of the regulars. He and Lala had now fallen into a groove, the results of many previous sessions. Vitalee closed her eyes, visualized "troubles with my man" and sang the blues to everybody's delight. On the dance floor, which was any space not occupied by a table or chairs, bodies were grinding belly to belly. The smoke was heavy and good times were rolling.

Martha entered and Phillip followed. She stopped inside the door. Planted like a rock in the middle of a stream of traffic, she was roughly jostled from one side to the other. Phillip did his best to avoid blocking the constant flow by stepping from side to side. Never before in Martha's life had she experienced the shock of what now bombarded her senses. The commingled smells of liquor, smoke, and sweaty bodies assailed her nostrils. The cacophony of blatant vulgarities and blues music, each trying to drown out the other, brought an unwelcome harshness to her ears.

She was in a foreign place. She stared through the veil of smoke toward the sound of the piano. She reached back, assured that Phillip would be within arm's distance, and grabbed his hand and pulled him alongside. She leaned over instinctively, trying to be heard over the noise, and shouted into his ear, "There she is." She could hardly believe her eyes. Here was her precious Lala in a den of iniquity. Everything that Martha had always regarded beneath her now surrounded her daughter. The gut-bucket music, smoking, drinking, and the niggers. All of it was here laying siege to her own flesh and blood. And she knew Johnny was responsible. There was nothing in Lala's upbringing that would lead her to this low life. It was her uncle. He had encouraged this behavior just to get back at her for all of the disagreements they had ever had. Martha's thoughts were traveling a mile a minute. She had not yet decided who should be the foremost recipient of her rage, but first she had to rescue Lala from this evil.

As foreign as this scene was for Martha, it was not so for Phillip. He had experienced before the feel of good times in the air, the aroma of sexy sweat, and the suffocating effects of smoke. As he focused on the dancers moving to the beat of the blues, he remembered the body-rub with Alicia in Port Allen. It was not, as he had briefly felt the first time, objectionable. This renewed experience seemed more familiar, and he surprisingly did not object to his daughter being here. If there was any reluctance at all, it was for her safety. But because it was Johnny's tavern, and not the proverbial "bucket of blood," he knew that she would be safe. He also knew that there was no way he could explain to Martha what he thought or how he felt. Phillip leaned his head in close to Martha's ear and yelled, "Now that we've seen for ourselves, let's go."

This seemed the only motivation needed to spring Martha into action. She began pushing roughly through the dancers, headed straight for the sound of the piano. Phillip reached out to restrain her but she eluded his grasp. He quickly looked around to see if he could locate Johnny. He knew that he would need help to corral the storm that was about to break loose. Unable to spot Johnny in the sea of smoke-shrouded faces, he thought it best to stay with Martha. He sidestepped couples and excused his movements as he rushed to catch up. Martha was already climbing onto the small platform that served as a stage. Lala turned in the direction of the commotion. Their eyes met.

"Mama!"

"Come on, child, I'm taking you home."

Martha grabbed Lala by the arm and pulled her roughly from the keyboard. This abrupt termination of Lala's accompaniment caused Cleve White to stop playing. Without the spell of the music, all eyes turned toward the stage where Martha was dragging a struggling Lala away from the piano. Lala broke Martha's grip, ran back to her seat, and resumed playing. Martha momentarily searched her mind for a counter action. Scattered sounds of laughter and applause from the amused crowd incensed Martha to uncontrollable rage. She shoved Vitalee out of her path and stood between Lala's hands and the keyboard. Phillip had finally reached the stage but was too late. Martha slapped Lala hard, back and forth, across the face. Phillip was able to restrain her hand in mid-motion. Lala cried out, "Ohhhh, Mama!"

"Come on, I'm taking you out of here."

Martha's reach for Lala's arm was halted by Phillip standing between Martha's rage and Lala's distress. He pushed Martha backwards and away. She was not finished. She looked toward the bar, knowing that Johnny was somewhere in that direction. She yelled at the top of her voice as Phillip struggled to pull her toward the exit.

"You low-life, sinful devil, wait till I get my hands on you!" Fortunately LightFoot was not in her line of sight, because during the altercation he had worked his way to the backside of the stage and was now comforting Lala. Had he been, there was no telling what Martha would have done. She was mad enough to kill. Naomi moved to LightFoot's side as he embraced Lala's quivering body. She whispered in his ear. "That's an evil woman." As Phillip pulled Martha toward the door through the crush of people, a path miraculously opened and closed—an indication that the revelers were anxious for them to leave so they could return to the business of having a good time. Outside, Martha shook herself free of Phillip's grasp and walked majestically to the car.

They drove home in silence. Tears slid down Martha's face. Her daughter had disrespected her. Her daughter had lied. Her brother had embarrassed her again. Both of them would live to regret the pain that they had brought to her heart.

Phillip's eyes returned to the empty gravel road. His mind raced with the sound of the motor as he sped along, putting as much distance between them and the tavern as he could. Tonight he had witnessed a side of Martha he'd never seen before. She was possessed with hate. He knew she was strong-willed. He knew she was determined. But he had never seen her act so disgracefully. Public display of any kind was a demeanor that she detested. Yet tonight she struck their daughter in public. Embarrassed the family. Made a scene that was totally uncalled for. Why? He tried to figure it out. Was it because she disliked her brother? Was it because Lala had lied? Was it because of Lilly Ellis's gossip? Was it because she hated the blues? He didn't know what to think. But he knew what he felt. For the first time, he had seen that the beauty he had admired all of these years was only skin deep.

LALA WENT straight to Miz Julee's house. Vel surreptitiously dismissed her client, passing him off as her date for the evening. She then turned her attention to calming her sister's hysteria. It simply did not make sense to them that their mother disliked the blues so much that she would strike her own daughter. Neither one could understand nor explain the reason for their mother's actions. But whatever the reason, it was clear to Lala that she could not return home. Vel prepared for Lala to spend the night in Miz Julee's room, hoping that the rational light of day would bring other arrangements. Lester refused to leave, insisting that he spend the night.

The light of day did indeed bring solutions. During the passion of the previous evening Lester had made love to Lala. It was their first time. Because Lester was a good Catholic boy he now felt obligated to marry her. They decided to elope. Lala knew her mama would want a big wedding, but all Lala wanted was to get away. She wanted nothing more to do with her mama. As far as Lala could figure, leaving was the only solution to the dilemma. Over coffee Vel listened, in shocked silence, as Lala detailed their plans.

"Lester got up early and went to Frilotville to get some money he's had been saving in the hayloft. When he gets back we're gonna drive to Beaumont, Texas, and get married."

Vel said, "Well, all I can say is, the embarrassment of this elopement will certainly cause Mama a lot of pain. You should have just hit her back."

"But I didn't."

"If you go and get married that's exactly what you'll be doing."

"She'll get over it. It's not like I'm twelve years old. I'm a grown woman, and Mama has to realize that."

Since Vel's psychological ploy did not jolt Lala into an awareness of the gravity of her decision, she simply wished her luck.

The only regret she expressed, in anticipation of Lala's plans to run off, had to do with her father. "You should have seen Papa's face. He was so embarrassed by Mama acting like that in public. I felt so sorry for him." She took a long sip of coffee and looked off into space.

"He takes a lot off'a Mama. I just wish I could talk to him before I leave. He's going to take this real hard."

Early Monday morning Lester and Lala took off, headed west. That evening when Vel returned home from school she found two letters sitting on the table. One was addressed to the principal of the school, the other addressed to "Papa." Both were marked "Delivered through the kindness of Velma Fergerson." That was the last that Estilette would see of Lala for several years.

THE BLUES Tavern buzzed with various versions of the incident. Since this had happened on a weekend, there were only a few townsmen present. Usually the tavern was taken over by soldiers on the weekends, so the townsmen had to enjoy their blues and their women while the soldiers were in camp. Now they enjoyed "the story" and it circulated for many weeks. LightFoot had stopped telling what happened. But there were several all-too-willing storytellers eager to add their interpretation to the action of the "colored lady who wanted to be white." In one version the mother dragged the daughter by the hair through the crowd, and there was no lack of imagination in other scenarios. During this time Vitalee Johnson did her own creative styling. She composed a song that told the story of that "blues- hating woman who tried to slap the blues away. "

One night after Vitalee left the stage, a white hand reached out and pulled her close. Frank Miller was back. He had not seen her since the shooting. Every time her black ass and luscious tits flashed through his white mind, his "johnson" got hard. Frank figured that sufficient time had passed for it to be safe for him to return. Besides, he had missed his "poontang" and it was time to get back to his black gal. There was nothing much that LightFoot could do about Miller, nor much that he wanted to do. He wanted peace and was not about to antagonize the white hothead into shooting him as he had shot Bill. So LightFoot tolerated Frank, and so did Vitalee, even though her dislike for him was greater now than before.

Previously, the money that Vitalee was able to get out of Frank made up for the displeasure that she felt whenever he touched her. Now, heightened by the murder, her resentment had turned to hate. Ironically, Frank was too naive and biased to be aware that she would have any feelings at all about the fact that he had killed a colored man whom she knew and liked. Inside she was seething with thoughts of being free of this white man's fixation for her body.

In addition to her regular chores at the bus station, Vitalee periodically baked apple pies. One night she brought one with her to the tavern and gave it to LightFoot. It was still warm. LightFoot stopped chipping ice, got a glass of milk, and sat at the bar to enjoy his gift. Vitalee went on to the back room to change into her singing clothes. Before LightFoot could eat his first slice, Frank Miller entered. It was early. Miller usually came late. This meant he was very horny and

Vitalee would be leaving before the joint got jumping. Frank sat next to LightFoot and ordered his regular Jax beer. LightFoot abandoned his pie and began searching through the cooler to find a beer the right temperature. Frank dug his fingers into the warm delicious-smelling pie. He liked it so much that he pulled the pan over and ordered a glass of milk along with his beer. LightFoot stood helplessly watching his pie disappear into Frank's greedy mouth. Frank licked his thin lips and ordered, "Another one of these."

"There ain't no mo'. Tha's all there was. That pie was made 'specially for me by Vitalee."

Frank could not have been more delighted. He saw Vitalee enter from the back room and yelled, "Gal, you gotta make me one of them there pies. That's the best eating I had in a long time."

Vitalee smiled a quickly fading smile and nodded, "OK," as she continued to the stage. At first she was resentful of the fact that Frank was now insisting that she also be his cook. But as she rehearsed her first selection of the evening, "My Lover Man Was Mean and Evil, Now He's Dead and Gone," an idea came into her head. It was a sinister thought but one which brought a satanic smile to her face. Before beginning the set she sashayed to the bar, kissed Frank on the cheek, and said, "Baby, I'm gonna bake you a pie and bring it by your place after work tomorrow."

THE NEXT night Frank passed on peacefully in his sleep. Sheriff Bobineaux could not understand why Frank died so young. The coroner ruled that death resulted from heart failure. There were no signs of struggle or foul play. There was nothing to suggest anything other than a congenital heart condition that no one knew about. The one thing that the sheriff was sure of was that Frank died on a full stomach. On the floor next to the bed, along with a pile of chicken bones and six empty Jax beer bottles, was an empty pie pan. In the kitchen, dishes from meals eaten weeks earlier were still piled around, attracting roaches. The house was a mess. The sheriff went down to the tavern and got Frank's "nigger gal" to clean up the place so it would be presentable for the wake. And that is exactly what Vitalee did. She cleaned away any and every thing that could be considered evidence if anyone had a mind to look for any.

After the funeral Vitalee murmured a sigh of relief loud enough for LightFoot to hear. "Now I'll get some peace for a change."

LightFoot knew. He didn't know how she did it but he knew she had. He slid a bourbon and water across the bar and asked the question that had been on his mind. "Did you fuck him to death?"

"Lord, no!"

"What was it killed him, then?"

There was a long silence and slowly the satanic smile crept back onto Vitalee's face. She took a sip of bourbon and chased it with water. LightFoot broke the silence. "Arsenic?"

"Lord, no. That mean ol' heart just stopped beatin'."

LightFoot's curiosity had to be satisfied. He was one of the few people who knew how much hate she felt for Frank Miller over the killing of Bill Blue.

"You know we been friends a long time."

"I know that."

"So any secret you got is a secret I got."

The smile that had been on Vitalee's face turned to tears. She collapsed into LightFoot's arms and openly wept on his shoulders. He walked her to the back room, leaving Naomi to care for the few regulars at the bar. The casual observer might think that Vitalee was overcome by the death of her white lover, but LightFoot knew better. In the privacy of the back room he asked, "What happened?"

Vitalee dried her eyes and blew her nose. She crossed her arms and looked far away into the past.

"Remember when my daddy come back from Alaska?"

"Yeah, just in time to get lynched. He'd'a done better staying there with his gold money."

Vitalee crossed the room to her purse and began talking as she searched for a cigarette. "He was tired of freezing his ass in them gold fields. But he had gotten used to bein' treated like a man."

She lit a cigarette and blew the smoke into her past memory.

"He brought him back a little jar of some crystals. He told me he was saving it for the first white man who didn't show him respect. They hung him before he got a chance to use it."

LightFoot stared in silence. He stirred his Early Times with his index finger and whispered inaudibly, "Cyanide."

From that time on LightFoot and Vitalee were as one, in spirit and knowledge of how Frank Miller died.

15

BOBBY WAS NOW twenty and in his second year at Fisk University. He had managed to stay out of the military draft by making good grades. In spite of his impulsive decision to leave Southern College and go to Fisk, he had not yet accomplished his purpose for wanting to be in Nashville. Alex had said on more than one occasion, "I wish it were possible for us to get to know each other better." Being in the same city had not been as conducive to getting together as they had hoped. Vanderbilt and Fisk, although separated by only a few miles, were still worlds apart. For some reason that even Bobby's fantasy knew better than to believe, he hoped he would be able to date Alex.

For no other explanation, except possibly wishful thinking, he also felt that being in Nashville would be different than being in Estilette. It was not. There were no places where he and Alex would be tolerated socially. So they had to be content with seeing each other at Fisk during public programs, like the touring Margaret Webster Shakespearean Company or concerts of the Jubilee Singers. Alex could attend these functions without arousing suspicion. On these few and far-between occasions they expressed wishes that things were different and they could enjoy each other's company more frequently. Ironically this inconvenience encouraged the bond growing between them. They wanted to be together—alone.

Finally they had a chance. Alex was living off campus. It was spring and Alex's roommate decided to go home for the break, so she invited Bobby to dinner and to listen to Bessie Smith records. Bobby and Alex looked forward to this opportunity. Alex was hopeful it might provide as exciting an experience as the situation in Shakespeare's *Othello*—the exotic fascination of Desdemona's forbidden relationship stirred her imagination. But she was not so foolish as to imagine that the same nobility that existed in the relationship between the Bard's characters existed between her and Bobby. However, she did feel that to discount the possibility of this relationship simply because of skin color would be a mistake. Like Bobby she also thought of people as human beings rather than objects of color. After all, that was the primary point of the beautiful relationship in the play by Shakespeare.

The time for the event finally arrived. Bobby bathed, shaved, and scented early so he would not have to hurry the long walk. Just to be sure he knew how to get there, he had made a trial walk south on Eighteenth, to West End, then to Twenty-first Avenue; it took him forty minutes. Before he left the Fisk campus he picked a bunch of crocuses from the west side of Jubilee Hall. He wrapped his present in a sheet of newspaper comics.

The table was set and the wine had breathed. The Shrimp Creole was done and Bessie Smith was singing, "Nobody Knows You When You're Down and Out." Alex waited. At last there was a knock so slight that Alex thought she was imagining it. When she opened the door there stood Bobby. He stepped inside quickly, presented his flowers, and received his first warm gentle kiss.

Alex had just put the flowers in a vase and placed them in the center of the table when there was a jarring knock on the door, followed by a loud voice calling, "Mary Ann." Alex recognized the voice of her roommate's ex-boyfriend. Alex thought it wise that Bobby hide in the space between the sofa and the wall. She remembered that Chuck was a persistent, boorish redneck, which was the reason that her roommate had cooled on their relationship. Alex opened the door only wide enough to speak to the intruder. Bessie Smith still sang in the background.

"Hi, Chuck. Mary Ann is not here."

"Where did she go?"

"Home."

"Home? She didn't tell me."

"I thought you guys had broken up."

"Yeah, well . . . this is Carson."

Chuck pointed to a friend standing nearby. He said, referring to Alex, "She's the one whose daddy owns a newspaper."

Alex could tell by the remark that she had been the subject of an earlier conversation, and it did not sound complimentary. She began to feel uneasy.

"Look, Chuck, I'm expecting a friend. I'll tell Mary Ann you came by."

"Who's that singing?"

Chuck pushed past Alex into the room, as if in answer to his own question. Alex protested but her demands fell on deaf ears. Chuck went directly to the phonograph, took off the record, and read the label.

"Who the fuck is Bessie Smith?"

"Will you please leave my records alone?"

"Just like I thought. This is nigger music. You're a nigger-lover!"

Carson, following Chuck's intrusion, wandered into the kitchen and began tasting from the pot on the stove. Alex rushed furiously at Chuck and gave him a push toward the door. She yelled, "Get out!"

Chuck's response gave justification for his intrusion. "You got a lot of nigger music here."

With that pronouncement he began flinging records against the wall. Alex sprang on him like a tiger, hitting, scratching, and kicking. Chuck warded off her attack. Carson ran to help, and together the two men were finally able, after her noble defense, to restrain and overpower her. They tore off her clothes, forced her down, and each held her arms while the other had his way with her.

Alex's cries filled the air. Bobby lay on the floor behind the sofa, afraid to say or do anything. The vulgar remarks from the assailants turned Bobby's thoughts to the fate of his friend PeeWee. He knew and understood what was destined for him if he interfered. So he lay there, knowing full well that he was saving his own life by remaining invisible. He felt he should make some effort to rescue his friend from the fate of rape. Yet he did not have the courage to be the Negro defender of white womanhood. He rationalized that if Alex thought it wise for him to help she would have called his name.

Finally, after satisfying their lustful appetites, the two men left with the bottle of wine. The weeping of Alex was the only sound that broke the silence. Bobby looked out from behind the sofa. There she was, stripped of her clothes and quivering on the floor. Tears filled Bobby's eyes. He picked up the ripped skirt and blouse and covered her nakedness. Alex looked up and whispered softly, "You'd better get out of here, or you'll get blamed." This reality hit like a clap of thunder. Bobby knew she was right. He left her surrounded by shards of the broken records, lying on the floor like a pile of soiled linen.

Bobby did not stop running for ten blocks. He felt compelled to get as far from the scene as possible. He sat on the curb of Charlotte Avenue to catch his breath. He was not guilty of anything, so why was he running? In his mind's eye were scenes from a book he had read in literature class—*Native Son*, by Richard Wright, that had been published four years earlier. In this story a colored man, Bigger Thomas, had accidentally killed a white woman that he was chauffeuring. He ran. He was guilty. Bigger was afraid; so was Bobby. Bobby was not guilty, but he ran also. They had both reacted to their different situations by running away. Bobby's comparison of their responses was a sobering thought. He was awakened to more levelheaded action and walked, instead of running, back to the Fisk campus.

The distance back was filled with questions. The ones about himself, with impossible answers, echoed most in his mind. What kind of man would hide behind a sofa while his friend was being raped? Was it the color of the attackers that had caused his fear? Why was he afraid to take a stand against injustice at any cost? Whatever his response to these questions, he knew that he would never be able to look into Alex's eyes again. He had failed her.

He lay on his bed in the safety of his room. He remembered the days and nights in the attic of Alex's house. He remembered how Mr. Estilette had protected him from whatever unknown fate those men had in store. He remembered how faithfully Alex had prepared his food and left it outside the door; how she had introduced him to the music of Bessie Smith. He remembered how he had cried on her shoulder when he read the news of PeeWee's death. Not one of these thoughts made him feel very good about himself. As the darkness of night choked off the shadows of the fading day, Bobby could still hear the echoes of Alex's whispered warning, ". . . *or you'll get the blame.* " There it was! The reason he ran—away from blame. He jumped from his bed, turned on the light, and found *Native Son.* His fingers raced through the pages until he found the section that had passed through his mind earlier. He read Wright's words again:

> They'll say you raped her. Bigger stared. He had entirely forgotten the moment when he had carried Mary up the stairs. So deeply had he pushed it all back down into him that it was not until now that its real meaning came back. They would say he had raped her and there would be no way to prove that he had not. The fact had not assumed importance in his eyes until now. He stood up, his jaws hardening. Had he raped her? Yes, he had raped her.

That was the reason this story had popped into his subconsciousness after running. Bobby now began to understand what he had not understood the first time he read these lines. He had not understood before why Bigger felt that he had raped her when he knew he had not. He continued reading:

> Every time he felt as he had felt that night, he raped. But rape was what one did to women. Rape was what one felt when one's back was against a wall and one had to strike out, whether one wanted to or not, to keep the pack from killing one. He committed rape every time he looked into a white face. He was a long, taut piece of rubber which a thousand white hands had stretched to the snapping point, and when he snapped it was rape. But it was rape when he cried out in hate deep in his heart as he felt the strain of living day by day. That, too was rape.

Bobby closed his eyes. Now he understood. He had not experienced all of Bigger's life but he certainly understood what he meant about feeling rape. He, like Bigger, now felt the guilt of a rape he had not committed. He was beginning, like Bigger, to feel the strain of living in a milieu that made a violation of everything good that he felt or tried to do. He was also now being stretched taut like a piece of rubber. Finally, he felt the tensions of Bigger's life.

16

IT WAS 1944. Lala had been gone for almost a year. She had written only one letter, seven months earlier, explaining that she and Lester were expecting a baby. There was no return address and no further communication. Martha was by now a grandmother but she knew little else about Lala's well-being. Martha had cried and prayed every day since her departure. Every morning she went to Mass. She was the first to arrive at the church and the last to leave. She kept her pain alive in her heart, and she did not feel any guilt for the chain of events that brought about Lala's decision to leave.

Now Martha had a second cross to bear.

It had been more than fifteen years since she suspected that Phillip had an affair. Martha had carried this in her heart through all the years. She had done nothing about it except pray that God would show her the way to handle the situation gracefully. Over the years her only response was a pretended enthusiasm to Phillip's lovemaking. She believed that God expected her to be submissive and respectful of her husband's wishes. But the suspicion of this one-time infidelity made her indifferent to any demonstrations of affection, and she went about her wifely duties bearing her resentment in silence.

But this new cross was different. Phillip was only a husband. Lala was blood of her blood and flesh of her flesh. Now she was gone. Martha had whipped and chastised her many times before, although never in public and never since Lala had grown into womanhood. Still, Martha could not understand why this should make a difference. Lala would always be her baby no matter how old she got, and as a mother she had a right and duty to keep her children in line. There must have been something else at work—the influence of that evil music. "Yes," Martha thought, "that was the cause of it all. Had it not been for Johnny, Lala would still be at home and single. Why had God imposed these burdens?" Perhaps if she prayed long and hard enough, the prodigal daughter would be shown the path home. These were her daily thoughts and prayers. A voice from above interrupted her meditation. "Would ye like to talk?"

Martha looked up from her knees. She furtively pressed away her tears then allowed her mantilla to drop from her face. Father Pat stood next to the pew. Martha slid into a sitting position and Father Pat could clearly see the red swollen stare of her eyes.

"It is not good to bear so much alone."

"Father, I didn't want to bother you with any more of my family problems."

"It is no bother. It is my mission to bring comfort where it be needed."

"I don't know where Lala is or how she is."

"Put it in God's hands."

"I have prayed and prayed that God would give me a sign so I would know."

Father Pat sat next to Martha and gently caressed her hand in his.

"And when that happens ye will know. He works in mysterious ways and it is not always so easy to know when He is pointing ye the way. Sometimes He shows a path that is not easy to follow, or a path that is not in ye nature to take. But always His paths lead ye away from the devil."

Martha felt relieved and at ease. Father Pat seemed so wise and all-knowing. There was no doubt that God was speaking through him. She began to share some of her inner feelings. She said, "I've often felt that all of this happened because of that devil's music."

"It very well could have been. Wasn't she playing in the Baptist church for a while?"

Martha had forgotten about that, and the fact her brother had also played the devil's music in the same church for the funeral of that boy. The connections were beginning to be made in Martha's mind. The music was the link. Lala was being punished because of it. Father Pat quickly added, "I'm not suggesting that music in itself is the devil's work. But sometimes it leads one into a sinful situation that would not have existed otherwise."

"Could that be the reason I slapped her?"

"Who am I to say? Only God can judge."

Father Pat softly mumbled his blessings in Latin, made a small sign of the cross with his thumb on Martha's forehead, and said, "Continue to pray."

The weight of Martha's burden had been lifted. She did not feel as guilty now.

"Thank you, Father. You have brought peace to my soul."

"Remember, God will show ye the way. He will answer your prayers."

"I know, Father. I believe."

After one last reassuring squeeze of the hand, Father Pat crossed the altar and disappeared into the sacristy. Martha was left alone in God's house.

After Martha had completed the rosary, she walked to the altar rail and knelt before the candle rack. She had decided to ask the Blessed Mother to intercede in her behalf. She was also a woman, so she understood the pain Martha felt over the loss of a child. She would light a candle. Martha deposited her nickel, reached into the candle box, and took out a candle. The only vacant spot on the rack was near the top. She reached up to place her candle in the empty holder. Her lace mantilla swept across the lighted candles on the lower rows. It caught fire. Martha tore the shawl from her head, threw it to the floor, ran to the fount, got some holy water, and poured it on the burning shawl. She stood looking up at the Blessed Mother. Her heart raced in panic. What did this mean? Was this a sign? Had her prayers been answered? Martha considered these questions on the way home.

BOOKTAU DANCED around the big trash fire that he fed with the rotting wood, broken branches, and discarded furniture from the Prudhomme place. They had finally decided to clean up the unsightly mess that had been lying there for months. Martha had often wondered what kind of people would allow so much trash to accumulate over so long a time. Now it was being cleared away. BookTau pursued his task with enthusiasm. If the blaze was not burning evenly on one side, he would douse that section with coal oil and then dance with delight at the burst of new flames. For several minutes Martha watched BookTau's antics from her parked car. There was something about fire that he enjoyed. Fire—a means of cleansing. Yes! An avenging instrument from the Bible. Fire and brimstone—Sodom and Gomorrah! Before she understood what she was thinking or why, she tooted the horn. BookTau hopped over the fence that separated the yard from the street and approached the car. Martha spoke, "How long it'll take you to finish up what you doing here?

"I'll be done by tomorrow, Miz Martha."

He spat out a wad of tobacco mixed with juice on the ground next to the car. It was all Martha could do to keep from throwing up.

"Come over to my house. I got some work I want you to do for me."

"Yes, Ma'am. I'll be there bright and early."

PHILLIP WAS pleased that Martha had decided to dig up the plot of ground in back of the chicken coop. It would make an excellent garden. There would be little need to add additional fertilizer to the rich soil. Phillip did not really understand the sudden motivation, but it didn't matter. He tucked his thumbs into his vest pockets and watched BookTau turn over several spadefuls of black dirt.

"What ya planting?"

BookTau stopped, wiped his face with the red bandana hanging out of the hip pocket of his coveralls, and spit out a mouthful of tobacco juice.

"Don't know, Professor. Miz Martha ain't told me yet."

Another voice said, "Figured we might plant some okra, since you like it so much."

Phillip turned in the direction of the voice. Martha was crossing the chicken yard with a pitcher and a glass. She seemed in better spirits than he had seen her in many months. No doubt she was putting her daughter's abandonment behind, and directing her energy to other things. If this was any indication, the garden was a good start. She poured a glass of lemonade and handed it to BookTau while saying to Phillip, "There's some in the house for you. I'm gonna leave this pitcher out here." This was a change for Martha. She had never before served anything to anyone working for her. Phillip didn't know what to make of it, but he headed for the house, leaving Martha laughing and joking with BookTau. It seemed she had reached a new level of pleasantness with a person she had always regarded as beneath her.

THE FIRE lit up the sky. The brisk breeze pushed the smoke and embers over the whole Southwest area of town. The heavy pungent smell attached itself to everything that it drifted past. People gathered in small groups and stood in the middle of the street, leaned out of windows, or crowded the doorways. It was the biggest event in Estilette since the soldiers came to town in truck convoys—the only other time when a crowd gathered for a single event. Although the fire had started in the Western Addition, some distance away, the flames were easily seen from the Fergersons' front porch. Rosa snuggled closer to her papa. This was the most exciting happening that she had ever witnessed, and her wide eyes took in everything. She said, "Papa, that fire looks like it's kinda close to Uncle Johnny's place."

"It sure does. I think I'll go over there."

Martha gathered her robe against the breezy night air as she advised, "You better leave that fire alone."

"I'll be back directly."

Phillip returned from the fire an hour later. Martha had made a pot of coffee and was sitting at the table reading a novena and waiting. Phillip reeked of smoke. His hands and face were stained with soot. He collapsed in a chair.

"That was Johnny's tavern. It's burned to the ground."

Martha seemed unmoved. She got up and poured a cup of coffee and set it in front of Phillip.

"Is he all right?"

"The place was closed. Nobody got hurt."

"What happened?"

"Nobody knows. It had just about burned down before the firetruck got there. All they could do was wet down the other places on the street."

"Well, I guess that's the end of that devil's music."

With that, she headed to the bedroom. Phillip sipped his coffee and wondered if he had detected a slight hint of delight in her statement. Perhaps it was only his imagination.

MIZ JULEE sipped her tea and always returned the saucered cup to the same spot on the table. She had recently returned home for the Easter break. Her visit with Martha was not going to be pleasant. She planned to reveal things about Martha's daughter that were not going to be easy. Martha chatted on about how much Vel enjoyed being on her own and how grateful she was that Julee had allowed Vel to "keep" her house while she was away. Miz Julee could stand the small talk no longer. She blurted out, interrupting Martha, "My house smells like a cathouse."

Martha was taken aback. She did not know exactly what to say or what to think. She and Julee had been friends all of their lives. Now it seemed that she was making an uncomplimentary remark about her daughter's hygiene. Martha looked into her dead gray eyes. The lids were opened wider than usual and her sightless eyeballs rolled uneasily back and forth. Martha could tell that Miz Julee was upset over something.

"She don't have a cat."

"I don't mean that kind of cathouse."

Julee drained her cup and reached out to place it on the saucer. She missed. The sound of the breaking china brought Julee to her feet. Martha put her hand gently on Julee's shoulder.

"It's all right. You missed the table."

"I'm sorry. That chile of yours got me upset."

"Have a seat. I'll pick up the pieces."

Instead, Julee turned to her left, took four steps around her chair and gently swept her hand back and forth until it touched the piano. She knew her way around this room. It was here that she had taught piano lessons to the girls and Bobby. She knew this space like her own house. Julee stopped in front of the lamp table beneath the portrait of Antoine Broussard that was on the wall next to the piano.

"These flowers dead now. You should take them out of here."

Martha, still busy with the broken cup, looked up from the floor. Julee was standing in front of the vase of withered hydrangeas.

"Dead flowers have their scent just like live ones do."

Julee turned in the direction of Martha as if expecting to see the expression on her face caused by her next statement.

"I was talking about the smell of sex, liquor, and smoke in my house."

Martha rose with her hands full of the broken china. The larger pieces broke into smaller ones when she dropped them on the table. Her voice shattered like the china as she whispered, "You mean to tell me my chile been smoking and drinking in your house?"

"I hear tell she's turnt it into a whorehouse."

Silence prevailed. Martha staggered across the room to the sofa. It was more than she could take standing up. Surely, she thought, there must be a mistake. How could a blind woman know so much about what went on while she was out of town? But why would Julee even mention this if she did not have proof of what she spoke? A hundred thoughts shot through Martha's mind in that instant. The fine clothes, the new car, the out of town trips, the infrequent visits, the gulf between Vel and her father. But not one of these thoughts gave the slightest credence to Julee's accusation. Martha felt the ever so slight pressure of Julee's hand as it pressed a handkerchief into her fingers.

"It's all over town. I even heard it in Scotlandville. So I came home to find out for myself. The smells in my house are like fingerprints to the sighted."

"Did you say somethin' to her?"

"No. She doesn't know I suspect anything."

"What do you plan to do?"

Julee moved across in front of Martha and sat next to her on the sofa. Her face was gentler now. She was sharing Martha's pain, which had now doubled. Julee knew about the situation with Lala and had thought long and hard about giving Martha another cross to bear. But it was best this way; truth concealed never helped anyone.

"I can't trust her any more."

Martha bit her lip because she did not want to engage her friend in a quarrel over Vel's reliability. She said, "She might be doing the things you say, I don't know. But even if she is, that's no reason to say you can't trust her."

Julee rose, moved across the room to the chair that held her pocket book and cane, and softly said, "She gave me three one-dollar bills for the rent."

"But I thought the rent was fifteen dollars."

"She doesn't know I can feel the difference between a one and a five-dollar bill."

Martha embraced her longtime friend and the moisture from Julee's sightless eyes met the dampness of Martha's pain. They held each other with a tenderness that seemed to have no end.

It was clear to both, although the words were not spoken, Vel would be asked to leave Julee's house.

WITH THE Blues Tavern gone there was not much for LightFoot to do all day. No one would hire him for big jobs, and since he had not recently been available for little jobs he got no work at all. He simply waited for the insurance money. Naomi had gone back to work as a maid in order to keep food on the table. So every day LightFoot sat on the front porch, played his harp, and waited for the mailman.

Finally after seven months the mailman put a check in his hands. There was not enough evidence for the insurance company to delay the payoff any longer. The company investigation could not link the smell of coal oil to the cause of the fire. It was concluded that the smell had come from the coal oil stove in the back room. The fire chief and the insurance investigator had tried all they could to establish a reason why someone they considered a nigger should not be paid the five-thousand-dollar insurance coverage.

LightFoot was happy. Now he could rebuild. He slapped the spit out of his harp and began playing "Happy Days Are Here Again." In the distance he heard a train. Knowing it was the wrong time of day for a freight, he stopped playing and listened. He quickly realized that the sound was coming from the path next to the side of the house. BookTau turned the corner and headed across the yard in his direction. He was playing a ten-inch harmonica inlaid with mother of pearl. BookTau danced happily as LightFoot examined the instrument closely.

"Where did you get this?"

"It were a present."

"When did you get it?"

"'Bout the time of the fire."

LightFoot wondered why BookTau used the fire to set the date of his gift. But it was only a passing thought and he did not dwell on the possibility of any connection between the two events. BookTau volunteered proudly, "I been practicin' yo' train." LightFoot picked up his harmonica and began playing. BookTau quickly joined in, and the double-volume train caught the wind and caused the dogs in the next block to bark and howl. LightFoot said, "That's a good harp you got there. Real loud with a good sound." This made BookTau feel good. He grinned and gleefully twisted his body, his hands behind his back, in the image of a kid accepting lagniappe. LightFoot laughed to see this

gargantuan, six-foot-ten, 270-pound giant behaving like a ten-year-old.

"I seen one just like it over yonder at Sandoz. It cost almost fifty dollars. Whoever give you this musta liked you a lot."

BookTau was quick to add, "And I got some money too."

"Damn, BookTau. What did you do to that woman to make her like you so much?"

"I ain't done nothin' but dig in her garden."

BookTau's response, which sounded like a subtle sexual reference, caused LightFoot to roll off his chair in laughter. He sank to his knees holding his stomach and was finally able to verbalize, "Well, you finally got yourself some pussy! Was it Little Sally Walker?"

BookTau's face changed to deadly serious. He yelled out in an irritated voice, "It weren't that way a'tall. Miz Martha gimme this for makin' her garden."

"Martha? My sister Martha?"

`BookTau grabbed his harp out of LightFoot's hand and began circling. He was mad. The kitten had become a lion.

"I ain't told you nothin'. You made me say that. You tricked me. I ain't told you nothin'."

LightFoot was startled and frightened. He watched BookTau back up and turn away with an explosion of anger that he had never witnessed before. LightFoot was thankful that the direction of his wrath was away and not toward him. He wondered why BookTau had gotten so upset. Was it the joke about pussy? Was the gift a secret he was told not to reveal? If so, why had Martha given BookTau such an expensive gift?

EVERY WEEK, on the seventh day at the seventh hour, Naomi invoked the spirits to bring a proper comeuppance to whomever set the fire that destroyed the tavern. She made an androgynous doll that she punctured in seven places with seven pins, thrusting each with a slow circular motion that would cause the greatest possible pain. She was determined that the one responsible would be amply afflicted by the voodoo gods.

LightFoot was not as bent on retribution as was Naomi. He saw the disaster as a blessing in disguise. With the insurance money they could build a larger and more attractive place. He began laying out the plans for the new club. Everything that he and Naomi had learned while running the Blues Tavern was incorporated into the new design. The main bar was in the center of the entrance wall, flanked on each side by an entrance door. The two doors could accommodate larger crowds entering or leaving. And with the bar located near the entrance, a person wanting only a drink didn't have to wade through a sea of people listening to music.

The stage was elevated and in the center of the back wall. So it didn't matter where anyone sat or stood, they could see the blues musicians on stage without any difficulty. A large dance space was in front of the stage, and tables were arranged around three sides of the dance floor. A railing separated the dance floor from the seating area. LightFoot was able to keep everybody happy in their own space by separating the dancers on the floor from the drinkers at the tables. The toilets were located inside, which was a great improvement over the outside toilets of the old tavern. And there was a kitchen. Naomi wanted a kitchen where she could fix fried catfish, chicken, potato salad, hush puppies, and cole slaw. That was her menu. Anyone who wanted anything else had to do without or eat someplace else. The walls would be unpainted and covered with placards and posters that advertised beer, liquor, and the blues singers scheduled to appear. All was designed so that the patrons would feel comfortable and have a good time. It was quite an undertaking. LightFoot and Naomi were proud of the progress they had made on the design. At the bottom of the plans LightFoot printed the new name—The Black Eagle.

Work began as soon as the insurance check cleared the bank. LightFoot got his friends in the construction trades to donate time after work and on the weekends. They were happy to pitch in. The work sessions had all the earmarks of a never-ending party. There was lots to eat. Naomi cooked the smoked loins and roasts left over from the fall butchering. Phillip donated *boudin*, cracklins, and hog-head cheese, to go along with red beans, rice, and collard greens. And there was lots of liquor. The last shipment of booze, not moved to the tavern before the fire, was still stacked in LightFoot's back room. And there was lots of beer for those who didn't want the hard stuff. Although the workers were not getting money for their labor, they enjoyed this endeavor more than the work they got paid for.

The only person conspicuously absent from the work party was BookTau. The other workers were frequently heard to ask, "Where's BookTau?" when it was necessary to move or lift something that required more than two men. Everyone knew he was as attracted to this kind of activity as a hog was to slop. So neither LightFoot nor anybody else could understand his absence. On one occasion BookTau was spotted on the vacant lot across the road. Somebody asked, "Why is BookTau peeping out from behind that pecan tree like that?"

LightFoot finished driving the nail he had started and said, "I don't know. But the last time I saw him he was mad at me."

Somebody else asked, "What'd you do to him, take his chaw away?"

This got a laugh from the group. LightFoot laid another board in place, "Naw. I jest asked him why my sister give him that expensive harp."

"But that's no reason for him to hide behind a tree. Maybe he's takin' a piss."

The group laughed and the discussion ended about BookTau's absence from the building project. But still LightFoot could not find a reason for BookTau's strange behavior. He shrugged it off and concentrated on the business of construction.

As the club neared completion, LightFoot thought about the blues artists that he would get to entertain. Of course he wanted the locals who were good and would attract a crowd. But he also wanted bluesmen who were up and coming and had a unique style of delivery. He made a list. The young Clifton Chenier from Opelousas headed his list, because his music was an innovative fusion of colored and Cajun rhythms. Some of the musicians that LightFoot put at the top of his list were Clarence "Parran" Garlow from Beaumont, Texas; Silas Hogan from Scotlandville; "Schoolboy Cleve" White from Baton Rouge; Otis "Lightnin' Slim" Hicks from Baton Rouge; and Roy "Professor Longhair" Byrd from New Orleans, who, while in uniform, had previously played at Blue's Tavern. These were his special attractions. And then there were the regulars, including Vitalee Johnson and, of course, LightFoot Broussard.

As the date for the grand opening approached, a sense of excitement and anticipation spread throughout the colored and white folks alike. The week before the opening, Naomi was in the back office glued to their new telephone, making last-minute arrangements for deliveries. LightFoot was behind the bar arranging and stocking shelves. The door opened. Silhouetted against the Indian summer light streaming in from the setting sun was a huge figure holding a gunnysack-wrapped object. It was BookTau. He paused, bedazzled by the new edifice. His eyes glazed, as if experiencing the wonders of an early Christmas morning. LightFoot stopped and focused his attention on his visitor. He said, "What you got there?" BookTau dropped the wrapped object on the bar and slowly pulled back the burlap to reveal the stuffed carcass of an alligator. He took several steps back, his hands swinging at his sides in rhythm, and then he pointed to a space over the bar.

"You kin put that right there."

"Where did you find this?"

This question triggered a sequence of movements, best described as squirrel-like, which were accompanied by a shy laugh.

"I took it from the old place before it burnt up."

"Were you inside when the fire started?"

"It'll go right up there jes' fine."

With that statement BookTau ran out. LightFoot yelled for Naomi. She came rushing out of the back office, heeding the urgency in his voice that something terrible had happened. She stopped and silently gazed at the gator peeking out from the burlap sack.

"Where did this come from?"

With a touch of sadness in his voice, LightFoot said, "I think I know who burned down the ol' place."

17

MARTHA KNEW SOMETHING was wrong. For several days Rosa had been picking over her food and going right to bed after coming home from school. And she had not been to early morning Mass for over a week. Martha decided to have a talk with her. She entered Rosa's darkened room and sat on the edge of the bed. Rosa opened her eyes and managed a slight smile. Martha reached over, turned on the lamp, and softly rested her hand on Rosa's forehead.

"You don't have a fever but you look peaked. What's the matter, chile?"

Rosa turned away while uttering almost inaudibly, "Nothing."

"Don't lie to me, chile."

With a rush of emotion Rosa threw her arms around her mother and unleashed a flood of tears. For several minutes Martha held her quivering body in silence. Martha was thankful there was no one else at home because she knew that Rosa was trying to hide whatever the problem was from the family. It was only mother and daughter at this moment and Martha felt this was as it should be. "Now, now, chile. Don't make yourself sick." Martha moved gently out of Rosa's grasp and went to the dresser. She poured water from the white porcelain pitcher into the matching flowered bowl, which were heirlooms handed down from Mother Broussard. She wet a towel and was headed back to the bed when her foot hit a chamber pot that was partially hidden by the counterpane. Martha was curious. There was little need for this convenience, since the toilet had been moved inside. She raised the lid and her face turned ashen.

"How long you been throwing up?"

"About two weeks."

Martha returned to her seat on the bed and washed Rosa's face with the cool wet towel. Rosa locked her arms around her mother's neck in the viselike grip of a drowning person and began crying again. Martha gently pried her body away and softly caressed Rosa's face in her hands. "How many months have you missed?"

"Three . . . almost four."

"Oh, my God. Why didn't you say something?"

"I was afraid."

Martha was angry and disappointed. Nothing was turning out as she had planned. She wanted to give her children—especially the girls—large, gala, church weddings, even surpassing the one that her parents had given her. Lala had run away, only for spite, with a boy she would never have otherwise married. Vel was leading a scandalous and wicked life for which wedding-white was not an appropriate color. And now this. What was becoming of her family? Had she been such a bad mother? Was God punishing her? What had she done or not done? She couldn't think clearly. Everything was running together. She was not able to sort it out. But at this time she had to deal with the problem at hand.

"Who's the boy?"

It came out blunt and harsh. Rosa turned away and hid her face under the covers. The bed shook with her sobs. Martha gently massaged her shoulder. "Tell me who the boy is. He'll have to marry you. You'll be showing soon and people will begin to talk." The bed continued to shake with the quivering of Rosa's body. She buried her fist in the pillow with one ultimate and definitive movement.

"I can't tell."

"Your papa will make him marry you."

"Please don't tell Papa."

"He'll know soon. Now who is he?"

"Mama, please don't make me."

"Chile, don't you understand? You can't have a baby and be unmarried."

"Then I'll go away."

"I can't lose you, too."

"Oh, Mama, what am I going to do?"

Martha wiped the tears from Rosa's face. Her eyes were like dusky agates surrounded by pools of scarlet dew that had been laced with bleeding webs. Martha knew that there was little point in pursuing the source of a pain that had been visited so frequently in so little time.

"Try and get some sleep. We'll talk later."

She turned out the light and headed for the door. In the darkness Rosa's voice reached out to her.

"Will God forgive us?"

"Baby, don't you know that God even forgave the people who killed His son. I'm sure He will forgive you and that boy."

Martha smoothed the wet hair away from Rosa's face and she looked deeply into what she could see of her eyes in the filtered moonlight. She realized that Rosa did not want to be alone, and she did not want to leave. Martha slipped off her shoes and stretched out next to Rosa, nestling her close.

IT MUST have been that she sensed it was time for Phillip to return from Southern College. Martha awoke to hear the car come to a stop in the yard below. Rosa was now sleeping peacefully. Martha slipped her arm out from beneath Rosa's head and carefully got out of the bed.

Phillip was washing his hands at the sink. Martha entered and turned on the fire under the pot of okra, tomatoes, and corn that was sitting on the stove. Phillip turned in her direction. "I thought you had gone to bed by now."

"No. Rosa's not feeling well."

"She's been acting kinda funny lately."

"It's the woman thing."

"I figured."

The conversation was headed in a direction that Martha was not ready to deal with. She knew that at some point Phillip would have to know what was going on. But she felt this was not the right time; she had not yet discovered the name of the boy responsible. She knew that would be the first question out of Phillip's mouth. She busied herself with heating the rice in the double boiler and setting his place at the table.

"How is Dr. Clark?"

"He sends his regards."

"You stayed mighty late."

Phillip had to be careful how he responded to this statement. Things were fine and he did not wish to create any suspicion that he was having an affair with "that woman" again. "After the meeting I felt tired, so I took a nap before heading back. I'm glad I did because the road was all torn up between here and Port Barre . . . and it took forever." Phillip thought, *That should do it. There's no way possible for her to know that I spent time with Alicia.* He had never lied to his wife before. But he had never needed the love and understanding of someone else before—as much as now. Martha had failed him. And he felt strongly that it had to do with what he heard her say to Julee about his leaving the church. And he knew there would never be a time when Martha would understand or accept that. So, at this point in his life, Alicia was exactly what he needed.

"The president died today."

"Oh, no! Lord have mercy."

Martha piled the okra on top of the rice and set the plate on the table in front of Phillip.

"What's going to happen to us?"

"Vice President Truman is now president."

"I mean . . . Roosevelt was good for the country."

"He didn't care that much for colored people."

"He had that nigger woman—what's her name?—in his cabinet."

"Mary McLeod Bethune was Mrs. Roosevelt's doing."

Martha sat at the table across from Phillip with a cup of coffee. He had successfully changed the conversation to one they could both discuss without a fuss. It was a rare opportunity when they could talk about a subject that both had opinions on without fighting. It was certainly better than the direction they were heading earlier.

"Don't get me wrong. He did a lot of good things for this country, and everybody benefited. But he was just a good politician. He wasn't out to help the colored."

"Well, it's a good thing his wife was there. She showed them DAR's a thing or two."

"Incidentally, I heard that the Lyceum Committee is trying to get Marian Anderson to do a concert on campus."

"Oh, that would be nice. I'd like to go."

Phillip closed his eyes and breathed heavily. He thought, *That did it. This conversation has gone too far. If Martha goes to the college she is sure to run into Alicia.*

Martha got the message from his demeanor. "You look tired."

"I am."

Phillip breathed a deep sigh of relief. He must have been more exhausted than he realized, because he had made two mental slip-ups in the last half hour. The increased sexual activity was taking its toll.

Then Martha provided the remedy. "Go on to bed. I'll put the things away." Phillip didn't waste any time taking his leave, and as soon as he was out of sight Martha headed upstairs to check on Rosa.

Martha was careful not to disturb Rosa's sleep. She pushed the door opened quietly. The bed was empty. Martha's ears led her eyes to the open window. Rosa knelt, silhouetted against the moonlight, saying her rosary. Martha listened, marveling at the pure, innocent faith displayed by her troubled daughter.

After Rosa had finished the last "Hail Mary," she began a confession. Martha stood in the darkness as a silent witness. "Please God, forgive Father Pat for breaking his vows, and me for loving him. You taught us love, and we learned to love each other. We care about what happens, so please help us to keep our secret. Please give me the strength to do your will. " Martha was so stricken with weakness that she did not know if she had the strength to walk down the stairs. A sharp spasm of rheumatism struck her knees. She ached all over. She clung to the banister as her soul cried out and her body screamed. She closed her eyes and cried quietly. There was no doubt in her mind that God was punishing her. The total impact of her baby—Rosa, being with child fathered by a priest of the church, was like a knife in the heart. She descended one step at a time, holding fast to the railing lest she tumble.

Martha finally made it to the front porch and collapsed into her rocking chair. She was acutely aware the every joint in her body ached, but could not decide if the cause was the rheumatism or what she had overheard. The physical pain joined the misery in her heart to create a feeling of despair that cried out for death. She stared into the darkness hoping to see an answer. A resolution. A solution. There was no explanation, no reason, no resolve. The sun rose on Martha in the same chair, staring into the same nothingness, and feeling the same emptiness that she had felt in the darkness.

Martha prayed. It was the same prayer that had brought peace to her soul in the form of the avenging fire that consumed the devil's music that had driven Lala away. And it would be prayer that would show the way to deal with Rosa's situation. She prayed while working, while walking, and while sleeping. She prayed standing up and lying down. She prayed on her knees until the numbness had overcome the pain of the rheumatism. She also read the Bible. There was a passage in Matthew, chapter 7, verse 15, that kept ringing in her head: "Beware of false prophets which come to you in sheep's clothing, but inwardly they are ravening wolves." Surely this description could aptly be applied to Father Pat, whom she felt was an evil and corrupt man.

There was not much time. As best Martha could figure, Rosa was ten weeks pregnant. In a few weeks she would begin to show. Whatever was to be done had to be done before then. She had to find someone to marry Rosa. But the more she considered this possibility, the more ridiculous it seemed. There were no Josephs in this life—no men who would knowingly marry a woman who was going to have a child by another man. The more she thought about this situation the more real it became. This was no Immaculate Conception. It was simply too much to expect one man to care for a child fathered by another man who failed to take his responsibility. Why then shouldn't Father Pat bear the responsibility of his own act? The questions in Martha's mind were as abundant as her prayers. Her thoughts regarding the priest were sinful and would be difficult to confess. But why should they be? Sins are confessed to be forgiven. Isn't that what confession is all about? To whom would Father Pat confess? Perhaps he would seek forgiveness from Rosa . . . or maybe Rosa's mother. The time of prayer had drawn to a close and the time for action was at hand.

MARTHA HEARD the window panel slide open, revealing the profile of Father Patrick O'Neill, which was fixed straight ahead. She intuitively began, "Bless me, Father, for I have sinned. I confess to Almighty God and to you, Father, that I have sinned exceedingly in thoughts, words and . . ." She stopped. Her breathing rate had increased and she could feel the beating of her heart in her head. Her body felt like a boiling kettle. Father Pat's profile did not change its bearing but his words came softly as he leaned his ear closer to the screen. "I'm listening."

"I need advice, Father. My daughter is in trouble and I don't know what to do . . . but I believe you can help."

"What do ye think I can I do?"

"You can marry her."

"If ye would like to arrange a marriage, ye should make an appointment at the rectory."

Martha was taken aback. She was sure that father Pat recognized her voice.

"Father, I am Martha Fergerson and Rosa is pregnant."

"Oh, I'm so sorry to hear that. So, that being the case, Mrs. Fergerson, it is she who must come to confession."

Father Pat's profile remained unmoved. Martha forced herself to continue softly in spite of the fact that she wanted to scream.

"She says you are the father."

"Yes, that I am in the image of God the Father."

"She means that you are the father of her unborn child."

"Do ye wish to make this your confession?"

Martha's body began trembling and her knees began to ache. Her voice grew louder and quivered with rage.

"Are you denying that you are responsible?"

"I am a priest with a vow to celibacy."

"Well, Father, you broke that vow when you had relations with my daughter."

"Ye are wrong to accuse a priest, a minister of God, of such a sin. Now if ye please, get on with ye confession."

Martha was exasperated. Tears slid down her cheeks. There was little to be gained by insisting that Father Pat take responsibility for his sin against God and Rosa. He was indeed shrouded in sheep's clothing. At that moment Martha knew what she had to do. For a long moment she was silent. Then she said in the most devout voice she could summon, "Father, forgive me for bearing false witness . . . I am truly sorry."

"Ye are forgiven, but ye should never speak of this again. Put this matter in the hands of God and pray that His will be done."

He then gave Martha absolution. As a penitence, he instructed her to recite the rosary three times. Martha left the confessional without further protest, but the matter was a long way from being settled in her mind and soul.

The following weekend Rosa appeared at the rectory, as usual, to resume her duties. After serving dinner and cleaning the kitchen, she waited until the other ladies had gone. Father Pat was in the library reading. She stood in the doorway timidly, uncertain about how or what she should say or do. He looked up from his research for Sunday's sermon.

"It is coffee time?"

"Yes, Father."

This was unexpected but at least it gave some relief and a few minutes more to think about what she was going to say. Rosa entered the library once more, this time with two cups of coffee on a tray. After passing one to Father Pat, she took a seat in the faded wing chair on the opposite side of the desk.

"Remember the time when I wasted coffee on you?"

Father Pat focused his gaze in Rosa's direction. The vague look on his face questioned the memory that she recalled.

"Did ye do that?"

"Yes. I remember it was shortly after Papa joined that other church."

"That was over seven years ago."

Rosa was quick to add, "And you didn't get upset."

"I'm sorry lass, I don't remember ye spilling coffee on me."

"That was the first time you kissed me."

Father Pat took a long sip of coffee and his stare penetrated deeply into Rosa's eyes.

"My child, I think perhaps ye are fantasizing."

Rosa was shocked. She could hardly believe her ears.

"But Father, you said you loved me."

"That I do. I love all of God's children."

"But this was different."

"In what way do ye mean, lass?"

Rosa could not believe what she was hearing. Tears welled up in her eyes. She put her cup on the desk and walked toward the crucifix hanging between the two curtained windows. She made the sign of the cross, walked back, and knelt next to Father Pat.

"Father, I am expecting your child."

"My dear lassie, if ye are with child, I am not the father."

"I have never been with anyone else."

Rosa was overwhelmed with an eruption of tears. Father Pat gently stroked her head of soft black hair and spoke softly.

"Sometimes when a person desires something so strongly, they can make themselves believe anything."

"But, Father, I am pregnant."

"Then ye have sinned with someone."

"I was only with you, Father, every time."

"Ye only imagined it was I. The passion of the body can deceive the mind into believing that which is not true. That is why ye must trust God to show the way. The devil is always at work twisting and turning the kindnesses that are shown by others into something vile and sinful. That has happened to ye." Rosa wiped her face with the back of her hand as his words slid into her consciousness and awakened uncertainty. Father Pat continued to intensify her bewilderment. "Do not ye know that it is impossible for me to have been with ye? I am a priest first, last, and always—a disciple of Christ. True I am fond of ye, lassie. True I do love ye. Ye are a fine lass. But ye have mistaken my good deeds and allowed the passion of ye flesh to carry ye to fantasy."

Father Patrick O'Neil's voice carried the same sincerity and honest conviction as it did in his Sunday sermons. There was little reason to question his belief of the words that flowed out of his mouth. Nor was there any reason to believe that his words were not inspired by God.

"I will consider this ye confession. And bound by the sanctity of the confessional, no one else but God will know what is in ye heart."

Father Pat extended his hand and made the sign of the cross on Rosa's forehead and began his prayer of absolution.

Hypnotically, Rosa began, "Bless me, Father, for I have sinned . . ." At the end of confession, Rosa left without another word. Cleansed of past sins, unburdened of the dark fantasy that she had imagined, and free to point the finger of guilt at someone else, she headed to the graveyard. Here she could think. A gentle, unsteady breeze swung the moss back and forth on the ancient oak branches. Rosa sat at the base of the huge crucifix and faced the reality of life, as it was marked by stone monuments stretching in every direction. Something did not seem right. She knew she was with child. She knew she had never been with another man. A voice in her head kept telling her that Father Pat had not been truthful with her. And yet another voice told her that he was a priest and could not lie. She was confused. She did not know what to do or think. She wished that she could disappear beneath one of the grave markers.

IT WAS the most difficult decision that Martha ever had to make. In addition she had to convince Rosa that it was the best and the only course to take. There was no question that a lifelong stigma, plus scandal, would be the result if Rosa had a baby without benefit of marriage. There was simply no respectable young man in town available to marry Rosa under the circumstances. Martha's experience with Father Pat's denial had caused her to believe that he would never take any responsibility for the life that he had helped create. As horrible as her decision was, it seemed the only solution to all the alternatives. Martha took the money that she had put away for a rainy day and told Phillip that she and Rosa were driving to Scotlandville to spend the night with Julee.

The narrow lane permitted the branches of the surrounding growth to brush the windows of the car. Finally after several miles of winding, wooded wilderness they came to a clearing. In the center was a shack surrounded by chickens, dogs, hogs, and cows. An old woman with a withered face sat on a sagging porch, smoking a corn cob pipe, her back propped against a post. Martha got out of the car and had a long talk with the woman. Rosa watched from the security of the car. Martha gave the old woman a rolled-up brown paper sack which the woman opened and examined. She then knocked the ashes out of her pipe, stuck it into her dress pocket along with the brown bag, and headed for the car. Martha opened the door.

"Rosa, this is Tante."

The ancient one extended her primeval bony hand and firmly but gently guided Rosa toward the house.

"Come on, gal, Tante's gonna take care you. Ain't nothin' to be scared of. Been doin' this pretty near my whole life and I ain't never lost a gal yet."

The smoked-smudged, newspapered walls reeked with commingled odors of tobacco, bacon, and the stale aroma of time. Martha thought, "If a person could survive breathing this stench, they can survive anything." Tante set about her work of preparation with skill and precision. In no time at all she had a roaring fire beneath two kettles of water, resting on the surface of the four-legged wood-burning stove. She placed several ancient-looking surgical tools into one of the kettles, and her manner took on a professional air that was decidedly different from the first impression Martha and Rosa received on the outside.

Tante gave Martha a crockery cup of coffee, the strength of which was foretold by the bitter smell of chicory. "Now, daughter, you jes' sit and relax. I know you used to helpin' that white doctor in town, but I don't need no he'p." Rosa was led toward an adjoining room. She and the old woman disappeared behind a creaky door held together by a cypress "Z" that seemed as ancient as the old woman. Martha tried very hard to remain calm but she was not in a relaxing mood. A million thoughts shot through her mind at the same instant. All brought worry and concern. It was difficult to keep her mind on the rosary, which she fingered with whichever hand was not holding the cup at the time. She kept her eyes fixed on the door, trying hard to see between the cracks which only allowed, from time to time, the voice of the old woman giving instructions to come through. It was impossible for Martha to sit still and she paced a path from the door of the bedroom to the window.

Martha thought of Naomi. Martha wondered if she believed that the directions to Tante's were for a patient of Dr. Rossini's, as she had been told. What if Naomi asked Tante whether a white girl had come for the cure? And what if Tante said "No, but Rosa Fergerson was here." In spite of the fact that she gave her an extra fifty dollars to keep the secret, Martha could not trust that Tante would not tell. Martha regretted that she had had to ask Naomi for directions, but realized there was no one else that she knew who could tell her exactly where to find Tante.

As if she did not have enough troubles, the sound of devil's music pierced Martha's ears. It sounded like the noise that Johnny made. She wiped away the grease and soot from the window pane and looked outside. She could barely make out the form of a man sitting on a log next to a small fire. He was playing a guitar and singing some disreputable song. Martha could never make out the words to that kind of music anyway. It all sounded the same to her—vile. She could never understand the attraction that gut-bucket music held for niggers.

That devil's music had taken Martha's mind away from her present anxiety. So the bony hand on her shoulder did not cause her to immediately question Rosa's condition. Instead she asked, "Does he have to play that music?"

"Don't pay him no mind, that jes' my ol' man, he play lik' dat every night. Go on in dere with your gal."

"Is she all right?"

"She fine. Jes' scared, dat's all."

Martha headed in the direction of the adjoining room, only to be stopped by the strength of Tante's whispered voice.

"Miz Martha."

The old one was now face to face, as Martha's dancing eyes searched for her motive.

"I done like you told me."

"Oh?"

"She won't be havin' no chillun."

A cold shiver passed through Martha's entire body. Hearing that her request had been carried out made her wish that she had not made it. For a fleeting instant, Martha wished that the old midwife had the power to take life from Father Pat just as she had taken it from Rosa. If only somehow there were a mystical power in the psyche shrouded by that wrinkled, dried, and withered skin that covered her face. A power that could deprive him as he had caused Rosa to be deprived. The moment vanished quickly. Now as before, Martha realized it was too late for second thoughts; this would have to remain a secret between her, the old woman, and God. She placed her hand lightly on the leathery fingers and said, "Thank you." With that, Martha walked into the bedroom.

Rosa slept, nestled in a fetal position, lulled by warmth from her mother's body. Martha remained awake. There was too much on her mind to allow her eyes to close. Anyway, it was impossible for her to sleep with the devil's music ringing in from the outside. It continued way into the night. The old woman's voice could be heard laughing and singing along. They were drunk. It reminded Martha of her no-good brother and all the trouble he had caused.

Shortly after the rooster announced the dawn of a new day, Martha and Rosa had breakfast of grits, bacon, eggs, biscuits, and lots of chicory coffee. Then they headed back to Estilette.

Phillip never knew what had taken place. He could tell by the unusual solitude that Rosa was not the same. But he did not suspect anything other than the monthly "women's problem." After a couple of days off from school because she had a "stomach ache," Rosa was back at her usual routine of activities, except early morning Mass. Going to church was less frequent than it had been. Sundays were the only times she went to church, but she did not receive communion. Since it was necessary to go to confession first, and she could not yet bring herself to face Father Pat, she received a spiritual communion. This situation continued for several weeks following Rosa's visit to Tante's.

Martha decided to take Rosa's place at the rectory. She volunteered to cook for Father Pat. He welcomed Martha's generous spirit because it showed that, as he told her, "Whatever evil thoughts that Satan had placed in ye mind have been overcome by ye good deeds."

"Father please forgive me; I am sorry for what I thought."

"Ye being here more than makes up for it."

Father Pat was convinced that Martha was indeed repentant and all ill thoughts toward him were gone forever. The subject of Rosa was never spoken. It was as if she and "the problem" had never existed as an event in Father Pat's life.

It was difficult to act one way and feel another. And Martha was surely not feeling too kindly about the wolf in sheep's clothing who had defiled her baby. Martha had a plan and a purpose and her actions were carefully plotted and rehearsed in her mind. It did not take long to discover that one of Father Pat's favorite foods was cornbread. Martha made a delicious cornbread, and she baked one every week for eight weeks. Always, Father Pat praised and congratulated her baking skills, "Tastes like a bit o' heaven." Martha agreed and assured him that as long as he kept liking her cooking she would be feeding him his favorite.

THE BISHOP sent a replacement from the white church when Father Pat went to the hospital. The report that Martha got from Dr. Rossini was that Father Pat was bleeding internally. It was a strange and mysterious malady; one for which the doctor had no explanation of origin and little treatment. Since his stomach could not process food any longer, he grew weaker by the day. The bleeding would not stop. It oozed out through his bowels to such an extent that his bed clothes had to be changed three times a day. Even the cotton packing that was used as a plug was a saturated bloody mess.

The news of Father Pat's death was received by Martha with closed eyes and an audible, "The wolf in sheep's clothing got what he deserved." Alone at the time of the phone call, she could vent, for the first time in many months, her true feelings over the fate that had befallen Father Pat. There was only one regret that she had—he died without knowing. There was a need in her soul, which she could not understand, that made her wish he had known that there was glass baked in his cornbread. She wanted to see the look on his face as he realized that he had been drained of the same life-giving fluid that had carried away Rosa's lost child.

With a smile on her face and a twinkle in her eye, Martha washed away all traces of the avenging substance from the mortar and pestle borrowed from Dr. Rossini's cabinet. She carefully and lovingly wrapped them for return. When Martha brought this news to Phillip's ears, he was more concerned about the news of the atomic bomb being dropped on Japan than he was about the news of a fellow Irishman, Father Patrick O'Neill, departing this life.

18

BOBBY WAS SO shaken by the thought of what could have happened to him in Alex's apartment that he did not attempt to make any further contact. With events in the life of Bigger Thomas still fresh in his mind, Bobby let that serve as a warning about what could happen if he became too friendly with white girls. He knew and understood that his relationship with Alex and what had happened in her apartment was in no way the same as the situation in Bigger's life. But because both situations involved relationships that had crossed the color line, he felt there was a warning in the book that he should heed.

He felt ashamed that he had not done anything to stop the rape. He had relived the scene in his mind many times and rationally he knew that there was little that he could have done to prevent the altercation. He remembered that Alex had also shared that feeling. At least he assumed that she had, because she had warned him that he would get blamed if he were discovered in her apartment. So as far as he was concerned, she knew even better than he did what fate he would have suffered had he tried to interfere. But no matter how he explained or rationalized the situation to himself, he still felt bad; he had been thinking only of himself, and he had failed his friend.

During the daytime he thought so much about the situation that he had nightmares when he slept: Chuck and his friend Carson had torn off Alex's clothes during her struggle to keep them from overpowering her. Bobby rose up from behind the sofa yelling, "Stop that, you redneck scoundrels." The assailants were so startled that they froze on the spot. Bobby jumped over the sofa and ran into the kitchen. He came out with a butcher knife, waving it in the air like a sword and yelling, "Get out!"

The assailants backed toward the door. Bobby advanced and they begged, "Please, Mister, don't hurt us. We're leaving."

At this point Alex cried out as she crawled to the safety of a distant corner of the room, "Thank you, Othello, the Moor of Venice, for saving my life." Bobby turned to look back at Alex and throw her a kiss.

Suddenly the closing door opened and slammed him in the back. He dropped his sword. The assailants pounced on him and drove him to the floor. They beat him senseless. They dragged his unconscious body into the hallway and threw him over the banister to the pavement below. Then the y dragged his body down the stair into the cellar; there they cut him into small pieces and burned him in the furnace.

Bobby sat up in bed yelling. The nightmare ended.

The week after the incident he went to a florist shop some distance from the campus.

"I'd like to order some flowers."

The lady looked at him suspiciously. Perhaps because she knew that there was a colored florist near the campus, and she wondered why the boy had come to her shop.

"What kind of flowers?"

"A dozen roses."

"My roses are expensive. You can get them cheaper somewhere else."

"I know. But I want them delivered."

"Where?"

He gave the address and the lady looked up at him. Although she did not say anything, Bobby knew she recognized that no colored people lived in that section of Nashville. He quickly added, "They're for my boss."

"And the name?"

"Alex Estilette."

The lady seemed a bit friendlier now, assuming that the name Alex was for a man.

"Do you want to send a card?"

"A card?"

"Yes, a card. To say who they are from."

"Oh, yes, ma'am."

"Just get one from that rack and write your message."

Bobby picked out a card and wrote "Hope you are feeling better. From Bobby." He was reluctant to write anything else. He suspected the lady might read what he had written and discover that he was sending roses to a white woman. He gave the card to the lady; she put it into an envelope and wrote the name and address that Bobby had given her. Bobby paid the lady and left.

Several times after that Bobby thought about calling to find out if she had gotten the flowers. But he did not. He was ashamed. What would he say? How could he explain that he had not come to her rescue? He tried to put the incident out of his mind.

He tried hard to forget about Alex. That was difficult. He liked Alex. He was in love with Alex. Although they had not been intimate and had only kissed that one time, he had the feeling of falling in love. Plus she had been nice to him. She had introduced him to the blues. She had encouraged him to come to Nashville to study medicine. He owed her a lot. Her kindness was hard to forget, but it was easier to forget about having a boy-girl relationship. *Native Son* had taught him a lesson that he would not soon forget. He was being stretched like a rubber band and he did not like the feeling.

A YEAR had passed since Bobby had sent the flowers. There was no further attempt to contact Alex. Bobby had come home for Christmas. He thought about calling to say hello but decided against it. He was in his room working on an assignment that had to be turned in when he returned to school after the holidays.

His mama's voice called from the bottom of the stairs, "Bobby, Alex is here." He was horrified. How could he face her? What would he say? He had not told anyone in the family about what had happened. Suppose Alex had come to discuss the incident? Had she told her father? And if so, had Mr. Estilette told his papa? He was afraid to go down; afraid to face Alex. His mama called a second time.

"I'm coming, Mama, just getting dressed." When he walked into the living room Alex was in a deep conversation with Martha. Bobby and Alex exchanged polite greetings and she continued, "So when I graduated, I went to Northwestern to study sociology."

"Tell me, chile, where is Northwestern?"

"In Chicago."

"How long you plan to be there?"

"It will take two years for me to get my graduate degree. And then I plan to write a book on the Creoles of Louisiana."

"Well, I can tell you a lot about that."

"When I start collecting information I'll interview you."

"That'll be nice. Now, I'll leave you two alone. I know you have a lot to talk about."

Martha headed for the kitchen. She stopped, turned, and said, "Tell your papa thanks for the Christmas present. Mr. Fergerson ain't here but Bobby will help you get it out of the car."

They were alone. Bobby did not know what to say. He smiled. He was standing close enough to smell the special Coty perfume that she wore. Her aroma overpowered the pine-scented Christmas tree and the kitchen smells that came from his mama's cooking. It was a seductive scent. One that brought back memories of her visits to the attic, and her visits to Fisk for the concerts, and his visit to her apartment. But he did not wish to allow Alex's desirable fragrance to awaken feelings that he had already put to sleep. After a moment of silence he said, "You have something in the car?"

"My papa sent over a case of wine. He put it in the car and it's too heavy for me."

"Oh. Well, I'll get it out."

He headed for the door. Alex said, "This is a nice Christmas tree. Did you help decorate it?"

"No. Mama did. It was up when I got back from school."

"How are things going for you?"

"Fine."

"When do you start medical school?"

"Come September."

There was another silence. Alex crossed to the door and headed out. Bobby followed. He took the case of wine out of the trunk of the car. Alex said, "My papa said to tell Mr. Fergerson 'that's the same wine we had the last time.' I don't know what that means but that's what he said to tell him."

"I'll tell Papa. Thanks! Merry Christmas!"

"Merry Christmas! And Bobby, thanks for the flowers."

Not a word was spoken about the rape incident. It was as if it had never happened and they had never been together in a circumstance where such an intimate occurrence had been witnessed. Alex got in her car and drove away. That was the last that Bobby saw of her. He put the wine under the tree. His mama stood in the doorway and watched. As he turned to go back upstairs she said, "Alex is a nice girl."

"Yeah, she sure is."

"Did you two see a lot of each other while she was in Nashville?"

"Some, but not too much."

"You might think about going to visit her in Chicago."

"Mama, I . . ."

Bobby paused in mid-sentence. He wished his mama would stop the talk about Alex. He wanted to tell her that there was nothing going on between him and Alex, that they were only friends. Or maybe he should just come right out and tell her about the incident. But he knew that would not be smart. So he decided to tell her as little as possible. He continued, "I'm so busy with my studies that I don't think I'll have the time."

"Y'all been friends since you stayed over at her house. And I know y'all talked together on the phone a lot before going off to school. It sure would be nice to bring our families together. I know it's kinda hard to get together around here, but up there in Chicago . . ."

"Mama, I got some homework to finish."

"I know. Just go on up and do your work. But don't forget what I said. And remember, your grandfather was Creole and that's as good as white."

Bobby mounted the stairs wishing that his mama did not go on so much about Alex, but in a few days he'd be gone and he would not have to listen.

WHEN BOBBY returned to college he enrolled in a biology class that was being taught by Ruth Frazier, a new professor. He fell in love. Ruth was everything that Alex was not. She was unromantic, practical, and the color of brown sugar. This brilliant twenty-seven-year-old Ph. D. from Columbia University was the object of desire for male faculty and students alike. She ignored all of her admirers, preferring to remain free and clear of romantic entanglements.

Why Bobby was attracted to her was a mystery even to him. Perhaps it was because she had a doctorate degree, an accomplishment he still had to realize. Perhaps it was because she was forbidden territory. The tendency to be attracted to women who were off limits was demonstrated by his desire for Alex. He was not able to discover why he was drawn to women who presented a challenge, nor did it matter. He only understood that he was determined to win Ruth Frazier over. Bobby was a good student, and with increasing frequency he found himself involved in discussions, special assignments, and committee work that also required Ruth's presence. With each occurrence their conversations became less academic and more personal.

Gradually she lowered her guard and became friendly; Bobby did not pose a threat to her single status. This was not the case with her more aggressive faculty admirers. Obadiah Mbola and Thomas Langston vied for her attention in different but intensive ways. She was not to be won or impressed by the traditional courting overtures or promises of domestic tranquillity. She was bored by their attention. The more they vied for her affections the more she sought the non-threatening relationship of her student—Bobby Fergerson. Soon their mutual attraction became more than a casual teacher- student relationship. They were in love. She now insisted that he call her Ruthie instead of Dr. Frazier when they were alone. An intimate relationship between a student and faculty member was cause for dismissal for both. Now their foremost concern was how to keep their passions in check. On special holidays they found themselves in Memphis, a large city away from the university where their romance could remain a secret.

It was 1945—the year of Bobby's graduation. Phillip, Martha, and Rosa piled into the car and drove to Nashville for the event. They were excited. Bobby was also excited and ready to enter medical school in September. Bobby and Ruth also planned to get married. But telling his parents in advance was not part of his plan. Nor were they introduced to her. Bobby knew his mother would do everything in her power to plan the wedding. That is, if she approved the bride. And there was another bit of information that had to be shared, which Bobby did not look forward to revealing—he did not intend to return home with them after the ceremony. He wanted to remain in Nashville to be near Ruth, but he told his parents he wanted to keep his job as a waiter at the King Cotton Hotel.

He told his mother, "I'll need the money for medical school, and it'll help take some of the burden off you and Papa."

Martha was slow to accept. She voiced her opinion, "But you need a rest and you haven't been home since Christmas when you saw Alex."

Martha had to get in the comment about Alex. Bobby tried his best to sidestep the subject that he would rather not face.

"If I'm going to keep this job I have to work through the summer."

"Well, maybe you can take off a weekend and go to Chicago for a rest."

Phillip came to Bobby's rescue. "Let the boy alone. He's a man now. He can work if he wants to."

Even Rosa put in her two cents worth. "The money you and Papa don't have to give him, you can give to me for my car. I need one to get back and forth to school."

All were surprised to hear that Rosa wanted to buy a car. Phillip saw a chance to take away pressure to have Bobby come home or go to Chicago. He said, "Well, if that's the case, Bobby should stay here and work. And we'll have to find an extra job for Rosa in Estilette."

Phillip and Bobby were the only ones to enjoy this humorous proposal. After tearful good-byes, Martha got in the car along with Rosa and Phillip and headed back to Estilette. Two weeks later Bobby and Ruth were married in a quiet ceremony by a justice of the peace in Memphis.

NINETEEN-FORTY-FIVE was also the year that the war in Europe ended, and Phillip was thankful that Bobby would not have to go and fight. The newspapers reported in large headlines that Hitler was dead and the Nazis had surrendered. Every person, regardless of color, welcomed this news. Phillip, like others in Estilette, was glued to the radio for the latest news. One evening after returning from Nashville, Phillip heard a special broadcast, *On a Note of Triumph*, which celebrated the Allied victory. It was written and produced by Norman Corwin and expressed the anxieties, fears, and prayers that were on everyone's lips. Phillip found a common identity with the ideas of the program. He remembered that it said:

> The price of peace was high. It cost over 400,000 American lives. Many soldiers who once flipped newspapers from their bicycles are alive only in their mothers' memories. The international character of America's newly discovered love of all human beings is not to be overlooked. A new awareness for people of color is in the minds of white America. After all, it was the Emperor of Ethiopia, Haile Selassie, who went to Geneva and gave the warning of the threatening war. He was not listened to at first; but later the events of which he spoke were finally understood. He foretold that war was easy to come by, but it would take many years to discover peace. Some men would fight for power but all men would fight to be free. The value of freedom is not something to be forgotten; like soil, it must be renewed after each crop. Free men who forget this are likely to lose their freedom, so the renewal of freedom must be remembered, in the summer of prosperity as well as the winter of drought.
>
> Every man is urged to do his daily homework. It is required that civil thinking take place in the voting booth. The demands that representatives represent should be constant, because freedom is never granted outright, but rather it is leased and there is a price to be paid.
>
> And finally there are prayers. The Lord God-Fire is asked to assist in forging swords into plowshares; and the Lord God-of-the-Living-Wage is asked to bring his sweet influence to bear on the assembly line of plenty, so men can eat today without fear of tomor-

> row; and the Lord-God-of-Blueprints, who taught the worms and the stars to live together, is asked to measure out the new liberties so that none should have to suffer for his father's color. And all these things are asked in God's name.

All these things that tumbled out of that radio speaker were expressed in the poetry of common sense. This appealed to Phillip, and he prayed that all of the promises of peace would indeed be turned into blessings that could be enjoyed by all men, Negro as well as white. He believed that the message of this program was speaking to him personally. And his hope was for the time when he too would be able to do his homework and vote.

19

IT WAS A STORMY night in 1946. Alicia cried while she read the letter. Phillip looked at the book sitting in the middle of its wrappings on the table. He picked it up. Beneath the title, *The Foxes of Harrow*, stood an aristocratic, redheaded man holding a scepter at arm's length across his body. In the background were two women, elegantly dressed in antebellum fashion, standing beneath a moss-covered oak growing in front of a plantation mansion. In the lower right-hand corner was the author's name—Frank Yerby. Phillip concluded that the letter had something to do with the book; apparently they had both arrived in the same package. He was curious about the reason for the tears. When Alicia finished reading, she handed the letter to Phillip. He read:

> My dear Alicia,
>
> Enclosed is my first successful novel, a gift for the kindness shown during my brief stay at Southern. I know that my leaving left unanswered questions, which I feel friendship requires explaining. My decision to leave was based on the growing conviction that by temperament and inclination I was unsuited for the profession of teaching. Specifically, there was an incident in which my car was blocking the work of white telephone linemen and Felton requested that I apologize to them for the incon-

venience. This, and the fact that I bitterly resented Mr. Posey keeping a list of teachers attending Sunday school, made me realize that Southern calls for humility that I do not by nature possess. I did not know it at the time, but leaving motivated me to once more concentrate on my writing.

I trust that this copy of my book makes up for my mysterious disappearance and the many unfulfilled hours of friendship that we were not able to add to those we had already enjoyed.

With fond memories, Frank

Phillip folded the letter and tucked it inside the front cover. It rested on the distinctive penmanship inscription, marked by small circles for dotted *i*'s. He looked around and found Alicia sitting on the sofa; her eyes were still bathed with tears.

"The author of this book taught here?"

"Yes."

"When?"

"Five years ago."

"Were you lovers?"

"No, we were good friends. He was married."

"Then why are you crying?"

Alicia rose from the sofa, put her arms around Phillip's neck and kissed him with a long-forgotten passion. A flash of lighting knocked out the power and left the room in darkness, except for the flickering flames from the fireplace. However, the raging storm did not dim Alicia's passion or the fervor of her memory.

"Like you, Frank is a sensitive, caring, and talented man. I was crying for his joy—his success."

Her path was lit by flashes of lighting as she walked into the hallway and got a lamp. Phillip was determined that neither the stormy night nor the absence of light would discourage his curiosity.

"The picture on the cover tells a story about white people and a slave plantation."

The flickering light of the lamp revealed impatience on Alicia's face—resentment that Phillip should dare question, which also carried in the tone of his voice, the subject matter chosen by her friend.

"So?"

"I just find it strange that a Negro would write about what it seems this book is about."

"Neither one of us has read the book, so I don't know that you know what it is about."

"I was reading the picture on the cover."

"I have a picture for you to read."

Alicia crossed to the mantel and picked up a snapshot. She handed it to Phillip with the enthusiasm of a schoolgirl on her first date.

"Thought you might like to see what you used to look like."

Phillip held the snapshot over the lamp to get a better look. The laughter of fond memories escaped his smiling lips. Alicia wrapped her arms around his waist as she recreated the pose of the two lovers with dreamy inclined heads resting together.

"I found that the other day while going through some things from Iowa."

Phillip kissed her with the remembered passion of the time recorded in the picture. Their growing desire was interrupted by a knock on the door. Alicia checked to be sure that there were no tell-tale marks of lipstick on Phillip's mouth. She opened the door to find Ben

Morgan, a roly-poly man with wrinkled blue-black skin and bloodshot eyes.

"Good evening, Miss Wallace. I was just passing and thought I'd stop by to see if you was all right."

"I'm fine, thank you, Mr. Morgan."

Ben strained his eyes to see if he could make out the face of the man silhouetted against the firelight. He continued his conversation but kept his eyes focused in the direction where Phillip stood.

"Nasty night out. But I've got to make my rounds anyway."

"Will the electricity be off long?"

"No telling. If they turned it off at the power plant it'll be back on soon. But if a transformer was struck, there's no telling."

Ben slapped his rain-soaked hat against his leg as his alcohol-soaked eyes looked past Alicia. He turned to leave. At the edge of the porch he stopped and turned back.

"Tell your friend to be careful. It's easy to get stuck on the road out."

"Thank you, Mr. Morgan."

"I take it he's not from around here."

"Thank you, Mr. Morgan."

The slam of the door joined a clap of thunder and the two sounded as one. It was Alicia's way of saying that she did not appreciate Ben's intrusion, and she hoped that he had gotten the message.

"I've got to move out of this campus cottage."

Phillip had witnessed a side of Alicia that he had never known existed—discourtesy.

"Who was that?"

"That was the superintendent of Buildings and Grounds, also known as the watchdog of night-time activities—the caretaker—the blabbermouth."

"I can tell he's not one of your favorite people."

"He's one of the reasons Frank left. This plantation is filled with darkies who run and tell Massa Clark everything."

Phillip could tell that Alicia was upset and no doubt exaggerating. After all, she was talking about a college of education; an institution where the pursuit of learning took place, not slave labor. And she was taking about Dr. Joseph Samuel Clark, who had spent his entire life giving hope for a better life to Negroes through education. Yes, she had to be upset to think that Southern came even close to being like the place she described.

"This is the kind of thing that Frank was talking about in his letter. I know that drunk fool came over here just because he saw your car out front."

"Drunk?"

"He's always drunk. But he sobers up when he reports to the massa."

"I think you're wrong about Dr. Clark."

"Oh, you do, do you? I'll bet anything that before this storm is over Dr. Clark will know that you were here."

Alicia's speculation seemed a bit far-fetched but Phillip could not rule it out entirely. He could not run the risk that somehow Dr. Clark might find out he was having an affair. He knew, without a doubt, that both Felton and the old man would look upon his having a mistress with disfavor. A lot was on the line. His program of teacher education, his image as a faithful husband and devoted father. Many relationships were being threatened since that Morgan fellow dropped by.

They did not continue the discussion of Frank Yerby. Alicia slid the snapshot into Phillip's inside coat pocket as she slipped off his coat. She turned her attention to other matters. She cranked up the Victrola and placed the player-head in the groove of a recording by Ma Rainey and Louis Armstrong.

"Now, I know if Ben Morgan hears this gut-bucket music he will definitely run right over and tell the massa."

Alicia's mockingly sarcastic description of the music brought Martha to his mind. But Phillip did not want to think of Martha or Dr. Clark or Ben Morgan. He would rather keep his mind on desirable things—Alicia, and the sharp rhythms of raindrops on the tin roof, accented by the rumble of distant thunder and the romantic feel in the air. Or on the delicious roast pork waiting to be eaten. He did not wish to have any of these desirables interrupted by drifting thoughts. But they were there—and these thoughts had to be pushed away and out of his mind.

The storm raged on. The dinner of pork, sweet potatoes, macaroni, and mustard greens was enjoyed by lamp and firelight. The cream sherry and cherry liqueur left Phillip feeling relaxed. Alicia also felt snug. Phillip could tell by her passionate kisses that she was ready to make love. But Phillip's thoughts were jumping from Morgan to Clark to Martha. No matter how he tried, he could not rid his mind's eye of their images. He could not get sexually stimulated. The earlier events of the evening had put a damper on his passion. He continued to feel guilty when he thought of Martha. The music that she hated so much kept playing on the Victrola and in his mind. On top of all, he was fifty-six years old and it naturally took a little longer and more stimulation for his "johnson" to get hard. Everything was right but nothing was working. The more he tried the worse it got. Alicia was aware that something was wrong.

She slid her hand down between his legs and found a soft limp roll of biscuit dough. Phillip was embarrassed. This had never happened before when he was with Alicia. He thought of leaving but the storm was still raging. Flashes of lightning revealed Alicia's sensuous body alive with passion and wanting. She said, "I can fix this." She slid his body to the edge of the bed, assumed a kneeling position, and spread his legs wide apart. She gently pushed him down on the bed and murmured, "Just relax." The warm, moist embrace of her mouth encircling his penis sent an electric tingle through his entire body. The blood rushed to his organ and it sprang alive. His thoughts were now on nothing else but making love to Alicia. He had never experienced anything like this before. He could feel the firm sliding friction of her teeth as the movement of her mouth grew faster and faster. He exploded in ecstasy. The elation of the moment carried with it his wish that time would stop and the moment never end.

The aromatic musk of sexual desire filled Phillip's nostrils. His tongue tasted the nectar that saturated the entire abyss, as Alicia's legs wedded his senses to her sanctuary of pleasure. Phillip was lost in the oneness of carnal desire. He had experienced for the first time that special something that drives lovemaking to another dimension. It was total. It was complete. It was the ultimate enjoyment of passion that, when interwoven with spirituality, sweeps one to a level of pleasure never before realized.

THE STORM had ended. In the early morning light Phillip skillfully maneuvered the muddy ruts of the road that led away from Southern. He dreaded the possibility that Ben Morgan might happen to be up and about. When he reached the tar and gravel highway to Baton Rouge he breathed a sigh of relief. The trip into Baton Rouge would delay his arrival in Estilette by a couple of hours, but he must have a copy of *The Foxes of Harrow.* He planned to find out for himself how this Yerby fellow wrote about the plantation owners pictured on the cover of his book.

He thought back over the previous night. There was much to adjust in his thinking. He had never experienced oral sex before. His memory of men-talk labeled what he had done "eating pussy" and what she had done "sucking dick," which was only done by a Jezebel. This of course was not at all how Phillip felt about Alicia. The term she used, "mouth music," was closer to how he preferred to remember the evening's activity than the terms used by men-talk. He had indeed experienced a symphony. Consequently his attitude about his new lovemaking experience changed with each passing mile.

The closer he got to Estilette the more his thoughts were occupied by Martha. She would never stand for a divorce. No one in her family had ever been divorced. Being Catholic made such endings to a loveless marriage unthinkable. And this is exactly where he found himself—in a loveless marriage. He could not remember when the absence of love was first apparent. Perhaps it was many years ago when he had his first encounter with Alicia. He could not remember whether it was sexual desire or the lack of love for Martha that had driven him to Alicia. Now it did not matter which. The only question was, what could be done about it? He would like very much to spend his remaining years with Alicia. The children were grown. Bobby would soon be out of medical school. Rosa was the only one still at home and it was beginning to look as if she might grow to be an old maid. He did not have to concern himself with raising children any longer. But a divorce was out of the question. On the other hand, maybe Martha would die a premature death. He quickly shut this possibility out of his mind as he turned into the driveway of his home.

It was not long before Martha found the forgotten picture in his coat pocket as she prepared his suit for the cleaners. All hell broke loose. He explained the picture was nothing more than a casual friendship. He denied any intimate relationship. Martha did not believe him. They fussed. They fought. Martha slapped him. Phillip slapped back. Phillip threatened to get his pistol. It was only the presence of Rosa that made these idle threats. As in previous years, she was the peacemaker and stood between the two, pleading, praying, and crying for an armistice. Each of these occurrences resurrected in Phillip's mind the notion of premature death. Each occurrence widened the gulf between them; by this time they were only going through the motions of being husband and wife. They slept in the same bed but did not talk. All of the differences that were once tolerated were now forces for separation. Martha hated the thought, idea, influence, and smell of "that woman." She blamed her for all the problems in their marriage. And Martha was determined not to give her the satisfaction of victory by freeing Phillip with a divorce.

Phillip compiled his own list of blame. Martha's vindictive and evil nature that was seen on the night she struck Lala. Her color prejudice, hatred of her brother and religious intolerance combined to form the basis for his reasons of feeling trapped in a marriage that no longer worked.

THE BLACK Eagle had been open for two years and word of mouth was spreading like wildfire. Lightnin' Slim and Schoolboy Cleve were regular blues artists from Baton Rouge, along with Vitalee and LightFoot himself. Perhaps because he knew Martha would not like the fact that he went, Phillip began to frequent the Black Eagle. He had formed a real liking for the blues. It seemed to be in his blood. It set him apart from other "high class Negroes" of whom he was considered a member. It set him apart from his wife, who insisted that "gut-bucket" music was nigger-music. In spite of the labels, he enjoyed the feeling that he got from the sound. He had a special table at the Black Eagle.

LightFoot usually sat with him between songs or duties and inquired about the family. Phillip was the only remaining link between sister and brother. LightFoot had not spoken to Martha since he found out that she had paid BookTau to burn his place down. However, he was still concerned about her well-being. He never forgot the good times, the fun times they shared when they were young. The nursing care she gave after his accident, and letting him live in with her and Phillip for ten years. There was never a time when he failed to ask, "Who's Martha hatin' now?" Phillip kept LightFoot fully informed about all family activities except his own relationship with Alicia. She was never brought up or brought to the Black Eagle. Whenever they did go to a blues club, it was in Port Allen or Baton Rouge. This was the one facet of his life that he shared with no one else. Sometimes LightFoot would ask, "Did my sister ever find out about the property?"

Phillip assured him she hadn't, but he knew it was only a matter of time before she did. Whenever that happened he knew it would create a storm the likes of which they had never seen before.

Phillip was curious about other matters—the blues.

"What makes the blues so special?"

LightFoot looked at him like he thought he was crazy. He shrugged his shoulders and said, "I dunno. I jest like 'em. Never really thought 'bout it like that. Jest makes me feel good."

"Anybody around here know anything about how the blues got started? I can't find anything about it in Carter G. Woodson."

LightFoot looked at him. His mind was going a mile a minute. He wondered, *Now why would Phillip ask me a question like that? I know he don't feel as strongly as Martha about hearing the blues, but for him to ask a question like that throws me off base.* LightFoot decided to try to get Phillip off his back.

"Go talk to Mr. Bobo."

"Mr. Bobo?"

"Yeah, he know all that stuff, and he remembers it, too."

Phillip drained his glass and got up.

"Thanks."

LightFoot watched him exit the door. He shook his head and smiled. He said out loud to himself, like he was talking to someone across the table, "I guess a little of Lala done rubbed off on him."

Mr. Bobo watched the Ford pull to a stop near the well. He had watched the car ever since he noticed the dust cloud a mile down the lane. He knew it was the professor but he didn't figure that he was going to turn into his place. The professor had business over at his farm further down the lane, so he was accustomed to him passing by. Phillip got out of the car and walked over to the porch where Mr. Bobo sat rocking.

"How you doing today, Mr. Bobo?"

"Right tolerable, 'Fessor. And you?"

"I feel better now that the war is over and we don't have to ration any more. Maybe things will get back to normal."

"Ain't that the truf? I feels the same way. Have a seat, 'Fessor."

Phillip took a seat on the edge of the porch above the steps. He realized that Mr. Bobo had offered him a chair on the other side of the porch, but he wanted to sit close to the man. He wrapped his hands around his knee and looked up at the map of time etched in the old man's face.

"Mr. Bobo, do you know anything about the blues?"

"Whatcha wanna know?"

"How it started way back? Where it came from?"

"I can't rightly say, 'Fessor. But I 'member somethin' about a nigger woman blues singer."

"Bessie Smith?"

"Naw, 'fore that, I thinks, but I ain't sure . . . I thinks she taught Bessie. Her name was Ma Rainey. Course dat's what people called her. Her real name was . . . lemme see, it's been a long time since I remembered somethin' like this . . . yes, dat's it . . . Gertrude . . . Gertrude Pridgett. She was born in Georgia, but she sung all over the South. They jes' call her Ma 'cause she married Pa Rainey, so she took his name. Dey was a pair, Ma and Pa. She called herself da Mama of the Blues . . . maybe she started it all."

Mr. Bobo began laughing. It was the most animated that Phillip had ever seen him. Usually Mr. Bobo was solemn and somber. Phillip asked, "What's so funny?"

"Jes' 'membering dat song she used to sing . . . call it da 'Black Bottom.' She used to sing dat song and then she turnt round and slap her behind and wiggle it a little . . . dat sho' was funny . . . she had one of dem *bigggg* asses.

"Where did you see her?"

"Lord, I don't remember. I think it was Miss'ippi, someplace. I used to go up there to pick cotton, and one time I go over to dis here little ol' joint and she was there . . . don't 'member where dat was. So much done happen, it's hard to keep it all sorted out sometimes. But she could sing . . . Make you feel good, like the blues suppose to do. Course she could make ya feel blue too . . . She could sing dem sad songs . . . She could sing 'em all. And the peoples loved her, 'specially dem womens . . . Ohhhhhh yes, she like some womenfolks . . . they jes' hang 'round all the time . . . Now don't get me wrong, she like some menfolks too . . . she like 'em all."

"You know any bluesmen around here?"

"Yeah, they sure got enough of 'em. Yo' brother-in-law one of de best."

"Is that right?"

"Sho' is. Everybody like his playin'."

Phillip felt that he had heard enough oral history for one day. He got up and stretched, and then he extended his hand to Mr. Bobo.

"Thank you for the stories."

"Anytime you wanna hear some mo', jes' come on by."

"Sure will. See you."

"So long, 'Fessor. Thanks for the hog."

Mr. Bobo watched the dust settle behind the car. The quiet returned, and the crickets and the birds.

20

THE INTERVENING YEARS, 1947 to 1949, were filled with events that Phillip had thought he would never live to see. In the spring of 1947 Jackie Robinson broke the color line in baseball. Phillip was glued to the radio, just as he was whenever Joe Louis fought. But this was a different fight. It did not last fifteen rounds in one night; this was a fight that was going to be fought every day of the season for as long as Jackie could hold out. Phillip knew what Jackie had to endure to win. As he listened to the broadcast he filled in the voices that he couldn't hear but knew were there. The voices of hatred, filled with taunts and threats, brought on the wind from the stands to Jackie's ears; and sometimes even from other ballplayers. Jackie would have to be a strong and dedicated person to hear and not hear. Phillip hoped that this champion would win this challenge, which was even greater than the Louis fight with Schmeling.

That same year, the Freedom Riders were challenging the bus segregation laws of the South. And the Archbishop of St. Louis announced that he would excommunicate any Catholic who continued to protest the integration of parochial schools. It was not a surprise to Phillip that there were Catholics who did not want Negroes in their churches and schools. He had experienced this first-hand. He realized that social changes were happening so fast he could hardly keep up. He read his newspaper every day, but in a way he felt left out. He had made efforts to improve the educational training of colored teachers, but he was no longer as fully involved as he had been years earlier. He felt empty. He wanted to do his "civic homework," as he had heard that time long ago on the Norman Corwin radio broadcast.

The 1948 election was six months away. There had been talk around town that the NAACP was trying to get a voter registration drive started. Most colored people in Estilette were afraid to challenge the status quo and Phillip was one of them. Since the poll tax had been repealed in 1934, under the political leadership of Senator Huey P. Long, very few colored voters in Louisiana had registered. Now there were stirrings about registration drives in places like New Orleans, Baton Rouge, and Alexandria. Finally the word got to Estilette.

Leo did not expect that Phillip would be an eager joiner of such a movement, and he suspected that neither could he stand to lose his state paycheck. But he was curious about Phillip's thoughts on the matter. He turned off the blacktop onto graveled Academy Street and headed to the conversation porch. Phillip lowered his *Times Picayune* when he heard the truck.

It was difficult for Phillip to tell that the original color of the Chevrolet truck was black. But he could recognize Leo's mud-colored truck any place he saw it. Phillip said to Leo after he slammed the door, "I got a hose on the side of the house if you wanna shoot some water on that caked-up mud."

Leo laughed as he made his way along the brick walkway up to the porch. "If I did that, them dirt daubers wouldn't have no place to live."

"You mean to tell me you riding around carrying wasp nests all over town?"

"Right under that spare tire."

Leo pulled up an empty chair and sat down.

"Where's Martha?"

Before Phillip could say, "She's in the house," Leo was on his way to the door. He cupped his hands around his eyes as he stared in through the screen. He said, "Hey, Martha, I'll take some of your good ol' lemonade."

He settled into the porch rocker and propped his feet up on the railing at a right angle to Phillip's.

"I was over by McGee's place the other day. I'd just picked a few watermelons and they was setting in the truck bed. A couple young boys come by and decided to mess with my melons. Before they could decide which ones they wanted, them yellow jackets got after them boys and chased them down the lane."

The screen door banged shut as Martha hobbled out of the house, carrying a pitcher of lemonade on a tray with two glasses and a plate of teacakes. She placed the tray on the table in back of where the men sat and covered it with the towel she had draped over her arm. Without pausing to wait for a greeting, she directed a question to Leo.

"Catherine still suffering with lumbago?"

"Not as much. She's been using that Vick's salve you gave her."

Martha, feeling the pain of her own persistent rheumatism, limped back the way she had come. Her voice could be heard from inside the house. "Tell her to keep taking them Doan's pills and using that hot poultice."

Leo poured two glasses of lemonade and handed one to Phillip.

"You got a fine woman there."

Phillip nodded, knowing that appearances could be deceiving. To most eyes, Martha's light skin and beautiful face bespoke a kind, gentle, and loving soul but Phillip knew better. Leo returned to his story as if there had not been any interruption at all.

"I laughed at those boys and yelled after them, 'That'll teach you to mess with my melons.'" Leo's face suddenly turned very serious. "McGee tells me they looking for somebody to go register."

"Register for what?"

"To vote. That's for what."

Phillip stared off in the distance while he pulled at his eyebrows. Leo could tell he was deep in thought. He had seen that pensive mood many times before. He wanted to find out what was going on in Phillip's mind.

"What you think about that?"

Phillip cleared his throat. "Well . . . it'll be a good thing if they could get a group of people together."

"Hell, man, they can't even find one. And that guy who's organizing things for the NAACP—that Alvin Jones fellow—he ain't from around here so he can't register. He's just setting it up."

"There're not many people 'round here who'll chance it. It's gonna take somebody with nothing to lose. Somebody who's not afraid of white people. 'Course, you never know . . . there could be somebody round here like that. Well, I know one thing. It won't be you or me. We wouldn't have our jobs two minutes after that."

Leo had finally gotten Phillip going on the subject of voting. He had no idea where the subject would take them, but he could tell it would be a long conversation.

The pitcher of lemonade had vanished and the plate with the teacakes was empty. It was getting dark and the mosquitoes had begun to feed. So Leo figured it was time to go home. When he left, nothing was any more resolved than it had been when the pitcher was full. It was still summer and the election was months away, so there was still time to talk again.

OCTOBER 1948 came quickly and the election was only six weeks away. There was talk on the radio and in the newspapers that it would be tough for Truman to win a full term. After Roosevelt died, Truman finished his remaining three years, but he had never been elected president on his own. It was Truman who had ordered the atomic bomb to be dropped on Japan that brought war in the Pacific to an end. Most Americans were happy and praised him for doing that.

But it was the other thing that he had done that was causing him trouble. He had ordered the military to be desegregated. The Southern states were up in arms. The Democratic Party was splintering. A faction of "states righters" formed a separate party called the Dixiecrats and nominated Strom Thurmond, governor of South Carolina, as their candidate. At the Democrat convention they united against Truman, claiming "he wants to reduce us to the status of a mongrel, inferior race, mixed in blood, our Anglo-Saxon heritage a mockery." And as if this were not bad enough, Henry Wallace, recently fired by Truman as secretary of Commerce, was nominated to run for president by the Progressive Party. It did not look good for Truman's reelection. The Democratic Party was now split three ways. Phillip felt that Truman needed every vote he could get. The thought of Strom

Thurmond, or even the Republican nominee, Thomas Dewey, becoming president was too much for Phillip to ignore.

Alicia told Phillip, "They'll never let you register." Her voice was strong with conviction and fear, but she went on. "Why do you want to do this?"

"I don't know, really."

"Then you shouldn't. The time is not right."

Phillip got up from the bed and began dressing. For a long while he was silent. Alicia stared up at the bedroom ceiling as if reading the future in the stars. Phillip's somber face echoed her concerns as he knotted his tie.

"Maybe it's because I know that the NAACP group is not gonna find anybody willing to do it. Or maybe it's because I haven't really stood up like a man for what I believe. Or maybe it's simply because I remember the look in your eyes when you read that letter from Frank Yerby."

Alicia sat up in the bed as if startled from a dream.

"I didn't feel . . ."

Phillip's expression as he turned from the mirror took the wind out of her sails. She could tell that he wanted to continue without interruption. She sat silently waiting.

"I could feel your admiration for Yerby when he took a stand. I mean, in leaving the school and against all of the attitudes about humility and stuff, and then taking up his writing again. And later on, when he left all of this racial stuff and moved to France where he could write and feel like a free man; you were happy about that, too. But he didn't stay here and fight. He left. And maybe that's why I have to do what I've decided to do. Somebody has to take a stand here and fight for what's right."

Alicia rose and wrapped her arms around his waist and buried her head in his chest. She dared not cry. It would not have been what Phillip needed or wanted. Her lips rose slowly to embrace his.

"I understand."

The drive back to Estilette got longer each time. This time it was no different. He had not told Martha what he was thinking of doing. He simply did not want the distraction. He knew he would not be able to convince her of the reasons even unknown to himself, as he had been able to do with Alicia. Martha was no longer the source of understanding or comfort that he needed. So it was just as well that she didn't know beforehand. He would simply walk in with his registration paper, or whatever they give someone who has registered to vote, and lay it on the table in front of her and watch the expression on her face.

Martha's beauty was still evident. The strands of gray in her hair blended more completely with her eyes, which were now showing a slight nesting place for crow's feet. Except for this, and a few folds of loose skin below her chin, she was as beautiful as ever. Even Phillip could not deny her beauty, although he had stopped loving her after seeing the not so beautiful images she kept hidden beneath the skin.

Martha crocheted late into the night when Phillip was out. Having been taught by Julee, it was the perfect busywork. In spite of the pain in the joints of her fingers, which she ignored as being required suffering from God, she could crochet without thinking. Her mind was allowed to wander freely over the godless lives of Bobby, Lala, Vel, and Phillip, all of whom were headed to wrack and ruin, according to her reckonings. The only person in the family she did not have to worry about was Rosa who, after the one slip with Father Pat—the "wolf in sheep's clothing"—never did anything without praying first.

As usual, the sound of a car driving into the yard was her signal to stop crocheting, put out the light, and get into bed. She pretended to be asleep when Phillip slid under the covers next to her.

The next day Phillip was up early; bathed, shaved, and dressed. As usual Rosa brought coffee to his reading place at the window. He was nervous and ill at ease. Although he held the paper in the usual reading position, he did little reading. He finished his coffee and left.

He parked the car across from the courthouse. He noticed more people than usual standing and sitting on the steps and benches around the front entrance. He did not like the looks on the faces of the rednecks, but then he had never liked the looks on the faces of rednecks—the ever present hate-etched slant of the lips and slit of the eyes. So this was nothing new. No doubt they were there for the same purpose he was—to register. And no doubt they would vote for the Dixiecrats.

As he walked past a group of four men, who had appeared from a distance to be engaged in a lively conversation, there was silence. Out of the corner of his eye he recognized Clovis Hicks and Lee Jay Clary, the two who had abducted PeeWee. Phillip's body went limp. His legs wanted to turn around and go back the way he had come. He suspected trouble. He knew that they knew what he was coming to do. He could feel their eyes burn into his back as he mounted the steps. Once inside he went directly to the door with the sign "Registrar of Voters," which he had seen many times before on trips upstairs to the superintendent's office. There was no one waiting in line. A man was behind the counter. He held his cigarette in the corner of his mouth with his index and second finger. He challenged, "What you want, boy?"

"I came to register."

Phillip heard the words rush out of his mouth but was not aware of saying them. They had been rehearsed in his mind so many times they came tumbling out unconsciously.

"Niggers can't vote in this town."

Then he addressed his next statement, with a nod of his head, to the space behind Phillip's back. "Ain't that right?"

The voices behind Phillip squawked like a chorus of buzzards: "That's right," "Niggers can't vote here," "This nigger musta forgot where he was," all punctuated with laughter. Phillip turned to face the ten or so men he had passed on the way in—now a mob. There was little doubt in Phillip's mind they had been waiting for him; someone had tipped them off. He could not even guess who it might have been. There had been dissension in the NAACP-led discussions over how, when, or even if such an attempt should be made. So the tip could only have come from someone in the meetings who did not feel that Phillip should go on his own. With little else said or done, the hate-filled mob surrounded Phillip. The voice of Lee Jay snarled above the rest, "Come on, boy. We gonna show you where to register." Phillip felt himself being dragged in the direction of the back door. The last thing he remembered was tobacco juice spattering in his face just before he felt a sharp pain in the back of his neck.

PHILLIP OPENED his eyes. The blurred figure standing over him slowly came into focus. He felt Alicia's tears strike his left arm. He hurt all over. His face felt like a tight balloon ready to pop. He attempted to turn his head to see where he was, but the pain in his neck was as piercing as the last blow he remembered. Another pain stabbed him in the chest when he took a breath to speak, but no sound came out. Alicia leaned over and spoke softly into his ear.

"Don't try to talk. You are in the hospital. I was parked outside the courthouse waiting. When I saw those men run to their cars and speed off, I knew something had happened. I went around back and found you in the bushes."

She kissed him lightly on the forehead. It felt as if she had slammed a hammer into his brain.

"I've got to go now. I called Martha, anonymously. I don't think she would be too happy to see me. I love you."

Phillip watched her disappear from the corner of his eye and he listened to her footsteps fade away. A nameless face with a head bandage came into view. Phillip remembered seeing the man on many passings-by outside the Sugar Patch Cafe.

"'Fessor, I sho' am sorry."

The man was still shaking his head when he was abruptly moved out of view. His face was replaced by Martha's. Stoic with a slight hint of mercy, her nurse-trained attitude gave way to questions.

"What happened?"

Phillip tried but could not speak. He heard the voice of the man in the head bandage. Martha turned in his direction.

"I hear tell them crackers beat the daylights outta the 'fessor when he went to vote."

Martha examined Phillip's face closely; then his arm. She pulled back the sheet, opened the gown, and examined the bruises on his chest and the rest of his body—all the while chiding, "I thought you had better sense than that. You know these crackers not gonna to let you vote. I can't imagine what got into your head. Thank God, they didn't take you off and leave you in some bayou like they done that boy."

She ended her cursory but thorough examination with, "I'm going to get the doctor."

Dr. Rossini had just completed his examination, sighed, and looked across at Martha when the hospital chief came storming in.

"Dr. Rossini, this is irregular. It's against hospital policy."

"What policy are you talking about, Dr. Doucette?"

"This patient was admitted and treated in the critical ward. We have other doctors assigned to care for our colored patients."

Martha's body stiffened and she could see the blood flush in Dr. Rossini's face. He began slowly and his tempo increased until he was almost screaming. "In the first place, this man was not treated in the critical ward. He has a broken arm, which was not set or cast. He has at least two broken ribs and possibly more. He has a concussion from a blow to the head. His body is covered with abrasions, contusions, and lacerations, and there is some evidence of internal bleeding. In the second place, Professor Fergerson has been a patient of mine since I have been practicing in this hospital. Now you just get the hell out of my face and let me treat my patient!"

Dr. Doucette was too embarrassed to even move. By this time every one of the twelve colored patients in the ward was listening to the dressing-down that one white doctor was giving to another in the interest of a colored patient. They had never witnessed such an unheard-of event as this. A hundred possible responses flashed through Dr. Doucette's mind. Finally he decided that a hasty retreat was the better part of valor. As he cleared the door, the twelve patients began to stomp the floor with feet, crutches, or chairs. It was a jolting sound that rocked the ward and shot into the hallway behind Dr. Doucette.

After giving the medical care that was initially denied, much to the displeasure of the staff, Dr. Rossini released Phillip to the home-care of his wife. Phillip's recovery was now in the rheumatoid hands of a woman who no longer loved him.

21

THE HIGH-PITCHED voice of Robert Johnson popped and crackled as he sang, "I got a kind-hearted woman, do anything in the world for me." Then LightFoot lifted the needle head from the grooves of the seventy-eight and sang the same words, picking out the matching chords on his guitar. He repeated this over and over until he could play and sing "Kindhearted Woman Blues" from memory. This was the way he expanded his repertoire of blues songs for the club. He had acquired the Johnson recordings from a Pullman porter on the Southern Pacific—those enterprising men kept suitcases full of hard-to-find platters that they peddled up and down the run from Chicago to New Orleans.

LightFoot was fascinated by the life and death of Robert Johnson as much as he was by his music. He had heard the story of Johnson's life from Lightnin' Slim, who had heard it from Muddy Waters. The story goes that Johnson was a traveling ladies' man. Born in Hazelhurst, Mississippi, in 1911, he lived a short, full life of hard drinking and fast women. He was playing a juke-house outside of Greenwood, Mississippi, and took up for the evening with a woman who, unknown to Johnson, was the houseman's wife. The jealous houseman, who knew that Johnson also loved his liquor, set him up with a half-pint of whisky that was laced with strychnine. Johnson was only twenty-six when he had his last drink. LightFoot likened the way that Johnson died to the way that Vitalee got rid of Frank Miller. Vitalee's last name was Johnson. LightFoot wondered if there was more of a connection in the same last name than just a talent for the blues. At any rate, he continued learning the songs of one of the early and most impressive country bluesman—Robert Johnson.

BookTau swayed to the rhythm of the guitar as he swung the mop across the liquor-soaked floor. Now in his late thirties, he had added cleaning up the Black Eagle to his regular odd jobs around town. This was his way of making up for burning down the Blues Tavern. He would not accept money for his labor after he told LightFoot, "She made me do it," meaning of course Martha.

The appearance of two people in the open doorway caused BookTau to drag his mop, leaving in its wake a wet trail, as he crossed to where they stood. He said, "The place ain't open yet."

"BookTau, where's Uncle Johnny?"

The sharp crack of the mop handle hitting the floor brought the music to a stop. LightFoot turned in the direction of the door, expecting to see the smoky discharge of a pistol. Instead he saw BookTau lift a man off the floor, whirl in circles like a child playing ring-around-a-rosy, and shout at the top of his voice, "Bobby, Bobby, where you come from?"

LightFoot set his guitar on the floor, jumped off the stage, and ran to the door.

"Bobby—or should I say, Dr. Fergerson? What are you doing here?"

"Come to see about Papa. This is my wife, Ruth. Ruth, my Uncle Johnny, and this here is BookTau."

"Your wife? Your mama know you're married?"

"No! That's why I came here first."

"Ohhhhh, man . . . BookTau, go get Naomi and tell her to cook us up somethin'. Welcome to the family, Miz Ruth. Come on, have a seat."

BookTau ran toward the back door and LightFoot led the couple to a nearby table. Bobby immediately asked, "What happened to Papa?"

LightFoot filled him in on all the details of the assault and continued, "Your papa's coming along slowly. 'Course, them white folks still mighty upset 'cause he tried to vote. I goes over there once a week to see about him, and your mama still walks outta the room when I come in. She gonna have a fit that you got married and didn't tell her first."

Bobby told the events that led to their marriage, as if a prelude to the questions he would have to answer when he got home. The courtship during his days as a student, although told to Uncle Johnny, would be left out when the story was told later. Ruth was quietly pleasant. She had large gentle eyes set in a face of Yoruba sculpture. Her nose curved down from her forehead and came to a rounded point from which her nostrils flared back into her high-set cheekbones. Naomi liked her light brown, friendly face immediately; except for the obvious difference in book-learning, they were a sisterhood. Naomi prepared a meal fit for a king and queen. It was several hours and many drinks later when Bobby and Ruth walked out of the Black Eagle and got into the car. LightFoot leaned into the driver's side window and said, “Good luck. You gotta be either crazy or drunk to see yo’ mama, so it’s a good thing you’re drunk.”

THEIR RECEPTION at the family home was cool, as Bobby had expected. He knew that as soon as his mother got a whiff of the liquor on his breath she would start fussing. However, she was too happy to see him to start in on him the minute he walked through the door, no matter how disgusting she thought his breath smelled. Martha was civil until she was told that Ruth Frazier was Mrs. Robert Fergerson, and then she turned to ice. She left the room without another word. Bobby had prepared Ruth to some extent, but not completely.

Ruth knew that Martha would be upset that they had gotten married without letting her know first. She knew that Martha looked forward to having big weddings in the family, and so far that hadn’t happened. But Bobby did not and could not tell Ruth that the main reason for her exit was because she was not his mama’s favorite color. He also suspected that his mama was disappointed because he had not married Alex. Bobby knew that the time would come when he would have to explain his mama’s jaundiced eye, but this was not it. He led his wife to his papa’s room where the reception was great and the atmosphere more congenial.

Early the next morning there was a soft knock on the door of Bobby’s room. Bobby turned over and looked at the clock. He expected that it was his mama wanting him to go to eight o’clock Mass.

“Yes?”

“Bobby, Mama say breakfast is ready whenever you and your wife get up.”

He was wrong. It was Rosa calling him to breakfast. This was the signal that his mama was sorry for her chilly reception the previous evening. He had seen this apologetic behavior many times in the past. He rolled over, on top of Ruth, and said, "Time to get up and have breakfast."

"Why so early?"

"You're in the country now. A new day is in the making."

"If you don't get off me that's not all that'll be in the making."

He was grateful for Ruth's attitude. She had hardly noticed his mama's slight. For all Ruth knew, what she had seen was Martha's personality, so she did not perceive that there was any expression of resentment toward her. Bobby had not told her much about Martha except that she was very beautiful, a portrayal with which Ruth agreed. Ruth took the comments made by LightFoot as a reference to one of her peculiar personality traits known to her and Bobby. That was the way Ruth was; she did not assume anything about anyone until she knew for sure.

In the center of the table was a large arrangement of hydrangeas and roses, still wet with dew from Martha's garden. This was surrounded by fresh-squeezed orange juice, a large grits, bacon, and egg casserole dripping with butter, stacks of two-inch thick biscuits, and fig preserves. Bobby knew that his mama had considered this a special occasion because she had opened her treasured fig preserves. Rosa helped Phillip to his seat at the head of the table. It was rare to have the family around the dining room table again, so Phillip made the supreme sacrifice to get out of bed for the first time since coming home from the hospital. Ruth's face brightened like a chocolate sun as she admired and complimented the beautiful arrangement of china, silverware, and crystal laid out on the linen tablecloth. Martha received her comments with a warm hug and a lingering arm around the waist, as she gently guided her to the place of honor next to Phillip. Martha could be charming when it suited her purposes, and Bobby wondered exactly what purpose his mama had in mind. However, this thought was quickly erased because Bobby did not want to spoil what had started out as a beautiful day.

During the breakfast, which lasted until noon, the main conversation centered on Ruth, her doctorate degree, and her family. Rosa was most inquisitive, asking probing questions about how and why she had made certain decisions and achieved what she had in so short a time. All were spellbound as Ruth described the long hours of research, study, and writing, complicated by the inability to find housing or convenient eating arrangements. And the racial slights and insults coming from professors and students who did not believe she, a woman and a Negro, should be in a doctoral program at Columbia University.

Martha had never known a woman like her; aggressive, smart, independent, and the color of brown sugar. Ruth defied, in Martha's mind, all of the traits that she believed people with dark skin possessed. In Martha's way of thinking, dark skin was the outward mark of ignorance, dependence, servitude, belief in the occult, and a passion for gut-bucket music. Now this dark-skinned person sitting at her table, as a member of her family, in the likeness of her loathing, was the sum total of the contradictions to her long held beliefs. This was another subject that Martha would have to take up with God.

The second part of the conversation was about Phillip's experiences. His left arm was still in a cast, and although the swelling in his face and body had gone and the abrasions had almost disappeared, he was still a sick man. The broken ribs had not completely healed and there was still a danger that a shattered bone could puncture a lung. He spoke with lethargic tones about his feelings. There was an absence of the emotional anger that Bobby had witnessed years earlier when PeeWee was murdered and when his father was thrown out of the Catholic church.

Now it was like the beating had convinced him that he lived among evil people with evil thoughts, and no effort from him was going to make a difference. He sounded defeated. The determination to continue the struggle in the face of trials and tribulation was lost. This loss, like blues blown away by the wind, signaled a change. Previously, his perseverance had been spread, like nourishment, sustaining others with hope for the future; Bobby, his students, Leo, and everyone with whom he came in contact. But now what Bobby heard in his papa's voice and saw in his eyes was the loss of willpower. Like a deflated balloon he had lost the ever-driving force of the message from the blues—to keep on keeping on.

The same week that brought the news of Bobby's marriage to Martha's ears now brought sadness to Martha's eyes. Vel came home from Chicago. It was her first time back in Estilette since Miz Julee had asked her to leave her house four years ago. At that time there was nothing else Vel could do but leave town. She could not return home, especially after what had happened between her and her father. Plus it was known all over town that Vel had been running a cathouse in Miz Julee's house. So she had to leave. Now she was back. She had heard about her papa's crisis.

Martha embraced her and then stood back to look at her wayward child. She was beautiful. Long sparkling jewels dangled from her ears. Curled ebony threads, formally eyelashes, framed her gray eyes. Her hair was long and flowing, a duplication of Lala's.

"Your hair's got good, and it's grown out."

"Oh, Mama, that's a wig. A human-hair wig—the best."

Martha had never heard of people wearing store-bought hair before. The sparkle of light reflected from Vel's diamond-filled, painted fingers, as they stroked her long tresses, caused Martha's eyes to blink. Vel's face was bright and alive with varying shades of pink, applied so expertly that it seemed her skin had been reborn white. She shed her mink coat with its matching hat and tossed them on the sofa, revealing a silk fuchsia dress that clung seductively to every curve of her body.

"It's a lot warmer here than Chi-Town."

"You must be doing all right up there in Chicago."

"I get by."

"You buy them kind of clothes on a teacher's salary?"

"Oh, Mama, don't start. Look what I brought you."

Vel opened the largest bag of her set of tapestry cloth luggage. She unwrapped a silk Chinese shawl filled with hand embroidered, multi-colored landscape designs set on a dark blue background, fringed by tassels echoing the colors. Martha's eyes overflowed as her arms enveloped Vel once more. At that moment Vel was again her sweet innocent little girl who brought her joy. Although, deep down inside, it saddened Martha's heart to imagine how she came by all the money for so many nice things.

"How's Papa?"

"He's getting better. I didn't know where to reach you. How did you find out?"

"Viola. The others know?"

"I haven't heard from Lala since she left. Bobby's here."

"He a doctor yet?"

"One more year to go. He got married."

"To Alex?"

"No. To a nigger, looks old enough to be his mama."

"He and Uncle Johnny love to scrape the bottom of the barrel, don't they? She here with him?"

"Yes. They went to the store. Rosa's in there with your papa."

Vel stood in the doorway watching as Rosa wiped the remaining lather from her papa's face. Phillip ran his hand first over one cheek then the other and down under his chin.

"You did a good job. No blood this time."

Vel said, to get their attention, "I'd like to shave you the next time."

Both of them turned in the direction of the familiar voice. Rosa ran to the door. "Vel! Vel, it's so good to see you."

As soon as she was free of Rosa's embrace, Vel knelt beside her papa's chair and kissed his freshly shaven face. Phillip pulled her close with his good right arm. He said, "Thanks for coming, daughter."

"I brought you a present, Papa."

Vel opened a small velvet case and took out a golden pocket watch attached to a chain. She pressed the knob on the top and the intricately engraved cover flipped open, revealing the face of a Bulova timepiece with roman numerals. The second hand swept around the full circle before Phillip could speak and look into her eyes.

"It's the best present I've ever received."

"Read the inscription."

Phillip looked at the inside of the cover. It was engraved *To Papa, Everything in Its Time. Remember, Keep Time for Everything. Love, Vel—1948.* Phillip brought her close once more. The moisture from his cheek smudged Vel's painted face and transferred its color to his own. She did not mind the smudged makeup any more than she cared about the tears leaving trails on her own cheeks. This was the first time that either of them had ever cried in the other's arms. Rosa, aware that the embrace should not outlast the moment, said laughingly, "Oh, come on you two. Break it up."

Phillip responded, "I was just getting used to her perfume again."

That brief moment of levity was exactly what they needed to free them from the memory of the pain that each had caused the other.

RUTH ENTERED the kitchen with an armful of groceries. Vel was taking a drink from a flask, which she quickly capped and slipped back into her purse. She looked Ruth over and asked with surprise, "Oh, are you the new house-girl?"

"No. I'm Ruth Fergerson.

"Bobby's new wife?"

"That's right."

"Bobby was always impulsive."

"And you must be Velma."

At that moment Bobby walked in, loaded down with the rest of the shopping. He said, "Vel, I didn't know you were coming."

He dropped his packages on the table and swung Vel around by the waist. She was still holding the perfume spray bottle that she used to cover the smell of gin.

"Ohhhh, Bobby, you've gotten so strong. I was just telling your little ol' wife here how full of surprises you are. You could have at least let someone know you were planning to take on a new dandruff scratcher."

The last remark was puzzling to Ruth, but it served to set the tone of the encounters by the two women for the remainder of the time Ruth was to spend in Estilette. Meeting Bobby's family was an eye-opening experience. Never in her wildest dreams could she have imagined such an odd assortment of females.

Vel was not in Estilette more than two hours when the phone rang. It was Viola. They made arrangements to get together. Viola had given up the fast life after Vel left town and had now settled down to one special boyfriend, Al. The next night Al took them to a night club in Lafayette, where the usual Creole clientele, dancing, and having fun was the order of the evening. After a couple of hours Viola got restless and wanted to leave. She ordered steamed crayfish to go. She really wanted to spend time alone with Vel, so she had Al drop them off at the Fergersons' because, as she said, "I plan to spend the night."

The two women settled on the porch, in the swing, in the warm autumn night, to enjoy their crayfish feast. It was like old times—lifelong friends drinking, smoking, giggling, and sharing secrets that no one else in the world knew but them. Viola told the intricate details of the happenings, during Vel's absence, that were too complicated to explain in their letters. The most compelling was the first time that she and Al had tried to make love in the rumble seat of his deuce coupe.

She described the twisting, turning, and various gyrations that he went through trying to "get his thing in."

"So, finally, I just cradled it in the cup of my hands and he pumped away. Honey, he never knew the difference."

The hysterical laughter of the girls turned into a coughing frenzy that then turned to tears. This acted as an alarm to Martha who, not able to sleep, was in the kitchen making a cup of tea. She hobbled in the direction of the laughter, cracked open the front door just enough to be sure that the girls were alone, then went back to the kitchen to tend her tea.

Vel quieted down after a drink from her flask and lit another cigarette. Viola was anxious to hear about life in Chicago. "Now tell me about your operation in the big city." About this time Martha returned to the front room with a cup of tea and made herself comfortable in the dark, where she could hear. Vel was describing her "blind pig," a place that sells unlicensed liquor, located in Hyde Park. It was a five-bedroom house formally owned by some rich white people who had moved north to Skokie. It was in the same first-class condition as when the former owners lived there.

"The present owner is a meat-packing man who is also one of my best customers. Girl, he passed the word to his friends and acquaintances who are high in city government, jewelry, furniture, insurance, and the clothing business. They are all hard-working, rich white men who put in long hours and are not satisfied at home. I've got five girls working and two of 'em live in with me."

"You must be making lots of money."

"More than I can count sometimes."

Martha had wondered about the source of the money that had bought the clothes on Vel's back and the expensive presents for the family. And she had figured it might come from some man Vel was living with. But now she knew better. It was worse. Martha's first impulse was to give her back the Chinese shawl and put her out of the house. But an inner voice said no. Vel was her daughter. Her oldest child. And she did not want Vel to know that she had discovered what she did for a living. There was no way to measure the sadness that this eavesdropping had brought to her heart.

Martha tried to get up from the soft cushioned sofa; her knees were not working, but Naomi's hex was. The cup slid off the saucer and she plopped back into the seat. The crashing cup brought the girls from the porch. Vel turned on the light to see Martha shielding her eyes from the instant brightness.

"Mama, what's the matter?"

"I fell asleep and the cup fell, that's all."

"You fell asleep a long way from your bed, Mama."

"Help me up."

Vel helped her to a standing position, knowing full well her mother had overheard some, if not all, of what was said on the porch.

"Don't you girls sit up too late. Good night."

On the way back to her bed Martha wished that she had not heard what she heard. She wished that she still had to guess about the source of Vel's money. At any rate, she thanked God for her blessings—Vel was beautiful, her skin was clear and white; her hair was long and gorgeous even though it was store-bought, which no one would know unless they were told. She said to herself, "She looks a lot prettier than that black thing that Bobby brought home." She vowed, "That's something else I have to take up with God," as she closed her eyes to receive the sleep that had eluded her earlier.

As the days since her arrival passed, Ruth was more convinced than ever that this household contained a strange assortment of females. Martha was indeed beautiful, but Ruth had a feeling that lurking just below the skin, waiting to be released, was an ugly demon. Ruth could hear its presence in chance remarks that were made regarding people unknown to her. One in particular was about a man named Lester who, Martha said, had, "lured my youngest daughter away from her family and into a life of sin. And I haven't heard from her since. But one day he'll get his comeuppance and I pray to God I'll be the one to see that he gets it." Martha was not the kind of woman that Ruth wanted to have angry with her for any reason. Anyone who prayed that God would make them the instrument of his justice was someone to be leery of.

Velma fit the image of fraud in Ruth's mind. From the top of her head to her high spiked shoes, she pretended to be what she was not. She wore expensive clothes and jewelry, ostentatious and tacky, like a lady of the evening claiming to be a lady of good breeding. Ruth did not believe Velma was sincere when she uttered sweet nothings that seemed, more often than not, like words of a first-rate con artist. Still, it was difficult to perceive her motivation. Why did she frequently say things like, "I know Bobby will love having you to mother him" and, "I bet you people really know how to care for spoiled brats." Ruth tried hard not to draw any conclusions from such remarks. However, during the short time that Ruth was around Velma she was able to conclude that Velma was a hypocrite and could not be trusted.

Rosa was quite a different matter. Ruth felt she could be trusted. She was sweet and generous and never seemed to be able to do enough to make Ruth feel at home. Ruth liked Rosa from the beginning. But she felt there was something "sub rosa" about her— something hidden. She didn't know exactly why she felt this, but she sensed a sadness, and concluded that whatever caused this sadness was a dark secret hidden away in Rosa's heart. In moments when Rosa was not aware that she was being observed, Ruth had perceived that Rosa's mind traveled to distant places; perhaps the past, or perhaps wishful thinking, but always surrounded by a cloud of melancholy.

Ruth had not known these ladies long enough to be sure about her first impressions. But she did know they all had to be taken with a grain of salt.

On the seventh day, Velma boarded the train back to Chicago.

Ruth and Bobby returned to Nashville. He with relief that his papa was on the road to physical recovery, she with distress that her reception into the Fergerson family was, at best, at arm's length.

THE VISIT from William Fontenot was not what it seemed. It began friendly, with Fontenot's best wishes for Phillip's recovery. This was followed by his admiration for the enormous outpouring of concern, evidenced by the vast display of cards and flowers that occupied every available space in the room. The room was saturated by the scent of a florist shop.

As Fontenot gazed around the room, a photograph of one of Phillip's ancestors caught his eye. He inquired the identity of the man. Phillip told the story of his great-grandfather from Ireland. How his grandfather, the son of a slave woman, was raised and educated by

James Fergerson, his father, along with his white sons and daughters. And he told of the event that had threatened his grandfather's sale into slavery, thereby causing his flight to freedom. Fontenot had always been curious about Phillip's heritage because of his appearance. Although Fontenot suspected these situations existed, there was a part of him that resented the fact that the source of Irish blood that gave Phillip the name Fergerson was only three generations removed. And it was that same part of Fontenot that made him feel justified for delivering the message that he had come to bring.

"The members of the board have instructed me to tell you that you are suspended without pay until further notice."

This was the last thing that an injured man needed to hear. Phillip tried to get a more complete explanation by stating the obvious, "I know that I can't go back to work just now, but I do have sick days coming, and I should be up and about in a couple of weeks."

"Please try and understand, Phillip. I'm just the messenger."

"They said suspended? But why?"

"I don't know."

"Mr. Fontenot, you must have some idea about why I'm suspended without pay."

"Phillip, I think it has to do with breaking a state law."

"There was no state law involved. I was trying to vote in a federal election, under federal law."

"I know, Phillip. And until the board can figure out what to do about all of this, you're suspended."

Phillip was silent. He didn't know exactly how to respond. Finally, he cleared his throat and said, "Let me ask you, Mr. Fontenot . . . how do you feel about all this?"

"I don't let my personal feelings get mixed up in decisions made by the board. Phillip, as far as I'm concerned you've always been a good, law-abiding colored man, I'm just sorry you saw fit to go and get mixed up in this voting thing."

Phillip was too disheartened to make further argument. Plus he detected a tone of irritation in Fontenot's voice that caused him to figure that he was stating his own position as well as that of the board. Phillip decided further discussion was useless. After an awkward silence Fontenot stood and said, "I've got a lot of work to do, Phillip, so I guess I'd better run along. Hope you feel better soon."

Fontenot was out of the room before Phillip could turn and look in his direction. He heard Martha bid him good-bye and the door slam. A heavy weight of tiredness descended like night, and Phillip closed his eyes and welcomed sleep.

MARTHA HAD overheard, from her station in the hall outside the bedroom, the message that Fontenot had delivered. Realizing that another source of money would be needed in order to meet the bills, Martha decided to take matters into her own hands. The next day she went to the bank seeking to borrow on her portion of the inherited property. After checking with the assessor's office, Mr. Mayer revealed that the property was owned by no one other than her and her husband. She questioned the disposition of the half ownership held by her brother. When told that she and Phillip had bought out her brother's share of the property several years earlier, she was furious. Her blood boiled but she was clear-headed enough not to allow the bank president to see her displeasure, so she pretended she had forgotten that transaction, and completed the business of a loan against the homestead.

On the way home with a note that had to be signed by Phillip, her anger grew to resentment. Phillip had completed the purchase of the property from her brother without her signature, but she had to get his signature on the mortgage note before she could borrow on land given to her by her father. Martha knew that the Napoleonic Code of Louisiana made the husband and wife community owners of property, but she did not like the fact that, because Phillip was a man, he could complete a transaction without her signature, but she could not do the same without his. She decided not to take up this matter with Phillip at this time. Phillip signed the note without question. He figured that Martha must have found out about the land transaction, but unless she brought it up he was not going to say anything. However, he did wonder how long it would be before this would be the subject of a disturbance. He knew she would not let it go without "fixing" him for not consulting her.

More important than vengeance was the fact that Martha finally knew where Johnny had gotten the money to buy the Blues Tavern. She regretted that she had not figured it out years ago. She should have known better than to suspect that his nigger woman would have money in the first place. This did not make her happy. The very thought that John had used money from his inheritance to go into business with that black witch, providing a forum for the devil's music, was more than she could stand. She tried not to think about it. That was also pushed into the back of her mind to be settled at a later date.

ON NOVEMBER 3, 1948, Stephen Estilette brought news that Truman had won the election for president in the biggest political upset in American history. Stephen even had a copy of the *Chicago Tribune* that had prematurely run a headline that Dewey had defeated Truman. He thought this news would bring some measure of comfort. At least Phillip would feel better to know that Truman did not lose the election for want of his vote. Stephen was right. Phillip was pleased.

From the moment Stephen had learned about the beating, he had been a frequent visitor and supporter of Phillip's right to vote, and was not afraid to say so. He had written an editorial, the week after the beating, that praised Phillip for his courage. After Huey P. Long led the fight to eliminate the poll tax in 1934, the only requirement to vote was registration, and any restriction to prevent that from happening was against state law, especially in a national election. There were many letters to the editor disagreeing, threatening, and canceling subscriptions because Stephen had "taken the side of a nigger." The abrupt drop in circulation was a blow, but he felt good about the fact that supporting his friend was the right thing to do.

It was now six weeks since Phillip had been suspended without pay and he had not heard another word. Stephen turned his attention from the news of Truman's election to the matter of legal action. He urged Phillip to sue, as he put it, "the men who beat you up, the registrar who denied you, and the city for allowing it to happen." He also suggested that Phillip sue the school board and demand his back pay and reinstatement. Convinced that there was not a lawyer in Estilette willing to take such a case, they decided to look for representation from the outside.

The cards and flowers signed with the full name "Alicia Wallace" usually got the response "Who's this?" from Martha. But it would not be long before Martha met the person she had always called "that woman."

It was unbearable for Alicia to stay away from Phillip during his period of suffering. It took all of her willpower to keep from calling or coming to Estilette to see and comfort him. Phillip understood the reason Alicia had not made any obvious effort to contact him. He also knew that Leo Roberts was providing her with regular reports of his condition. However, this was not totally satisfying, and the desires of the heart overruled Alicia's wisdom of restraint.

On Thanksgiving Day, Leo and Catherine appeared with an extra guest for dinner. Alicia Wallace was introduced to Martha as the faculty coordinator of the teacher training program that Phillip had initiated. Martha's initial response was, "Haven't we met before?"

To which Alicia gave the polite and diplomatic response, "No, but I feel that I know you because Phillip has often spoken of how beautiful you are." That was all that was necessary to stop any further verbal probing of the subject. However, it did little to keep Martha from continuing to wonder why this woman's face seemed familiar.

As the dinner wore on, Phillip felt uncomfortable having the two women with whom he had shared sexual intimacies sitting at the same table. However, they laughed, joked, exchanged stories, and had a pleasant time. In an unguarded moment Leo tried to refresh Alicia's memory of an event that had taken place at Iowa. Martha was quick to ask, while looking directly into Alicia's eyes, "Did you meet Leo and Phillip at Iowa?" A sudden chill came over dessert. Alicia ignored

Martha's question and answered Leo's ill-timed query by saying, "Leo, your memory is fading. That was in Ohio, not in Iowa."

"You're right. That was Ohio, and Phillip wasn't there."

However, enough was said to arouse Martha's suspicions, and Phillip could see it on her face. He was on pins and needles for the remainder of their visit, expecting at any moment an unpleasant scene from Martha. It didn't come, and the day ended as it had begun, with many things to be thankful for.

22

IT WAS A THICK, swirling fog that made it almost impossible to see more than three feet ahead. After a moving body passed through, the space was quickly and quietly swallowed up. In the fall, a light fog usually hung low to the ground as the cool night air met the warm bayou heat. But tonight the fog rose to a greater height, was thicker, and covered a wider area. Adding to the eeriness of this night was the distant croaking of bullfrogs and the hooting of owls that pierced the stillness like daggers.

The only way Lala could tell she was walking in the right direction was to follow a path where the gravel of the roadway ended and the ground began. If she strayed too far to the middle of the gravel, she was afraid that she would follow a road that led in the wrong direction. As long as she stayed between the *crunch* of rocks beneath her feet and the *swish* of the sucker weeds on her legs she knew she was headed home. It had been five years since Lala was on this road, but she remembered that if she stayed left after leaving Frilotville, she would eventually come to the moss-covered oak at the corner of the turn into Estilette.

Lester Jr. had not said a word for thirty minutes. He clung to the strap from the small bag in Lala's hand and was half dragged, half guided along the path. He was four years old and his sister, bundled in Lala's arms, was fourteen months. Lala had been walking with her children for over an hour but it seemed like days. She had estimated that it would take about five hours to walk the ten miles to Estilette.

A small voice said, "Mama, I'm tired." Junior had broken his silence. Lala marveled at what an excellent little trouper he was because he had not complained since they left the Martel farm. She also felt it was time they rested. She looked around to find a place to sit. The fog was too thick to see anything, so Lala sat in the roadway on the small case. It was so late there was little danger of being hit by a car, and, since she had not seen one during the entire time, she knew that she was the only one crazy enough to be out on a night like this. As soon as she was seated little Ann began to cry. Walking had lulled her to sleep and now that the motion had ceased the baby came awake. Lala tried to shush and comfort her but to no avail. The croaking of the frogs and the screeching of the owls, combined with the crying of Ann, caused Junior to be scared, and he added his cries to the chorus. Lala did not know what to do. She regretted that she had decided to leave Lester in the middle of the night.

The distant sound of footsteps on gravel came from behind. Lala stood and stared into the mist. The sound grew closer. She was afraid it might be Lester. But then she realized that she left him so drunk he would not be able to walk until noon the next day. She watched as billowing wings moved on each side of the misty image that began to appear in the distance. It was an angel. She wiped her eyes. She stared at the sound of the approaching image. It became more distinct. It was an angel. The image stopped and looked at the mother and children. The disturbed fog surged and swirled in waves around the statue-like form, and then it began to slowly settle. Lala could see more clearly now. It was a man. He walked slowly in their direction. He was dressed in a well-worn leather jacket over bib overalls and a red plaid shirt; on his head was a knitted sailor's cap. Slung across and tied to his shoulders was a not-too-neatly wrapped bedroll.

"You folks need help?"

Lala was not familiar with the accent of his voice, so she figured he was a stranger passing through.

"My little boy is afraid. We're trying to get to my papa's house in Estilette."

"I'm going there to catch a train."

"I'd be obliged if you would help."

The stranger picked up Junior and the suitcase, and the travelers continued their fog-bound journey in silence. He did not ask questions or volunteer information and neither did Lala. Several hours later, about five in the morning, Lala knocked on the door that she had not entered for five years. She turned to thank the stranger but he was not to be seen. All she saw was a swirling white mist. She rushed to the edge of the porch in an effort to catch sight of him. She could not. She called out into the fog, "Thank you, Mister!"

"Lala, that you?"

A voice from the open door brought Lala back from the edge of the porch. Martha flew out of the door to welcome home her baby daughter, squeezing Ann between them.

"Oh, my baby. And you got two babies! Come on in this house out of the cold."

Lala guided Junior inside. Martha picked up the suitcase and asked, as she looked out one last time before closing the door, "Who was that you talking to?"

"An angel."

"Chile, did you say an angel?"

"Yes."

"Girl, you come back talking all outta your head."

Lala heard the distant sound of a train. At first she thought it might be Uncle Johnny coming home drunk, playing his mouth harp; then she realized it was the 5:30 freight; the train that the angel-stranger had planned to catch. She knew she was not talking out of her head. She was talking out of a miracle.

While Martha put the children to bed, Lala made coffee. There were a thousand questions that Martha had on her mind to ask. She settled at the table in the kitchen, her eyes taking in every aspect of Lala's being. She was still beautiful but looked a little tired and overweight. Martha did not know what to ask first. There was a five-year gap of information that she wanted filled all at once, but she remembered their parting at the Blues Club and thought it wise to proceed slowly.

Lala filled Martha's favorite cup, set it on the table in front of her, and dropped exhausted into a chair. She said with a sigh, "I left Lester." The silence that followed was the interval of Martha's mental process trying to decide a response. There were many comments to choose from: "Good," "That doesn't surprise me," "You shouldn't have run away with him in the first place." The thoughts went on and on but she could not select the right one that would express her feeling.

Before she could decide, Lala continued, "I just couldn't take his drinking and beating anymore. After we got back from Kansas City he got drunk again, so last night I decided to leave. When I got outside it was all fogged up. I couldn't go back so I just kept on going. I hope it's all right for us to stay here a while."

Martha's prayers had been answered. The story had already been written. The prodigal had returned to be forgiven and was welcomed with open arms. It was difficult for Martha to listen without saying anything, but she forced herself into silence as she heard for the first time the details.

"Me and Lester went to Kansas City when we left here. His mother's cousin Gussie lives there."

"I know Gussie . . . She . . ." Then Martha stopped. She promised herself that she would be quiet and let Lala talk. "Go on, chile."

Lala continued. "She helped us find a place and everything was fine. I was in love with Lester and he was in love with me. Lester got a job selling insurance and I waited for the baby to come. Then he lost his job. I didn't know what happened . . . but something happened, and he wouldn't talk about it. He'd go out to look for work and come home drunk, and we'd fuss. And I was about to lose my mind. I was washing diapers, nursing the baby, trying to stretch the little food we had, and Lester was drunk. I fussed so much he went out and got any ol' job . . . as a mechanic. That helped a little. We could buy a few things. But I was cooped up in that house, that wasn't that big . . . not much bigger than any little ol' shotgun you see around here.

"Anyway, I was grumpy and tired all the time. I wanted to go out and have some fun like I used to . . . But no! I had to stay with the baby. I fussed so much, me and Lester always got into a fights. Then he'd say he was sorry and we'd make up, and that went on and on. One night I got Gussie to keep Junior, and me and Lester went out and had a ball. For the next few weeks everything was fine . . . just like old times. Then I found out I was pregnant again. I didn't intend to have another baby; it just happened. And the two children just got to be too much. Then we started fussing again. He would blame me and I would blame him. Then he'd go out and get drunk and we'd fuss, and then he began hitting me. I loved him but I just got tired of being hit. His papa couldn't manage that place with his eyesight getting worse, and he called and asked us to come back, so that's why we're here."

Lala took a deep breath and a sip of coffee; after a few seconds she continued.

"That time when you slapped me in public, I got mad and I never wanted to see you again. Then when Lester hit me, I thought that was how it was supposed to be between a man and his woman. Like you and Papa. Y'all love each other and you still fight. So I thought it was all right. But I got tired of being hit and I went back to feeling angry like I did when you slapped me that time. I'm sorry, Mama."

Lala collapsed in the security of Martha's arms, like she had so many times in the past. Phillip appeared in the doorway of the kitchen.

"Lala?"

"Papa!"

"I was having a dream, and I dreamed you were in the kitchen talking to your mama, and I woke up and here you are."

Phillip buried her in his arms for a long while. Lala looked into his eyes and saw something she had not seen before.

"Papa, you been sick?"

When told of the events that had taken the fire out of his eyes and left the sunken vacant stare, she was horrified, disheartened, saddened, and angry. Each emotion came like a charge of electricity.

"I'll never leave you again, Papa. I've brought you some grandchildren as a Christmas present."

That was also a charge of electricity—a pain through Martha's heart. It jolted her mind into another place. All the remorse, compassion, pain, and regret that had grown with Lala's story a few moments ago had now vanished when she said, "*I've brought you some grandchildren as a Christmas present.*" In its place were Martha's revengeful, vindictive, selfish words—"What about me? Don't I count as grandmother—*grandmere*? I just put the *cheries* to bed. And where was your precious papa?—asleep! Things have just picked up where they left off. I resent it. This bond, this affection, this unholy alliance . . . You didn't think of me when you left your letter addressed 'To Papa' . . . You were always his favorite . . . I wish you had stayed gone and never come back!" She stood up abruptly from her chair, slapped Lala across the face, and said, "Now that you're back you can fix your precious papa his breakfast."

With that, Martha walked out of the kitchen and went back to bed, leaving them to God.

Phillip tried his best to justify the frustration that had prompted Martha's behavior. He explained that, for the last few years, things had grown bad between them. Martha had found a picture of a woman in his coat pocket. The same woman had paid a visit on Thanksgiving and Martha accused him of having an affair. Phillip continued, "She's tired from nursing me these last few months. And on top of that, your statement about the children and Christmas was too much for her.

She's angry, jealous, and resentful of anybody and everything that has anything to do with me."

He explained that because of the constant pain of rheumatism she wasn't herself. "Your beauty and youth remind her of how she used to look. All of that makes her afraid of growing old. So try and understand your mama and forgive her."

Lala listened and said she would try. But she knew it would be difficult, especially since the memory of why she left had just been vividly brought back to mind.

AFTER CHRISTMAS Martha had another anger to add to her growing list. LightFoot gave Naomi a brand new 1949 white fishtail Cadillac. It was something that Martha could not stand. She said to her friend Julee, "She looks like a fly in bowl of milk driving that thing." Miz Julee reminded Martha that since she could not see, she relied on her description of what Naomi looked like. Then Miz Julee put the question, "Why do you dislike her so?"

Martha did not hesitate one breath with her answer.

"'Cause she's a nigger."

Miz Julee figured that her dislike also had to do with other matters, like being married to her brother, and being an in-law, whether Martha liked it or not. And also because Naomi and John were rich and getting richer. The Black Eagle was raking in money hand over fist. It was the biggest and best club for the blues for miles around. People from as far away as Baton Rouge and Alexandria were being drawn, and the word was still spreading. Martha could not tolerate all their success. Her mind was made up about who should and should not be rich. And no amount of money in the world was going to change her mind about accepting the blues. Miz Julee knew it was hopeless and summed up her feelings with, "Chile, you may as well get used to it. There's a new day a'coming."

IN THE summer of 1952 Bobby was near the end of his second year internship at Homer G. Phillips Hospital in St. Louis. Ruth was still teaching at Fisk. It was not the most desirable arrangement, but one that both had agreed would be best for this short transition. When Bobby's internship was completed, and after a permanent location to practice had been chosen, Ruth planned to give up teaching and they would make one move rather than two. They were together in Nashville or St. Louis whenever their busy schedules permitted. So the call for Ruth to come to St. Louis for a visit was not out of the ordinary.

When she arrived, Bobby was in bed with a headache and dizziness. It was not a fun weekend and Ruth regretted that she had made the trip, leaving so many papers to grade piled on her desk. She was short-tempered, believing that Bobby had been drinking and his illness was the result of a hangover. She left one day earlier than planned and returned to Nashville.

Early the next week Ruth got a call from Dr. Thompson, chief of Intern Residency. Bobby had been admitted to Homer G. Phillips as a patient. He had passed out in the corridor while making rounds. He had a high fever, dizziness, and was vomiting. They were not yet able to make a diagnosis but she could tell from the doctor's voice that he was worried. He suggested that she come as soon as it could be arranged. That she did.

Ruth arrived to discover that her husband of six years was a very sick man. He was being fed by tubes because nothing would stay on his stomach. His neck was stiff and it was difficult for him to turn to either side, which required that Ruth lean in directly over him so he could see her. Bobby grew weaker by the day and Ruth grew more despondent. His doctor could not discover the source of his illness, and it was as much a mystery to the hospital staff as it was a frustration to Ruth. She was determined to remain with him even if she was being exposed to an undetected contagious disease.

Finally, after several days of tests and speculations, the doctor came up with a diagnosis. Bobby had meningitis. It was fatal. There was only one known treatment. But because the meningitis had gotten a running start, it was doubtful that the treatment would be effective. It was not.

Bobby's death was hard to take, especially because of the suddenness and mystery surrounding the disease. Everyone in the family looked to Ruth for answers and explanations. She did the best she could with the information that she had, but it did not satisfy all the questions. Each member of the family created his or her own sanctuary of comfort.

Phillip and Lala's thoughts were the least complicated—"The Lord giveth and Lord taketh away." Yet they did not understand why, since Bobby was so young and still had so many years of giving as a doctor. But this was God's work.

It was not as simple as this for the others.

Rosa remained in a state of mourning. She cried hysterically at every thought, mention, or reminder of Bobby's face, presence, or actions. Her rosary was a faithful companion, and her attendance at morning Masses increased to include evening novenas, benedictions, and Litanies. All for the repose of his soul and penance for marrying outside the church.

For Martha and Vel, blame had to be assessed. Together they pointed fingers. For reasons they themselves did not understand, they blamed Ruth for Bobby's death. "If she had been with him when he got sick he wouldn't have died. It was her duty as a wife to be with him. He was not eating right. She neglected his health." The more these speculations were expressed between them, the stronger their convictions grew. This became their unifying force. When Vel returned to Chicago two days after the funeral, Martha was left with an unshakable belief that Ruth had somehow caused Bobby's death.

After the funeral, Ruth decided to remain with the Fergersons. To share her sorrows with the family, rather than grieve with her relatives or alone, seemed the right thing to do. In a manner of speaking it was her way of making up for his loss. Also she wanted to get to know the Fergersons better. She took a leave of absence from her job and moved into Bobby's room, thereby extending, in the presence of his spirit, the short time they had been married.

PHILLIP NEVER fully recovered from the beating. He frequently had pains in the chest, and his left arm had not regained its former strength. There were times when he would disappear for hours and no one knew where he could be found. He would go off by himself to walk along the bayou or fish. Sometimes he would just sit, look into the muddy water, talk to God, and wait for answers.

"Why, of all people, would You take Bobby? A good boy. He had never done a mean thing in his life. Sure he was weak in some ways.

He liked to have things done for him and he liked to depend on women for things he could do for himself. But basically he was a good boy; and he was smart. He studied hard and made good grades and he was going to be an excellent doctor."

Few knew that Phillip had kept up with Bobby's studies and grades at Meharry. He called Dean Hambrick once a month for a report on Bobby's progress. Phillip was pleased with his development and he was proud of the fact that Bobby was fulfilling his father's unfulfilled desire.

He and Bobby had often fished for catfish from this very spot. Today while preparing the hook with the rotten meat that Bobby used to hate, Phillip remembered his voice: "Papa, do mine, this meat's as stinky as dirty feet." Phillip cried. He prepared two hooks and two poles. He dropped both into the muddy water and held them in place with two rocks as, as he and Bobby had done so often in the past. He leaned his back against a pecan tree and closed his eyes. In his mind's eye he could see Bobby picking and shelling pecans and popping them into his mouth. He could hear his voice as clearly as if yesterday: "These pecans are giving me the shits." Phillip smiled.

He was brought out of his daydreams by a soft voice. "Why are you smiling in your sleep?"

"Ruth? What are you doing here?"

"Looking for you."

"Looking for me?"

"Thought you might like some company."

"How did you know where to find me?"

"I went to the farm and the man that was plowing told me you went fishing. He told me to follow," she mimicked, "'dat dare road till you get to the gas station, and turn right and go on down the gravel road to the sign that say Hadacol, and turn left and go till you see 'Fessor's car. He'd be under that big ol' pecan tree.' So you were exactly where the man said you would be."

Phillip's body shook with laughter. The sadness was gone. He invited Ruth to sit and tend Bobby's pole. It was good fishing. They didn't catch any catfish, but they discovered the need that each had for the other to fill the absence left by Bobby.

PHILLIP'S LEGAL cases against the city and the school board were still pending. With the help of Stephen Estilette, he had been successful in getting the legal counsel of an up-and-coming Negro lawyer named Trudeaux from New Orleans, who was joined by an ACLU advisor named Kinksler from New York. Together this team prepared a case that charged the assailants with depriving Phillip of his civil rights and named the city officials as accomplices. The second case provided that the school board show just cause for the dismissal, and requested that Phillip be reinstated immediately with all back pay.

While this was pending he was a full-time gentleman farmer, and Ruth was invited to accompany him on his daily trips to the farm. She was delighted. She helped him feed, water, and tend the livestock and look after the many odd jobs that farming required. On the long treks through the fields to check the plowing, planting, or cultivation being done by the hired hands, they talked of everything— God, nature, politics, and the plight of colored people. Ruth talked about personal matters—her family and growing up.

"My mother is the God-loving and faithful director of the AME church choir. And she also teaches elementary school."

"Is your father also a teacher?"

"Yes. You remind me of him. He loves teaching but he only teaches one class now. He's head of the English department.

"So you grew up around educators."

"We were campus kids. All of our life was spent on the campus at Virginia State. We even went to the College Laboratory High School, where the would-be teachers got their training. We were around for everything, and had to go to all of the programs on campus . . . people like Roland Hayes, Marian Anderson, and Mary McLeod Bethune. We were right there sitting between Mama and Papa on the front row."

"You have sisters and brothers?"

"Just a sister. She's in music. Still hoping to be a pianist like Hazel Scott. She's teaching now at Central State College in Ohio.

"Why did you go into biology?"

"I didn't have any better sense."

She laughed and was joined by Phillip. Then she got serious and continued, "I wanted to get a Ph. D. in the most difficult subject I could think of. It was a challenge. I had a tough science teacher in college."

"At Virginia State?"

"No. Hampton Institute. That's where I got my B. S. For my graduation present, my parents took my sister and me to the Olympics in Berlin to see Jesse Owens. My dad had followed his career all the way through college."

"That must have been exciting."

"Oh, Papa Phillip, you have no idea. That was the most thrilling experience of my entire life. To feel the explosion of cheers for one of our own . . . it was indescribable. I still get chills when I think about it. And Ralph Metcalf, Archie Williams, and John . . . what's-his-name . . . John Woodruff . . . they also ran and won. But Jesse was the fastest human in the world, especially after he beat those Germans. After that we went to Paris, Rome, and London."

"You've jammed a lot into your young life."

"Everything . . . except children."

"Yes, I was looking forward to grandchildren."

"And so were my parents. My father was looking forward to a grandson. Now it doesn't look like they are going to have any grandchildren."

"You're young, you could still . . . well . . . but they wouldn't be my grandchildren."

"It's not very likely that I will get married again. Most likely I'll bury myself in my work. Now that Bobby's dead . . . I don't know how to face Daddy to tell him . . . because he doesn't know about this . . ."

After a pause she said, "My sister doesn't like men, so she won't be getting married either. You know what I mean?"

Phillip knew. And now he understood more clearly why Ruth needed to be with them during her period of mourning.

During this time they became close. Phillip discovered why Bobby had fallen in love with this brilliant, sensitive woman six years his senior. Phillip had found a friend and confidant in his daughter-in-law. He invited Ruth to accompany the family to a dinner given in his honor by the teachers of the parish. They were gathering to honor Phillip's pioneering efforts in education—the establishment of two schools, the teacher-training program, and his courage for attempting to vote in the face of overwhelming odds. The guest speaker was to be Alicia Wallace, director of Educational Services for Southern College.

THE MORE that Martha thought about Phillip's invitation to Ruth, the more she resented it. She could not bear the thought of sitting at the same table in public with the black woman she believed was the cause of her son's death. In addition, the main speaker was Alicia. And no amount of denial from Phillip could convince Martha that nothing had taken place between them. As the time for the event grew near, the more Martha's mind was made up that she should not attend. On the morning of the event she said to Phillip that her knees were hurting too much to walk.

The event was well attended and enjoyed by all. Ruth saw an image of Phillip as a well-liked and respected leader of the community who encouraged the growth of ideas. So it followed that their well-meaning exchanges in front of the fireplace continued until well into the night. Ruth sat on the floor at the feet of the older, wiser sage; learning, challenging, and debating matters of interest to both. It was for Phillip a return to the time when ideas had not yet been so bent out of shape by actual events. Ruth said, "I'm sure Bobby would love to hear you now. You're so alive with conviction. When he left here after our visit he was afraid you had lost your 'keep on keeping on' spirit."

Rosa started crying.

"Stop it. I can't bear to hear anyone talk about Bobby . . ."

There was immediate silence, except for Rosa's sniffling. Then she dried her tears.

"I'm sorry. I just miss him so. I do this every time I think about him or hear his name."

This was one of the few times that Rosa and Lala had joined the discussion around the fireplace. Phillip wanted them to feel comfortable, because he hoped that by their presence and participation they would get to know Ruth.

"It's all right, baby, we understand. We all miss him. You just keep praying for him. We'll talk about something else. Ruth, did you hear about Annie Allen?"

Ruth was confused.

"Annie Allen . . . Annie Allen . . . Oh, you're talking about Gwendolyn Brooks. Yes! That's right. She was the first Negro to win the Pulitzer Prize for a collection of poems called *Annie Allen.* But that was almost two years ago."

Rosa asked, "What's the Pulitzer Prize?"

"That's an award of money and recognition for achievement in the area of literature and the arts. It was set up by a newspaper man named Alfred Pulitzer."

Ruth laughed. "Oh, Papa Phillip, you're getting your people mixed up. His name was Joseph Pulitzer . . . You're probably thinking about Alfred Nobel."

Phillip joined her laughter. "Yes, I am."

Lala did not want to be left in the dark. "Who is Alfred Nobel?"

"He's the man who invented dynamite and other explosives . . . I've got it straight now."

Ruth added, "And because of the destruction and all the killing associated with his inventions, he set up the Nobel Prize to honor people who contribute to world peace, and medicine, and things like that

that help people. They give away much more money than the Pulitzer."

Lala said, "Wow, you know a lot."

Ruth continued, "And the first Negro to get the Nobel Prize was Ralph Bunche. That was the same year that Gwendolyn Brooks got her Pulitzer."

Rosa's mouth hung open. She was soaking it up like Bobby used to do on the front porch.

"Who was Ralph Bunche?"

"A professor from Howard University who was appointed to the United Nations. He worked out the peace agreement between the Jews and the Arabs. That's why he got the prize."

"Ruth, you sure are smart."

Lala chimed in, "You're telling us that two colored people got these high-class prizes last year?"

"In 1950, almost two years ago."

Phillip went on with enthusiasm, "And that same year Roy Wilson was the first Negro admitted to the law school at LSU."

Rosa asked, "The white school in Baton Rouge?"

"That's the one."

Lala was in wonder again.

"Oh, wow. Colored people are making a lot of progress these days."

Rosa stood up and said, "Look, all this is good to know, but it's getting late and I have to get up early to go to Mass. And I still have to say my rosary."

Lala followed suit. "Yeah, I'd better get some sleep too . . . the children wake up early."

"You need to come to Mass with me?"

"How can I, with the kids?"

"Leave 'em with Mama. You ought to go—you've got a lot of praying to do."

The two left the room discussing Lala's need to go to Mass. Rosa's expressed pious devotion had an impact on Ruth. And now that the door had been opened, it seemed a good time to ask a question that had been troubling her. She said to Phillip after Rosa was out of earshot, "I believe that you are a religious person but you are not given to such . . . sanctimoniousness."

"Sanctimoniousness?"

"I'm sorry. It's the most descriptive word I know to use."

Phillip answered laughingly, "Don't apologize. Just tell me what you're getting at."

"It's really difficult to explain kindly. But I noticed that Rosa and Martha especially—not so much with Lala—usually announce that they are going to church or getting ready to pray. Is this . . ." She began to flutter her hands almost apologetically, searching for the right word, ". . . required by your church? I know that the Moslems are required to face the East and pray several times a day. Is this the same kind of thing?"

By the time she finished her question Phillip was on the verge of exploding with repressed laughter.

"No, it is not. They are what you might call overenthusiastic. Although some might call them religious fanatics."

"I'm sorry. I didn't mean to . . ."

Phillip interrupted. He did not wish that she feel in any way guilty for perceiving, and having the courage to point out, what he had known for many years.

"Don't be. Your description sanctimonious was exactly right."

Now that the ice was broken, Phillip told about his break with the Catholic church and the various reactions from the family. But he didn't stop there; he opened other closet doors. After all, Ruth was a member of the family and their mutual sharing, heart-to-heart, had the effect of clearing the air of many negative impressions made by other members of the family. It felt good to share feelings again. Especially since his visits to Alicia had been made infrequent by his recovery. But more importantly, he wanted Ruth to feel included.

He shared the pains of disappointment about Vel and her ill-gotten money, their inability to see eye to eye, her attempts to "be white" and her dislike for black-skinned people. He shared Rosa's preoccupation with religion, which he believed would lead to life as a spinster because, as he put it, "She is married to the church." He also shared Lala's unhappy marriage, the anticipated road to divorce, and his wife's jealousy over their relationship. He talked about Martha's obsessive dislike for dark-skinned people; how her hatred for the blues had, over the years, caused the alienation of her brother. Phillip told all of the closely guarded family secrets. However, he stopped short of telling Ruth about his own relationship with Alicia. Ruth's response to this outpouring of pain was, "It all sounds so . . . I don't know the right word . . . dysfunctional."

To which Phillip replied, "It is."

MARTHA HAD heard enough. She quietly closed the door at the end of the hallway and returned to bed. She now had another reason, in addition to her color, to dislike Ruth. She had "put a fix" on Phillip to make him tell intimate secrets about the family. Like most of the niggers she knew, Ruth was no doubt capable of placing hexes. So she must have also put some kind of a hex on Bobby. These were the thoughts that she went to sleep with. They stayed in her mind until they became obsessions.

Every morning, after having her coffee, Ruth gathered roses and hydrangeas from the garden. This was her way of doing something to be part of the family, which Martha did not mind, since she liked the smell of fresh cut flowers throughout the house. But several days later, while returning from Mass, Martha ran into Ruth with the car. Ruth's knees were smashed and she suffered a concussion and a broken arm. Martha claimed that she saw her too late and, because of pain from her rheumatism, was not able to stop in time. It was an accident. Deep down inside, however, Martha knew that Ruth would be in the yard and considered it a sign from God that she was powerless to ignore. The deep-down-inside part was not told to Sheriff Cat Bobineaux.

As soon as Ruth was released from the hospital she wanted to go home to Petersburg for Christmas. Phillip made arrangements, hired a hearse from Lastrap's Funeral Home, and rode to Virginia with her.

NAOMI NEVER gave up. After BookTau brought the alligator to the club, Naomi had enough evidence to warrant changing the features of the androgynous doll. The face of the figure was painted white. The hair was taken from Martha's comb. The body was filled and covered with material owned or touched by Martha—portions of a lace handkerchief; scraps from a discarded bodice, skirt, and stocking; fingernail clippings; and cuttings from unwashed underwear stained with dried menses blood. All made a strong and powerful gris-gris for the hex. Once a week when the owl screeched, she plunged a long sharp shaft into the body of the doll. The thrust was a slow circling motion executed to inflict the greatest possible pain in another body part. Naomi was intent on giving her victim the same pain that had been brought to her and LightFoot. She figured that if Martha ill-treated one black person, she had ill-treated others. This was Naomi's way of giving payback, just like her ancestors from the days of slavery had done. Little did she realize how far the effect of the doll's karma would go.

LALA WENT back to Lester after he promised never to hit her again. She really loved him but could not endure the abuse that was a reminder of her mama's actions. Although her husband was indulged because of the children—at least this is what she told herself—she could not forgive her mama. The offense was not as impossible to forgive as was the offender. In the case of her mother, the years of jealousy and opposition to "papa's girl" had taken its toll. In addition, she could not help but think that maybe the incident with Ruth was not an accident. For years she knew how her mama felt about dark-skinned people. This, along with placing blame for Bobby's death on Ruth, caused Lala to see her mama in a different light. It was not as easy to forgive her mother as it was to forgive her husband.

23

NINETEEN-FIFTY-three was a special year for the Black Eagle. It was the high-water mark in booking of talent. LightFoot had heard from the grapevine that an up-and-coming blues singer from Indianola, Mississippi, now living in Memphis, was touring the Southland. This bluesman had appeared under many different names —"Riley King," "Beale Street Blues Boy," "Blues Boy" and "B. B. King." He was different. He fused the sound of country blues with jazz. He favored the electric guitar because he could make the instrument sing by lengthening the duration of chords to create a whimsical sound that was strangely human. He was an excellent guitar player and soulful blues singer. His guitar, which he named Lucille, became a duet-voice that he talked to and sang with. Often he would let Lucille do solo blues talk.

LightFoot booked B. B. King for two evenings. People came from all over—Lafayette, Opelousas, Baton Rouge, and as far away as Alexandria. The place was packed on both occasions. Traffic was stalled. Parking was a basket of snakes. Sheriff Cat Bobineaux, who remarked to his deputies, "I'm getting too old for this shit," had never seen the likes of this in Estilette. The large number of white faces making their way to the Black Eagle was the only reason that Cat and his officers were involved in trying to unravel the mess that the traffic created.

Inside there was standing room only. The inconvenience did not seem to matter, nor did it put a damper on the spirit of enjoyment. The blues lovers danced, swayed, snapped their fingers, and clapped their hands in time with the music. B. B. was a master entertainer. His face was a visual mask of expressions bringing to life the stories that his songs were telling. He was tireless and his selections lasted so long the dancers wished he would take a break so they could rest. There was simply no rest for anyone within earshot. It was impossible. No one could listen to B. B. without moving some part of his or her body. Heels beating the rhythm, toes tapping the beat, shoulders moving, heads bobbing, fingers popping, palms clapping—and this was the people sitting down. The people dancing executed all of these movements plus the erotic hip gyrations of the lovemaking ritual. The essence of the blues was here. It was basic and earthy, yet uplifting and spiritual. It struck all the chords of human emotions at once. No one could listen and not be affected.

It was also music to LightFoot's ear. He was making money as fast as he could rake it in. And this was an event that Phillip did not want to miss. He had the best table in the house and he shared it with Alicia and her friends. (LightFoot had been instructed to bring the lady who asked for Mr. Phillip Fergerson to Phillip's table.) Alicia and Phillip thought it best they not come or leave together. Alicia talked a couple of friends from the college into driving over with her for the B. B. King performance. Not only did it look less suspicious for her to be with Phillip, but also it provided company for the drive back to Scotlandville in the wee hours of the morning. This was the first time that Phillip and Alicia had been together at the Black Eagle. LightFoot knew, when he looked into Alicia's eyes, that there was a special relationship between his brother-in-law and this lady. However, he was not resentful. Throughout the years he had suspected the denials that Phillip was forced to live with would someday lead to an outside woman.

Phillip remembered the first bluesman he had heard at the Green Light with Alicia—Lightnin' Hopkins. Lightnin's style was very different from that of B. B. King. Lightnin' was country, B. B. was urban. Lightnin' played an acoustic guitar, B. B. an electric. Lightnin' used his guitar to play chords, B. B. used his guitar as another voice with whom he sang duets. Lightnin' talked his way through his songs, B. B. sang melodies with a jazz flavor. Phillip liked B. B. King. But Alicia liked Lightnin' better because he was closer to the country blues—"like Robert Johnson. B. B. is too commercial," as she put it. But whatever it was that B. B. had, the people loved every minute of it. They rocked the place. Phillip thought he had seen a lively crowd at the Green Light, but there were no words to describe the response of the people to B. B. King at the Black Eagle.

IT WAS late, or rather early in the morning, when Phillip got home. He had stayed until B. B. and the piano player had packed and gone. Alicia and her friends had left an hour earlier. When Phillip walked through the door he knew something was wrong. The lights were on and the dinner dishes were still on the table. There was no disarray but what he found was unusual. Martha never left dirty dishes on the table and she always turned out the lights when she went to bed. Plus it was too early in the morning for Rosa to be up, even though she was now getting up in time to attend seven o'clock Mass. Added to this premonition of something being wrong was the smell of burning candles.

Phillip entered the bedroom to a scene that made his body tremble. In the corner opposite the bed, to the left of the chifforobe, was an altar, the place where Martha said her morning and night prayers. Above the altar was a crucifix. Below the crucifix was a statue of Mary with arms extended and palms outstretched to those on which her downcast eyes were focused. On one side of Mary was a statue of Joseph. On the other side was a replica of the Holy Family in flight from the wrath of Herod. Martha was kneeling nude in front of this altar. Lighted candles covered every inch of the altar. Some had burned down to the very bottom of the small glass cups and had forged circular pits through the surrounding wax. Others sputtered and flickered on their candelabra. The dozens of candles around the altar were echoes of the voodoo scene in Naomi's front room. The major difference was that the crucifix, Mary, and the Holy Family had replaced the dolls, charms, and fetishes.

Phillip stopped long enough to catch his breath and gather the strength to cry out, "Oh, my God, Martha, what have you done?" Her naked back and buttocks were crisscrossed with red lesions oozing blood. Her legs were in the same state of flagellation. Martha's head was bowed and she knelt, holding on to the armrest of the kneeler with her left hand. The buggy whip that Phillip used to urge Betsy along dangled from her right.

Never in his wildest dreams did Phillip imagine that he would ever witness a scene so reminiscent of the Middle Ages. He had seen paintings of flagellation—a medieval church practice of atonement for sins; but this custom had been relegated to history long ago. Phillip did not want to believe what he was seeing. He gently picked Martha up and laid her face down on the bed. He pried the whip out of her vise-like grip. At that moment Martha became aware of Phillip. She cried out, "God will forgive me now!"

Phillip gathered her disheveled salt-and-pepper hair from the bloody wounds on her back and gently placed it across the nape of her neck. The red-stained strands left their impressions on the white cotton pillowcase.

"Why, Martha? Why did you do this?"

"God will forgive me now."

Phillip dabbed away at the moisture on her face with his handkerchief and stared into the out-of-this-world gaze of her sunken eyes. There was nothing there. No awareness of present time, or the fact of his presence.

"Why, Martha? Why?

"God will forgive me now!"

That was the only response he got.

Phillip went to the bathroom and drew warm water in the antique washbasin. On the way back to Martha's bedside, Rosa appeared, robed and yawning, in the hallway.

"Morning, Papa. What you doing up and dressed?"

"Your mama's hurt."

Rosa thought she knew what had happened. Papa had shot Mama. But she didn't remember hearing the sound of a pistol. Maybe he didn't shoot her; maybe he hit her. They were always fussing and fighting. And she usually heard the fussing voices but this time she heard nothing. Maybe she was wrong about her first thoughts. She hoped she was. Rosa followed her father into the bedroom. Her knees buckled when she saw her mother's scarred body stretched out on the white bloodied sheets. Together she and her father washed away the blood from Martha's back and legs. Rosa wiped away the salty tears oozing from her eyes with the back of her hand before they fell on Martha's wounds. She joined the refrain begun by her father, "Why, Mama?"

And she got the same response. "God will forgive me now."

Phillip left the room to call Dr. Rossini.

DR. ROSSINI faced the picture of Joseph Broussard, his back turned to Phillip and Rosa, who were sitting on the sofa waiting for him to speak. It was ironic that he faced Martha's father but it was not by design; it was difficult to look into their eyes and say what he had to say.

"She's out of her mind."

Phillip recovered from the shock sooner than Rosa, who remained motionless with glazed eyes staring into space. Phillip asked, "You mean, she's crazy?"

Now that the word was spoken, Dr. Rossini turned to face them.

"She's in a self-destructive condition that shows itself by flagellation . . . and I'm afraid that she may do even greater harm to herself."

"Her papa committed suicide."

Rosa's face jerked to the right and faced her father.

"Grandpa was killed by that Silas man!"

"That's what your mama wanted to believe. But the truth is, he killed himself."

Dr. Rossini pulled a chair in close and sat between the husband and daughter. He felt it best to be within touching distance to say what he planned to say.

"I think we should put her in Pineville . . . at least for a period of observation."

Rosa rushed out of the room, almost knocking over Dr. Rossini. Phillip and the doctor completed the discussion of the details necessary for Martha's commitment to the state mental institution. An ambulance was called.

In a scene that was chillingly similar to one shared years earlier by Rosa and her mama, Rosa's body shook the bed as she sobbed in the arms of her papa.

"Please tell me Mama's not crazy."

"The doctor says she's only going there for observation. But, honey, we've got to understand that anyone who whips themself that way is not in their right mind."

"The doctor said it was because of guilt about something."

"It could very well be."

Rosa buried her crying face in her papa's shoulder. She remembered the old woman Tante and the smelly old shack. She remembered the secret that she and her mama shared about that awful night. She wondered if this was the guilt that had driven her mama mad. She wondered if she should tell Papa about what had happened. But she realized that she would have to tell him everything. About Father Pat and her; how it began and how it had gone on for all those years. And there didn't seem to be any point. Anyway, God had taken Father Pat and no doubt he had paid for his sins. She cried herself to sleep. Phillip left her in the dark room to rest. This was the end of a night he would never forget.

THEY TALKED more than they had in a long time. Martha asked questions and seemed interested in the answers. She wanted to be brought up to date about national news. President Eisenhower had ended segregation in the veterans hospitals, the Rosenbergs were executed in the electric chair, Senator Joseph McCarthy continued his search for communists, and the Korean War had ended. Now Phillip figured she needed to hear about the family. He began by saying, "As far as I know, Vel is still in Chicago."

"Vel? . . . Vel? I had a daughter named Vel once."

"Yes, and you have one named Rosa and one named Lala.

The expression on Martha's face changed.

"Lala is no daughter of mine."

"Yes, she is. You've forgotten how much she means to you."

"She means a lot to her papa, not to me."

"Mama, how can you say that?"

Martha stood up and looked at Phillip as if seeing him for the first time.

"Why you call me Mama?"

"I've always called you Mama."

"Who are you?"

She was now talking loud enough to alert the on-duty attendant. Phillip moved closer to the retreating Martha.

"I'm your husband, Phillip."

"I ain't got no husband . . . he left with that woman!"

She was now screaming at the top of her lungs. The attendant put his arm around the waist of the upset, yelling Martha and led her out of the room.

"You're no husband of mine . . . Be gone, Satan."

Phillip related everything that happened to Dr. Comeaux, who listened carefully and took notes. Referring to the file he said, "I noticed this is your fifth visit in the six months that Martha has been a patient. Has anything like this happened before?"

"Well, not exactly. She didn't recognize who I was before, but today was the first time she told me to go away."

"Does she have a reason to want you to go away?"

"She thinks there's another woman. We were having problems when this happened. I've told Dr. Hebert about all that."

"Yes, my assistant. Everything is here in the file. I was just trying to make sure nothing was overlooked."

Dr. Comeaux explained that Martha had created something of a social dilemma for the hospital.

"During her first weeks here, she would become agitated whenever she was taken into the colored ward. She shouted and screamed that she did not want to be with the 'niggers.' Since the administration did not want to upset the white patients or their relatives, and after conferring with Dr. Rossini, we decided to put her in a room isolated from both. This seemed to calm her down and on some days she showed real signs of progress."

But there were still areas of concern that worried the treatment staff. Dr. Comeaux hoped that Phillip could shed some light on matters that were still puzzling. The doctor explained that they had noticed some subjects of concern to Martha that possibly represented a key to her problem.

"She's makes repeated references to dead sheep and a child, Sodom and Gomorrah, an accident, blood being thicker than water, and the prodigal being sent away. "

Phillip did not feel he could shed any light on the first two subjects. But he did feel that the last three could possibly have some reference to feelings regarding an automobile accident, her brother John, and her daughter Lala. Dr. Comeaux said he would continue trying to get Martha to talk out her anxieties, and he suggested that visits from the two relatives Phillip had identified might help bring her problems into focus.

DRUNK. IT was the only way Phillip could handle the situation. He could forget and remember at the same time. And it seemed that painful memories were easier to forget while he was drunk. Yesterday he had seen Martha; now he wanted to be with Alicia. In the back of his mind, not shared with the doctors, was the suspicion that this was the main reason for Martha's breakdown. But he needed Alicia. He got in his car and drove the forty miles to Scotlandville.

Alicia had finally left campus housing. She had bought a house on Curtis Street just across the tracks from the college. It was a small white cottage with green shutters. It was a comfortable and homey place. A place where Phillip felt safe. He arrived at twilight and Alicia knew that he would be coming. He always came after his visits to Pineville and she expected that today would be no different.

But it was different. He had a lot on his mind. He was beginning to feel the guilt of having a wife in an asylum and a mistress in an institution of higher learning. He wanted to be free of all ties to his wife but he dared not think of or give any indication of his wishes. He had to get rid of these gnawing emotions. However, Alicia knew. She knew his needs and his thoughts. She had told him not to cause himself pain. And he certainly did not want to agonize as he was doing. He could not stay bottled up. He had to talk it out. Alicia listened as he rambled on, letting the liquor talk his thoughts.

"Martha's real problem is in knowing who her ancestors were—but not knowing who she is—in the present scheme of things. Did you know that Martha's grandfather was Creole?"

Alicia shook her head. Phillip poured another three fingers of Old Taylor, filled the glass with coke and ice, and continued, "He was of mixed blood but considered himself white. During the Civil War he was a Confederate sympathizer. Can you believe that shit? . . . A Confederate sympathizer."

Phillip seemed to scrutinize his own revelation. In the silence that followed, he shook his head as if he doubted the truth of what he had just spoken. Alicia felt that perhaps an awareness of the times in which they lived might help. She said softly in a matter-of-fact manner, "Well, if he was passing for white he might have been."

"He wasn't passing, he was a white Creole. He loved that way of life—slaves, wealth, plantations . . . and the pick of any slave wench he wanted at any time. And on top of everything else, he had the blessings and turn-a-blind-eye sanctions of the good ol' Catholic church. What more could any man want? So it was no wonder that during the war Antoine went back to his military blood and became a spy. Did you know his father, Antoine Sr., was a military man?"

Alicia shook her head. Of course she had no way of knowing this but she knew better than to start a conversation when Phillip was off and running. She had been through this before. Phillip needed to talk it out and he needed for her to listen. She also knew he needed something to eat. She got up and headed to the kitchen, knowing that he would follow. He did and continued.

"Yeah, the old man was a colonel in the French Army and he was married to a woman from Haiti. He was assigned to New Orleans in 1724, the same year Jean Bienville put the Code Noir in effect. And that's when all this shit started. Governor Bienville gave him a large charter of land for his loyal military service to France and he became rich. But Antoine Jr. didn't want to follow the old man's footsteps, so he became a spy . . . Well, that is . . . he had to be a spy. He had more than twenty slaves, and if a white man had more than twenty slaves he didn't have to fight. So Antoine Jr. decided to help the South as a spy. That bastard swam across the Atchafalaya River, which even to this day has the swiftest and most treacherous current in the country. Did you know that?"

He was now slurring his words and talking louder. Alicia knew the move to get some food in his stomach was well timed. "He was carrying a message to a Confederate camp near Baton Rouge. But he was captured by a company of Union soldiers who treated him like a prisoner of war. They beat him up, but he wouldn't talk . . . Then they tied him up and sat him under a tree. He watched those starving soldiers try to catch and hold a hog, and he laughed at them . . . That bastard laughed so hard, it finally got the best of those Union soldiers and they untied him and made him catch and butcher that hog. Well, that was right up his alley . . . He waited till they ate and got drunk, and then stole away and found his way to the Confederate lines."

During his talk about the hog, Alicia had heated up and put on the table smothered pork chops, rice, red beans, and cornbread. Phillip filled his glass again and continued his history lesson, while filling his stomach and drowning his pain. He went on to explain how Antoine carried the message about Admiral Farragut's plans to sail his fleet up the Mississippi from New Orleans to take Vicksburg, which was the linchpin of the Confederacy. It was believed that Farragut could be stopped at Baton Rouge. Although Antoine got the message through to the right people, the Confederates were not able to stop Farragut and he took Baton Rouge and Natchez.

"Needless to say, Antoine was very upset when the emancipation took away his free labor . . . and he got more upset later on, when Kenneth Estilette took away his land. His anger was passed on to his son Joseph, Martha's father . . . He tried hard to recapture the lifestyle that his father lived, with sharecropping, nigger servants, pomposity, and pretense. But the son of a bitch couldn't stand it . . . being poor and pretending."

"Didn't he have the land?"

"What was left of it . . . forty acres out of the four thousand . . . and a plantation house falling down around his fool head. The few acres of land that were left had been all used up; wasn't rich and fertile any more . . . and his share of the crops wasn't much . . . But the hardest thing of all to swallow was being colored. Then I come along . . . I was going to be a doctor and bring back the wealth and give them status."

"But you became a teacher instead."

"And that almost killed him . . . When he couldn't stand it any longer he killed himself. He'd rather be dead than be called a poor nigger . . . It happened on a make-believe hunting trip."

"How do you know that?"

"The sheriff told me . . . and so did Silas. He was with him . . . he used to say Mr. *Joe ain't nothin' but a po' nigger tryin' to be white.*"

By now Alicia had joined Phillip in having a drink. Sitting across the table from him, she could swear she saw a tear in his eye. But then again it could have only been her imagination, or a reflection from the light. However, what had come out of his memory was enough to make anyone cry. She did not think for one minute that being colored was an easy road to travel; she could understand why anyone might do anything they could not to be.

Alicia knew it was difficult for Phillip to be in the position he was in and have to make the decision he had to make. She poured the next three fingers and wondered how long before he would be too drunk to talk or remember.

"Martha's just like her papa . . . all that pretense, make-believe, and churchgoing done drove her crazy."

"You think that was all?"

"That and Bobby . . . when he died, all the hopes she had once had for me died too.

"You feel you disappointed her that much?"

"I do."

Alicia drained her glass and got up. She didn't want to hear his guilt. She put on a record. For a rare moment there was quiet and the only voice was Ma Rainey singing "Blame It on the Blues." Phillip did not know if this was coincidence or whether Alicia had purposely selected this to make a statement. At any rate, he knew that the blues had also brought a significant amount of distress to Martha's mind. As Alicia watched his heavy eyelids slowly descend over his tipsy, bleary eyes she knew he would soon put his guilt to rest. But that would only be for the night. Tomorrow it would be back, along with Phillip's other frustrations. The frustrations nourished by broken promises—the promise that all men were free and equal, and had the right to life, liberty, and the pursuit of happiness. She knew that he was not able to realize his full measure as a man because of these frustrations. There was not a day that he breathed that he did not think about the difference between being colored and what he was divinely promised as a human being. She knew this because she knew Phillip. She knew he believed that there was a difference, a big difference.

PHILLIP'S LEGAL problems were now behind him, five years after he had been beaten. Clovis Hicks and Lee Jay Clary were each given a five-year suspended sentence. Which was nothing, but it was more than they got for killing PeeWee, when there were no eyewitnesses and no charges filed. Phillip was his own eyewitness. He charged them with attempted murder and the rest of the mob with being accomplices. Since there were no name identifications of anyone other than Hicks and Clary, they were the only ones to get guilty verdicts. Stephen Estilette was furious and urged Phillip to appeal all the way to the Supreme Court if necessary. He pledged his financial support. But Phillip was tired of the hassles and relieved that it was over. The determination that Bobby had once seen lacking in Phillip's eyes was still lacking. Phillip was weary of the struggle and still suffered bodily pain from the beating. However, since he was injured on city property he was reimbursed by the city for his medical bills.

Phillip fared better with his suit against the school board. He was reinstated and the school board was ordered to pay his back salary. The court also ordered that a public apology be given for whatever embarrassment his suspension may have caused. Fontenot was especially sorry, in the privacy of his office, for allowing pressure from the board to cause him to take the action that he had against a teacher who, as he put it, "was only trying to practice good citizenship." He also took the occasion to say how grateful he was for the years of hog meat, chickens, ducks, and turkeys that he had received. When Phillip left Fontenot's office, he passed the registrar's door and wondered if any difference had been made at all. He had been teaching for forty-plus years. Now he was thinking about retiring; or should he go for fifty?

24

NO ONE COULD make Naomi believe that it was not her hex that had caused Martha's problems. Every week when the owl spoke, she had done everything according to her voodoo rites. She was convinced that her gris-gris had worked. Now it seemed there was little point for her to continue the hex. Her purpose had been achieved. Plus, she did not have as much time to practice voodoo as before.

Naomi was now busy with the duties of the club. Prior to this she thought having money would make life easy, but now she was working harder than she ever had in her life. It used to be that when she was off work, she was off. Now she was never off. There was always something to do. And on top of everything else, she had to watch the people who worked around the place: the cooks, the barkeeps, and the waitresses—She said, "Anyone could steal you blind when you not looking." It was a tough life but it did have its rewards. She drove the biggest Cadillac in town, had nice clothes a large, beautiful house, and money in the bank. She had little to complain about, even though she didn't have much time for voodoo.

LightFoot made his announcement as casually as he could, but Naomi's response was not what he expected.

"What you mean you goin' visit yo' sister?"

"Jes' that."

"She wouldn't come see yo' ass if you was sick."

"The doctor wants me to come see her."

"Oh, the doctor . . . Yeah, who told you that shit?"

"Phillip."

"That damn woman done caused us enough trouble in her lifetime . . . She got her comeuppance so let her be."

"She's my sister."

"Yeah, that's right. Blood's thicker than water."

Naomi said no more. She decided that no matter how busy she was, she was going to have to keep her hex going. She complained that she was not feeling well and had decided to take the night off. After LightFoot left to open the club, she lost little time in getting back to her sorcery. She retrieved the doll likeness of Martha and placed it in the center of her altar. With the candles burning and the aroma of the strong pungent orris root to appease the voodoo gods, Naomi made a very strong *wanga*.

During her incantations she poured chicken blood over the white face and hair of the Martha-doll. Then she wrote M-A-R-T-H-A F-E-R-G-E-R-S-O-N on a piece of paper that was pierced seven times, then dipped in chicken's blood. She split open a Gaspa Goo with a new razor blade and buried the paper with Martha's name on it inside the fish's abdomen. Then she filled the remaining space with a can of black pepper and sewed up the opening with black thread. She invoked the voodoo spirits with hypnotic movements accompanied by chants in the unknown tongue. She continued this ritual until she collapsed. When she had recovered sufficiently, she walked to the Fergersons' house. With the full moon as her witness, she dug a hole in the garden plot that BookTau had prepared and buried the fish. The *wanga* was complete. Several miles away in Pineville, at that same moment and under the same moon, a shriek vibrated the walls of the hospital. The night attendant went running to Martha's room. Her pain of rheumatism was unbearable.

THROUGHOUT MARTHA'S hospitalization, Vel remained in Chicago. Although she was aware of the situation, there was nothing she could do. She told Rosa by phone, "I don't want to see Mama like that." Vel had been in Chicago for more than ten years and the practice of her profession had provided her a comfortable and, by some standards, respectable life. After taking courses in education at the University of Chicago and maintaining her contacts with the powerful and politically connected, she was put on a ticket to run for the school board. Vel was through with Estilette and, except for the call of death, she never wanted to return.

This was not the case with Rosa, who was stuck at home. Still teaching at the Catholic school, she ran the family house. She did the cooking, shopping, and looking after all matters of upkeep. Phillip tended the farm during the week when he was in town. On the weekends he went to Scotlandville, and on these occasions he made arrangements to have one of his hired hands look after feeding the animals. Rosa knew and didn't know where he went and with whom he stayed while in Scotlandville. She had heard enough fusses to remember "that woman," so she accepted the inevitable and asked no questions.

Rosa had a long prayer list and her mama's was the first name on it. Her visits to Pineville were timed between those of her father's.

This way Martha saw someone from the family every week, even though she seldom recognized Phillip. This was not the case with Rosa, whom she always embraced and looked forward to reciting the rosary with. Sometimes Martha would join Rosa. Other times she would just sit and listen with a stare of distant bewilderment. At these times Rosa wondered what was going through her mind. She wondered if her mama was thinking back to the visit in backwoods cabin. She knew that what they had done was a sin and wondered if this was the price that God had imposed on her mama for the part she played in that decision.

Sometimes when she looked into her mama's vacant eyes, she did not think her mama knew who she was. And other times Rosa would recognize a slight smile or a knowing look that they had shared in the past, and she hoped that her mama knew that her baby Rosa was with her. Rosa had accepted her fate of punishment—spinsterhood. She would never know the pleasures and joys of being a wife or mother. She was married to the church. The rest of her life was a penance, dedicated to service and prayer. Except for the secular clothing, she was a nun in every other respect.

Lala, the beauty in Martha's image, had moved away. Phillip said he understood why she had not come back to see her mama in the hospital. After Lester's father died, they sold the sugar cane farm and purchased a large house in Kansas City. In addition Lala was still angry. The second slap was never forgotten. In spite of the request by her papa to try and understand her mother's problems, she could not. The only conclusion that came out of any attempt at understanding was a suspicion that her mama hated her. And Phillip had never told Lala that Martha had disowned her as a daughter. To hear that would have been a bitter pill. So it was just as well that she had not returned. At any rate her presence would not have helped Martha's condition.

THE PHONE rang early on May 18, 1954. Phillip hated when the phone rang early or late. It was usually bad news. The voice on the other end of the line was familiar. "Have you seen the morning paper?"

"I haven't gotten up yet, Stephen."

"Well, hell, man, get up and read your paper."

Phillip opened his *Times Picayune* to the headline: HIGH COURT BANS SCHOOL SEGREGATION 9 TO 0. Thurgood Marshall had successfully led his team of NAACP lawyers in arguing the case *Brown v. Board of Education* before the Supreme Court. The long-standing policy of separate but equal was now unconstitutional. Phillip thought it was good news to be awakened for. It had come near the end of the school term. Most schools would be closing for the summer in a couple of weeks and the nation's school boards would have three months to think about what to do. He was dying to find out what Fontenot and his board were going to do.

As was customary, each principal was required to schedule an end-of-term review meeting with Fontenot. Three weeks later, which Phillip decided was enough time after the decision to let the matter cool off, he scheduled his end-of-term meeting. To say the atmosphere was strained would be an understatement. Actually, relationships had never returned to what they were prior to his attempt to vote. Then, Fontenot had treated Phillip as his special above-the-other-niggers colored man. That is, he was given a place of esteem. However, unknown to Phillip, he was accorded this honor because of his yearly gifts. After his attempt to vote and after winning his legal action,

Phillip noticed a change in Fontenot's attitude. There was little doubt that the closer Phillip came to full equality the more distant Fontenot seemed. And now that the Supreme Court's action had made it possible that Phillip could be a principal of an integrated school, he expected that the prevailing attitude of estrangement would be greater.

Phillip noticed the chill in the air the moment he entered the office. The secretary let him wait for several minutes before she even attempted to notify Superintendent Fontenot that Phillip had arrived for his appointment. When she did, Fontenot requested that Phillip be shown in immediately. Reluctantly the secretary opened the door and Phillip was greeted by an eager handshake. Phillip was taken aback by the enthusiasm of the reception, and especially when Fontenot said to the secretary, "Bring Professor Fergerson a cup of coffee."

In the many years of receiving Phillip in his office, Fontenot had never offered him coffee. Phillip felt that the Supreme Court decision had made the difference. However, there was no doubt that the secretary resented being told to serve coffee to a nigger. It was certain to be the topic of conversation at her home that evening. She turned and quickly left to fetch the coffee. Fontenot leaned back in his chair, put his feet on the desk, and locked his hands behind his head.

"Well, what do you think?"

"About what?"

"The Supreme Court decision."

Phillip felt he was being baited. But he would speak his mind. He had been through so much, he no longer cared that white folks might be offended if he said something they didn't want to hear.

"It's a good thing and it's about time."

"My feelings exactly."

Phillip couldn't believe what he was hearing. And neither did the secretary, who had just re-entered the room. As she was placing Phillip's coffee in front of him, she did a double-take with so much surprise that a lot of the coffee spilled out of the cup, dripping into the saucer. A few drops splattered on Phillip.

Phillip ignored the coffee. He said to Fontenot, "But there are a lot of people who don't share your feelings."

"I imagine not."

"How does the board feel?"

The secretary slammed the door with a thud. Phillip turned in the direction of the sound and smiled as he poured the saucerful of coffee back into his cup. He waited to hear Fontenot's answer, now that they were alone.

"They're going to fight. As we sit here there is an appeal being prepared."

"I was hoping to be surprised by your answer, but this is no surprise. It's simply a delay. The Supreme Court vote was unanimous."

"Right. It's a waste of time and money. You know it and I know it. And it's going to be a nightmare. That's why I'm retiring."

Phillip was shocked. Fontenot had been in education as long as Phillip had; he was approaching his forty-fifth year of service. But most shocking was the fact that he had revealed it to Phillip.

"I want you to know that you're the first one I'm telling. I haven't even told my wife yet. The next few years are going to be hell. And I don't want to be around to go through it. What about you?"

"Well, I, er . . . don't know. I haven't really thought about it."

Phillip lied. He had thought about retiring. Even before the Supreme Court decision. He was tired of fighting, especially after five years of the legal battle that he had waged. Now there were new battle lines being drawn and, like the Civil War, sides must be taken. Fontenot was more honest about his decision than Phillip was. In an ironic way, Fontenot was helping Phillip resolve his dilemma.

"Well, you should think about retiring. It will be a long time and an uphill fight before this board will let you principal a school with white teachers and children."

Phillip knew he was right, but he did not want to discuss his future with Fontenot. He said, "What about the end-of-term report?"

"To hell with that, Phillip. I've got more important things on my mind and you do, too. If we're around next year, we'll take it up then."

As Phillip walked past the site of his last battle, the voter registrar's office, Fontenot's words echoed in his brain. If he stayed, there would be another fight. Change was not going to come easily. Maybe he should retire. The times were changing faster than he knew how to deal with. He had to make a decision.

AFTER ALMOST a year since the initial request was made, LightFoot was finally on his way to visit his sister in Pineville. It had been so long that Naomi had forgotten about the opposition she had raised when it was first discussed. In the meantime, two other factors compelled him to make the trip. Phillip continued to ask, "When are you going to see your sister?"

He continued to answer, "Soon as I get a chance."

When Phillip seemed convinced that LightFoot was not going, he stopped asking. Then LightFoot began to have dreams. In one dream, LightFoot and Martha, as children, were coming home from school.

Some mischievous boys began throwing rocks at them. LightFoot ran home leaving Martha alone to return the hail of rocks. When she got home and told their papa about what had happened, Joseph ordered LightFoot to go into the peach orchard and select the instrument of his punishment. His papa gave him a good whipping for not looking after his sister. "You should always stand up and protect your sister."

In another dream, LightFoot drank ice water and rested in the shade of a pecan tree. Then the devil appeared, a put a saddle on LightFoot's back, and rode him up and down the bayou roads laughing, while Martha burned in hell. His mother had always told him as a young boy, "When the devil rides you, somebody in the family is going to die." Feeling that the prophecies of his dreams were more than he wanted on his conscience, he decided that it was time to visit his sister.

LightFoot felt that Martha had created her own problems by years of hating and expressing her evil thoughts. He hadn't realized, until he knew for sure that she was behind the burning of his tavern, how much she despised blues music. But in spite of his thinking *She's lying in the bed she made herself*, she was still his sister. Blood of the same blood, being fathered and mothered by the same people, all counted for something. As he sped toward Pineville, all of his thoughts were about Martha. She had not always been the way she was as a grownup. He tried to remember the good things and the good times. How she had nursed him back to health after his accident. How she had given him a place to stay for many years. Her voice as a seventeen-year-old came screaming into his mind: "Johnny, Johnny, come quick."

He was twelve at the time and hidden away in his treehouse, learning to play his harp. He stuck his head through the hole in the floor and saw Martha at the bottom of the pecan tree looking up at him.

"Johnny, come on down here and help me."

"What's wrong?"

"Susie Mae's hurt."

"What happened?"

"Just come on down here, quick."

John and Martha ran across the freshly plowed rows of a field that was being prepared for planting corn. Martha headed for the barn with John running right behind. She stopped at the barn door.

"I got to catch my breath."

"What you doing way out here?"

"I was looking for you. Mama want you to come finish stacking that wood before Papa come home."

"Where is he at?"

"Went huntin'."

"Again?"

"We ain't got no time for that now. Come on."

Martha led him into the barn toward the horse stalls. Susie Mae, a twelve-year-old black girl, was on the ground, crying. Her left arm was wrapped with strips of white cloth forming a tourniquet; she had been bleeding badly. John knelt next to the young retarded child and asked, "What happened?'

"Her pa left her to unhitch the horse and he rode off in the wagon. The horse kicked her, she fell back on the plow, and it cut a gash in her arm. I think it cut an artery."

"You put that bandage on?"

"Yeah, I tore off my petticoat and stopped the bleeding. Help me put her in the buggy."

John and Martha placed Susie Mae in the back of the buggy. Martha wiped away her tears with her torn petticoat and said, "Don't cry. You'll be all right. We're gonna take you to the hospital."

They headed the buggy toward town with Martha driving. John looked back at Susie Mae and then turned to Martha.

"Good thing you come along when you did."

"I was looking for you and heard the commotion in the barn. I went in just when the horse kicked her."

"What you think Papa gonna say?"

"If he found out, he'll fire her pa from sharecropping. He had no business leaving a girl like that to unhitch the plow. So don't tell him."

LightFoot wondered what had happened to the caring, compassionate Martha in the intervening years. She had saved the life of a black retarded girl and kept it a secret so the girl's pa could keep his land arrangement to support his family. After Martha had grown up she could not even stand to be around black people, much less do anything to help.

He turned his white Cadillac into the grounds of the state mental institution and parked. He was shown into the visitors' waiting room where he was greeted by the strong smell of urine that permeated the air. Martha was still on his mind as his eyes drifted around the room. The dirty pea-green walls were in need of painting. He noticed a pair of roaches scurry pass on the windowsill near his chair. He knew that Martha's condition was serious, because one would have to be crazy to stay in such a place.

Martha was brought in. She was limping. The rheumatism had swollen her legs twice the normal size. She should have been in a wheelchair. Instead, her pride made her cling to the arm of the attendant. Her fingers were gnarled and knotted and the beauty had gone from her face. Her hair was no longer meticulously arranged. Now it was uncombed and tangled and hung down around her shoulders in a stringy array of black and white. Her mismatched and misfastened clothes hung loosely around her bloated body like moss on a tree. It took all of LightFoot's inner strength to suppress the shock of seeing his sister in this condition.

After a moment of hesitation, he limped in her direction when she headed towards his chair. Martha left the grasp of her attendant and hobbled the rest of the way, quickening her pace when she recognized him: "My baby brother."

LightFoot was thrown by her reception, but he returned her hugs and kisses. This was not the greeting that he expected. His immediate thought was, *Being in this crazy house has softened her heart.*

"Did Papa go huntin' today?"

He knew by that question she was living in the past, which explained the reception. He decided to relive the time that she was reliving. It was a time when they got on in a peaceful and loving manner.

"Not today. He's going tomorrow."

"Good. You go with him. Don't let him go with that nigger Silas."

LightFoot was not surprised to hear that the cause of Papa's death was still on Martha's mind. He felt sure that this might have been one of the events that brought her to Pineville. He continued to play along.

"I'm going with him."

"Johnny, you got your harp?"

"I left it . . . in my tree house."

She was now back in the time when he was twelve and she was seventeen. He used to leave his harp in the treehouse because his papa didn't like the sound of it and didn't want it in the house. At that time Martha would request, "Play the train . . . It sound so real." LightFoot didn't know where this would lead but he didn't want to do or not do anything that would upset his sister. Phillip had told him how fragile her mind was, and that since she had been returned to the general ward with the other colored patients the slightest thing could set her off. LightFoot excused himself to "get my harp from the treehouse."

When he returned, the attendant met him at the door. Martha was on her knees leaning against a table.

"She's waiting for confession."

"Confession?"

"She thinks you're her priest."

"But, I, er . . ."

"Why not. It'll keep her calm. Anyway, you're her brother; it can't do no harm."

The attendant left the room and closed the door. Martha looked up to greet LightFoot.

"Hello, Father. I'm ready."

LightFoot didn't know what to say or do. He moved his chair next to her kneeling position and simply listened.

"Bless me, Father, for I have sinned. It's been many years since my last confession. I just couldn't before . . . but I want you and God to know I'm sorry for all that I done."

LightFoot felt like he was about to look at his sister naked. He wanted to get up and run out but he wouldn't dare upset her. Like the attendant said, it would keep her calm. He looked into her eyes and saw the pain of what she was about to say slowly creep to the surface of her once beautiful but now wrinkled face. She continued, "I fixed it so my daughter Rosa would never have another baby, and I arranged to kill the baby she carried for that sinful Father Pat . . . And then I did another terrible thing. I made Father Pat suffer and die for what he did to my chile . . . I fed him glass that tore up his insides, and he died just like that baby that he ill-conceived with my Rosa . . . and I know I'm gonna have to suffer for what I did, 'cause God is the only judge. And Father, I was unkind to my brother . . . He's a good man when he's not drinking and playin' that devil's music. I paid BookTau to burn down his sinful place. I knew it was wrong but I was mad and he was livin' with that ol' black woman I hated. And I run over that other black thing called Ruth. She killed my baby boy . . . and I know that was wrong, too . . . and I know God said, 'Vengeance is mine,' but . . ."

There was a long silence during which Martha's water-filled eyes remained fixed on those of her confessor's. LightFoot remained frozen, afraid to say anything that might upset the delicate balance. Maybe she had recognized him. So he dared not move. Plus he was still in shock from what he had just heard. There was nothing in his entire experience that had prepared him to receive such grievous sins from one whose blood also ran in his veins. Finally her lips parted, her tone of voice remained the same as it had been throughout her confession, and she leaned in close to LightFoot's face and whispered, "Excuse me, Father, but I got to pee."

The excruciating look on her face told LightFoot it was urgent. He hurriedly limped to the door and summoned the attendant.

LightFoot entertained thoughts of leaving while she was gone. But he felt obligated to complete the confession. If she returned and found that her priest had abandoned her, it might upset her. He could not even begin to imagine what other sins she still wanted to confess. When Martha returned there was a tranquil look in her eyes. The attendant and Dr. Comeaux stood watching from the opened doorway. LightFoot looked at the doctor and lifted his shoulders in a gesture of helplessness, as if to ask, "*What do I do now?*"

Comeaux responded with a silent verbalization of "It's all right. Continue." Martha greeted LightFoot again with hugs and kisses, just as she had done when she first entered the room.

"My baby brother. Did Papa go huntin' today?"

"He's going tomorrow."

"You go with him. Don't let him go alone with the nigger Silas."

"I'm going with him."

"Good. You got your harp?"

"Right here."

"Play the train for me . . . but don't let Papa hear."

About the Author

WHITNEY J. LEBLANC, who grew up in Louisiana, has worked as a director, producer, designer, teacher, and stained-glass artist. He has also written scripts for film and television.

In addition to serving as Associate Professor of Theatre at Antioch College, Towson State University, and Howard University, he has been a visiting professor/lecturer at venues across the country. He has been a lecturer/panelist at many events, including the Tennessee Williams Literary Festival in New Orleans and the Black Arts Festival in Atlanta.

LeBlanc has directed *The Glass Menagerie*, *A Raisin in the Sun*, many other major stage productions, and has won three Outstanding Director awards. In Hollywood he has worked for network television and PBS, including *The Young and the Restless*, *Benson*, *Generations*, *The Redd Foxx Show*, *Good Times*, and many other programs.

LeBlanc has been listed in *Who's Who in Black America* and *Who's Who in American Education*. Today he is a stained-glass artist in the Napa Valley in California, and works with university and regional theatres as a director, teacher, consultant, and workshop facilitator.

Now available from River City Publishing!

The song "Blues in the Wind" by Wayne Perkins on a CD single.

Not only did WAYNE PERKINS audition to replace Mick Taylor in the Rolling Stones, he's worked with Eric Clapton, Leon Russell, Delbert McClinton, McGuinn/Hillman, the Everly Brothers, Bob Marley, Joni Mitchell, Levon Helm, Glenn Frey, Bob Seger, and many more top stars. Now he's written and recorded the song "Blues in the Wind" especially for this book.

"Blues in the Wind"

words and music written and copyrighted © by Wayne Perkins

Don't need much outta living, to keep my nature satisfied
Take the bad with the good, there's just too many women
I've got one at home and two on the side
Things look better than they've been, it's only the Blues in the Wind.

Down on everyone around her, put herself above her own blood
With the shade of her skin, she'd never wondered if she was ever one cut above
Painted herself into a corner, the source of her own sufferin'
How could she ever win with all of these Blues in the Wind
It seems there's no end to all of these Blues in the Wind.

She never liked my music, said it was a low-down sin
Playin' the Devil's music, that's where yo' troubles begin
She turned my world around when the Play House burned down
But I could never prove what she did.
Still hear flames ragin', it sounds like the Blues in the Wind
Her voice haunts me again, it sounds like the Blues in the Wind.

Black Eagle rose from the ashes torturing sister's dark soul.
Caught between her race and religion, that's where her nightmares unfold
Her deeds came back to haunt her and slowly started doin' her in
Seems like there's no way to win all of these Blues in the Wind
Only heartache for a friend when she hears the Blues in the Wind.